Copyright © Peter Chegwidden 2017

The moral right of the author has been asserted.

No part of this publication may be reproduced, stored in a retrieval system or transmitted in any form or by any means without the prior permission in writing of the publisher, nor be otherwise circulated in any form of binding or cover other than that in which it is published and without a similar condition being imposed upon the subsequent purchaser.

This book is a work of fiction. Names, characters, businesses, organisations, places and events are either the product of the author's imagination or are used fictitiously. Any resemblance to actual persons, living or dead, events or locales is entirely coincidental.

Formatted for Kindle and paperback by www.publishonkindle.co.uk

ISBN-13: 978-1981637485

ISBN-10: 1981637486

Contents

Contents 2
Introduction 4
Chapter One 5
Chapter Two 9
Chapter Three 17
Chapter Four 23
Chapter Five 28
Chapter Six 36
Chapter Seven 42
Chapter Eight 51
Chapter Nine 60
Chapter Ten 69
Chapter Eleven 76
Chapter Twelve 86
Chapter Thirteen 93
Chapter Fourteen 106
Chapter Fifteen 116
Chapter Sixteen 126
Chapter Seventeen 135
Chapter Eighteen 143
Chapter Nineteen 151
Chapter Twenty 159
Chapter Twenty One 168
Epilogue 175
Author's Afterthoughts 177
Appendix I - Off the beaten track 178
Appendix II - Other e-books by Peter Chegwidden 179
    Deadened Pain 179
    Tom Investigates 179

Tom Vanishes 180
Sheppey Short Stories 180
Kindale 180
To be published 181

Introduction

Murder comes to the Kent countryside and a quiet little unassuming village.

Everyone knew who the killer was, so why didn't the police do something?

A lovely old gentleman is slain in his back garden and everyone was sure his wicked stepson, Michael Martyn, carried out the dreadful deed. And Martyn has plenty of secrets he wants left hidden.

But it transpires there are other secrets in this rural settlement.

If you like your murder mysteries in a less than serious and more genteel and cosy vein, tinged with humour, set in glorious bucolic surroundings, and with just enough sauce added to make it spicy, then this tale's for you.

Village gossip takes hold, the police seemed baffled, a too-clever-by-half local reporter gets involved, and then, inevitably, another murder takes place. And secrets are uncovered.

One by one.

Chapter One

Everyone knew who the killer was.

Well, it was obvious, wasn't it?

Steve the butcher knew and was keen to tell anyone in his shop who would listen, and did so as part of his noisy humour-filled banter with his customers. Martha, who played the organ for church services and did so without any obvious skill, was aware of the identity of the murderer because, in her mind, there could be nobody else. Gillian, who drove for the local bus company, knew as she'd been told by so many of her passengers.

Dr Monroe was pretty confident too, but tried to suggest to his patients that they shouldn't be too hasty in condemning someone out of hand, despite the fact he himself had privately done so. Dave the taxi driver knew, because taxi drivers know everything and are always willing to share such knowledge with their fares.

Maud was as certain as certain can be, and told the owner of the florist shop she cleaned in the mornings she was certain. Keith, the newsagent, had his doubts but kept them to himself so as not to offend his clients. Harry, in his third year of retirement and enjoying part-time work as a jobbing gardener, was absolutely clear on the subject. Guilty!

Indeed, everyone knew who had committed the heinous crime.

So why didn't the police do anything about it?

* * *

William Kerbidge had died in his back garden while replanting some fuchsias which sadly also perished through subsequent lack of attention. Mr Kerbidge received all too much attention being strangled as he knelt in front of the flowerbed, and throttled rather coarsely, if appropriately, with his own gardening twine which had been wrapped around his throat four times.

The culprit, as everybody knew, was his good-for-nothing stepson, Michael Martyn, who now stood to inherit the property and much else besides. So, quite naturally, there could be no other malefactor involved. He had the only known motive. He possessed no alibi, and was laden with a wealth of opportunity as he was at the home he and the victim shared during that afternoon.

In truth it was he who discovered the body.

The public view was that it was no surprise he should find his late stepfather as Mr Kerbidge was lain where Mr Martyn had sent him from one world to another, if the public view was correct.

Michael Martyn's only alibi, and a slender one at that, was that he spent the afternoon in his study, a first floor bedroom overlooking the front of the house, and that he ventured into the rear garden later in the day to see if his stepfather wanted a cuppa.

The police had checked his computer records and were able to establish that, yes indeed, he'd completed quite a bit of work including the sending of various emails, and the computer timings seemed to demonstrate that the operator might've been busy all afternoon. Martyn was taken for questioning but had been released firstly on the strength of what his computer told the officers, and secondly because no forensic evidence was available to link him to the crime.

That created the following mystery:

The large rear garden was bordered by trees and shrubs and, beyond them, fences. Either side lay open fields. The garage was close to the house with a small passageway between guarded by a substantial gate.

The crime took place mid afternoon and nobody saw anything out of the ordinary and the police could find no evidence that anyone other than the occupants had been in the back garden.

A mystery.

But not to the local community.

There being no other conceivable explanation Michael Martyn must be the guilty party, especially as he was so unlikeable and so easily detested by just about everyone who knew him, and a few who didn't besides. There he was completely condemned, ready to be locked up forever with the key thrown away.

And that poor, poor Mr Kerbidge as well. Dead and gone. Slain without mercy by his wicked unloving stepson.

The police realised it wasn't as simple as that, even though they were faced with inescapable circumstantial evidence that put Martyn in the frame and then some more. But how to prove it? And, if not Martyn, who else, and where would the damning proof lie?

* * *

Chief Inspector Drype sat quietly at his desk and puzzled the conundrum, tapping his fingertips gently together as he held his hands in front of him, as if in prayer. Every now and then he blew onto his fingertips as if to suggest that he hoped some sort of genie would appear and bring him the solution.

Perhaps he was praying. Maybe he needed divine guidance. Possibly some magic.

Either way this murder was a tricky one.

DCI Drype had one problem that had accompanied him through life from birth without so much as a pause or brief intermission: the pronunciation of his surname, correctly 'Dry' with the p and the e silent.

He had often been referred to as Drip particularly during his years as a schoolboy and then as a police officer. It was not unusual for various verbs and adjectives to be added although not normally within his earshot.

Having said that, certain criminals had most definitely taken his nickname in vain and added, within his earshot, a colourful array of blistering suggestions and, usually inaccurately, observations and further personal descriptions of a foul, obscene and abusive nature.

That didn't bother him as long as he had the last laugh when they were sent to prison. He laughed less these days as prison was becoming not so much a last resort for the courts than something to be avoided at all costs. How times had changed!

From the beginning of this case he had not taken a shine to Michael Martyn.

He shared a mutual view with residents of the village that Martyn was probably the killer but proving it was both easy and difficult. It could be nobody else but a half decent defence barrister would tear the evidence to shreds. No, they needed something more concrete or something to point them in somebody else's direction, and they didn't have either.

* * *

Michael Martyn hadn't been an optional extra when his mother remarried, he came as part of the deal and one that the groom could well have done without. They found it effortless to loathe each other but somehow managed to co-exist for the sake of the bride.

The new Mrs Kerbidge, being considerably younger than her new man, seemed hell-bent on wearing him out quickly in all respects. It was the popular local view that she had married to get her hands on the gentleman's wealth, and an equally popular local view that she was working him to death from bedroom to garden in order to inherit his small fortune.

It remained unknown whether or not furious and exhausting nocturnal activities were being engaged in, although once again gossip felt this was highly likely. There were one or two men who considered Maisie Kerbidge an appreciable catch and who therefore envied William Kerbidge being worn out in such a presumably pleasurable fashion.

But it was elsewhere that he was rather more obviously kept hard at it.

The garden, which quite frankly was his pride and joy anyway, was transformed, and at the same time there was a similar makeover in the house, this being redecorated and renovated to Mrs Kerbidge's specifications by her husband. He might have been retired but he was now working all hours almost every day, and flat out to boot.

And in all of this neither she nor her lazy off-spring did anything to assist.

Whatever activities Mr Kerbidge engaged in at local level Mrs Kerbidge made sure that his physical toil was noticeably in excess of his previous involvement. A couple of hours now and then tidying up the church grounds on a voluntary basis was, by that medium, extended to three or four visits every week, all comprised of hard labour. Mrs Kerbidge supervising.

In fact she became known as the Foreman but that was one of the more polite terms applied to her.

Everybody felt sorry for William. Everybody was sure about what Maisie was up to. And everybody was certain Michael had killed him.

There might have been a revenge element too, it was widely accepted.

For it was actually Mrs Kerbidge who perished all too swiftly, possibly from a surfeit of overbearing command or an overdose of intimate gratification, depending on the viewpoint of each rumour-monger. Her son was distraught, at least for a few days, and quite publicly blamed his stepfather and did so with an air of annoyance, anger and bitterness in ever increasing quantities up to the day of the funeral.

It was Martha, the church organist, who told anyone willing to listen, that she had heard him issuing violent oaths aimed at William from the very graveside after Maisie was buried.

Village horror was complete!

So it was never going to be a surprise that Michael should be held to account for that terrible murder. Except that he wasn't being held to account at all.

Whatever were the police up to?

Chapter Two

Chortleford was an unassuming village in a very assuming county.

It was difficult, but certainly not impossible, for places to hide in Kent, and many had made sterling efforts to steer clear of the beaten track. This most astonishingly beautiful of counties had managed to tuck away some of the loveliest of countryside and with it secrete small settlements where they might not easily be found.

Anyone who believes Kent to be in any way fully industrialised, totally built up, all motorways, high speed rail links and busy seaside resorts, needs to visit the county and make a closer inspection. Yes, it can be all of the above, yet so much of it, so very much of it, is still gloriously rural, and there are many places one can go and see nothing but unspoilt countryside for mile after mile.

And the countryside itself is so varied and surprising.

Gentle rolling slopes, delightful hills, fabulous valleys, simple pastures, thick woodlands, even the flatlands such as the famous Romney Marsh; all are here. There are miles of blissfully happy golden sandy beaches, there are the mighty towering White Cliffs dominating the Channel and quite possibly the French coast beyond; there are shores of pebbles, there are rivers and inlets and creeks and islands.

There is more history than you could shake a stick at. Even in more recent times Kent showed its true mettle as the front line county in world war two.

There is the magnificent Dover Castle, and others such as Rochester and Deal, the Royal Military Canal and the Martello towers, all standing ready to repel boarders at various stages in history!

The visitor can locate peace and quiet, the silence disturbed only by birdsong, other wildlife and the occasional tractor or other piece of farming equipment. Oh yes, and the plague of skies everywhere, aircraft.

There are still hop farms here and an array of oasthouses (most converted to private dwellings), and the county has now added well-applauded wine production to its repertoire. Having been at the heart of the brewing industry (Shepherd Neame has been busy since 1698) it is comforting to know Kent can quench the world's thirst so decisively.

Kent can rival the best countryside of Yorkshire, East Anglia, the West Country, and more besides. The county has a coast no other English county can match, surrounded on three sides by water.

There are sheep by the hundreds. No mountains it is true, but the visitor will find hills a-plenty and scenic views to match. Add in the quiet and picturesque villages like Chortleford and Kent is the place to be.

Nothing much has disturbed Chortleford, and it has rarely contributed to the crime statistics. A village surrounded by farmland in the middle of nowhere in particular with only its village sign, and the road signs supplied by the County Council to advise the caller where he, she or they have arrived. Many of the few tourists that make their way here do not tarry as in any case most are en route to somewhere else, or are hopelessly lost of course.

Thus do many of Kent's little villages feature in the great itinerary of life, all too often visited by accident rather than intent, their attractiveness unlikely to delay the busy holidaymaker. This all being a very great shame.

Not that Chortleford ever worried.

In truth its residents preferred that kind of anonymity.

There had been an attempt by some of the local young things to organise a village festival but the concept had been stifled at birth much to the satisfaction of the elders.

A similar fate had befallen periodic attempts at forming a village cricket club.

For one thing the village green was deemed too small: a half-decent six off the meat of the bat, once it had cleared the boundary, would be sure to cause damage, especially to anything made of glass.

And suddenly Chortleford was in the national news, not at all where it wanted to be. Worse still, maps were produced online and in the press so that enquirers could pinpoint the heart of recent villainy in relation to Canterbury, Dover and Rochester, and the rest of the United Kingdom.

The village was exposed and found to be naked.

A local reporter, one step ahead of the media masses, had booked the village's only B and B, but the publican of the curiously named Log and Weasel quickly found a way to accommodate two more journalists, he being a man with a ready eye to business.

The circus did not stay long.

Other stories beckoned and there was little left to report. There was nothing likely to land in the realms of 'public interest' let alone 'reader or viewer interest' and so, like William Kerbidge, it all died a death, and did so in Chortleford.

It was as if the media representatives had concluded Michael Martyn was guilty. Game over, end of.

The police had been less than helpful.

One or two papers tried to make a story out of perceived police failings but it never really caught on.

DCI Drype and DS Penderfield stood in Mr Kerbidge's back garden and for the umpteenth time tried to make sense of it all.

Surely Martyn must've crept up on his stepfather and strangled him. Surely?

The one thing they had learned about Martyn was what he did for a living.

A thorough search of his computer revealed him to be a successful author writing under two different names and two very different genres.

The mainstay appeared to be his romantic novels penned under the name Glynis Parham. So far seventeen had been published and a quick Googling had shown them to be very popular and good sellers. There were ladies in the village who were avid fans and keen readers of these works, little realising they had been written by a local man they deplored.

Less successful were his murder mystery books, his nom-de-plume being Peter Quendon. Five of these were on sale but enquiries of the publisher had demonstrated them to be poor sellers that had attracted atrocious reviews.

The publishers were not enthusiastic about releasing any more, and had only gone as far as the first five to ensure 'Glynis Parham' stayed with them, 'she' being, as the Managing Director put it, a nice little earner.

And in all of this his fellow villagers remained in ignorance.

If he was ever brought to trial it would all come out, of course.

DS Penderfield had the unenviable task of reading the Quendon works and found them to be entirely awful, and expressed the thought that he wasn't in the slightest surprised they hadn't sold. Quendon was never going to be the new Ian Rankin.

But Glynis Parham? Seemingly 'she' was loved the book world over.

It had been an interesting and amusing task trying to find a female officer to try one of Parham's tomes, for the female detectives shied away from confessing to a penchant for such novels.

Eventually DC Emma Brouding admitted she'd actually read one or two (several had truth been told) and agreed to sample another two or three in a more objective and investigative vein.

Nobody was seriously expecting to find any valuable clues in these romantic novels (the murder mysteries appeared a better vehicle), but everything needed looking into. Emma concluded that only a typical male, such as Drype, would consider it important for a woman to study an example of romantic fiction. Why not a job for a man, she'd reasoned?

Michael Martyn, alias Glynis Parham, was currently working on his eighteenth book and it was this matter that had, apparently, held his attention throughout the afternoon of the killing.

Drype and Penderfield left the back garden and invited themselves back into the house, Mr Martyn having granted them, under sufferance, a free licence to wander wherever they might.

The main bedroom looked just as it had that sorry afternoon, everything neat and tidy and the bed made, all clothing in cupboards and drawers as appropriate.

Certain of Mrs Kerbidge's clothes were still there. Martyn explained his step-father couldn't bear to be parted from them although he had persuaded the old man to reduce the stock, piece by piece, and by such means had seen the bulk disappear.

So what was left represented the core memorabilia for Kerbidge to grieve over. Drype could appreciate the situation as he was sure Maisie Kerbidge would've looked positively stunning in a couple of the very elegant gowns, and seductively fetching in a red dress that was made of a shockingly small amount of material.

A couple of skirts and blouses and a wide variety of underwear, some of it racy by any means of definition, went towards completing the 'museum' as Penderfield had taken to calling it.

Michael Martyn was working on his novel in his study so the police officers checked his bedroom.

It was the antipathy of his step-father's. Bed unmade, clothes flung here and there, books on the floor, a cupboard door wide open .... both bedrooms looked today just as they had when the detectives had first arrived on the scene in the immediate aftermath of murder.

They thought to disturb Michael but thinking of nothing they could now reasonably ask him they left him alone, muttering their farewell's as they went past his study. Michael (or Glynis, as he presently was) ignored them and they let themselves out.

* * *

Of course, it was only going to be a question of time before the village's amateur sleuths set themselves to work on this most enigmatic of cases.

Gladys Frobisher, a widow for many years, was a Chortlefordian born and bred, proud of the fact and proud to be a maid of Kent too. In all her years she had rarely stepped outside the county's borders, her perfect holiday destination having always been Broadstairs. Her husband came from Faversham where, incidentally, he also died.

They were a happy if childless couple, content in their world, content with their lot, and never willing to venture far afield when they had all they could ever want on their own doorstep. Her sister-in-law, Edna Frobisher, had made a conscious and determined effort to remain a spinster, believing from childhood that men might be an almost necessary evil but could and should be avoided whenever possible.

Certainly don't marry one, and she'd never allowed herself to come close.

But she doted on her brother who visited her often, and it was there that he perished many moons ago. In their grief the two heartbroken ladies decided on a simple course of action. Edna moved in with Gladys at Chortleford, and two became inseparable.

Mrs Frobisher was a stout lady, rather more rectangular than regularly chubby, with an equally square face boasting eyes that could produce a flesh-piercing gaze. Her normal stance was firmly upright, erect as a guardsman, with arms folded in front of her appreciable chest in a pose suggesting power and defiance.

She had a booming voice, somewhere between baritone and foghorn, and a voice that required, nay demanded, listening to. Her sister-in-law usually did the listening.

Miss Frobisher was the opposite of Mrs Frobisher, being thin, shapeless and relatively short, and carrying a demeanour of surrender and subservience, nervousness and fear.

Gladys had always seen herself as a kind of Miss Marple. Her enthusiasm stemmed from the books, not the television series. She hardly ever watched.

Being the leader in their relationship, Edna being the follower, Gladys often referred to herself as Gladys Holmes and to her sister-in-law as Edna Watson. This might suggest that solving crime had occupied a fair portion of their time together in their late autumn years, whereas Gladys had only ever dreamed of it as a result of reading murder mysteries.

Edna did not share this great love for fictional crime, but always went where Gladys led, and made sure she usually nodded in the right places, and said yes or no as appropriate where the application of such words was deemed important.

And now 'Mrs Holmes' had something very real to get her teeth into.

A local murder!

Edna winced, afeared for her sister-in-law or rather what she might find herself tangled up in. Leave it to the police, she'd pleaded, her pleas readily dismissed. The police, according to Gladys, were worse than useless and were never going to solve this one.

Of course Michael Martyn did it! Arrest the man!

The entire village knew he was home alone with that poor Mr Kerbidge, and that there was no other suspect and no evidence to incriminate anyone else. How dare the police believe whatever feeble alibi he'd come up with!

What neither Gladys nor Edna realised was that their chief suspect was himself a crime writer, even if a very poor one, shunned by critics and readers alike.

* * *

Colin Nash-Perry was looking at his computer screen, his eyes darting alertly from item to item.

He had assembled a kind of chart in relation to Mr Kerbidge's sudden and violent passing, a chart that possessed all the knowledge of the event he had and a few reasonable assumptions and summations.

The chart showed the results of a thorough search of the news media and assessments of local gossip, but lacked the fine detail that police had not made public.

Consequently there were a number of question marks, colour coded in relation to their likely relevance and importance, dotted about the screen. He knew he would have to make do with his chart unless he could unearth some hitherto hidden matter, or find himself privy to inside information.

A great fan of the works of Edward Marston (the Railway Detective series was his favourite) he also adored Ellis Peters's Cadfael chronicles, clearly preferring the classic style of writing, and historical settings, of such period pieces.

Although he had ventured into the realms of today's authors he found them a little too blunt (particularly when it came to the overt and excessive use of filthy language).

He'd enjoyed Frances Brody's Kate Shackleton mysteries set, as they were, between the wars, as he felt they were the work of a true story-teller.

Ellis Peters, he believed, wrote with great beauty and expression without the need to sully her delightful prose with unpleasant words. And yet her murder mysteries were exciting and enthralling.

Such talent did not require dreadful language in the pursuit of "realism".

He'd even tried a book by that Peter Quendon but had given up by chapter three and returned it to the library. Littered all too liberally with disgusting comments, the brutal killings described in horribly gory detail, and the sex-obsessed nature of the characters had all contrived to produce utter revulsion in Mr Nash-Perry.

Neither he nor his wife had ever approached anything that could be remotely described as sex-obsessed and as a result had one child, Vanessa, who had married and produced four of her own, almost as a way of saying 'look mum and dad – it's easy and fun'.

Now in retirement Colin and Rita had taken to village life like ducks to water, moving to Chortleford to escape the city of Canterbury, having fallen in love with this glorious part of the Kent countryside years before.

The murder had been a real shock to Rita, less so to Colin, and she had remarked, as people so often do, that you read about these things happening elsewhere but you never expect them where you live. Colin was now indulging in his own investigation, work that he made no fuss of in front of Rita, for it was not her interest and he believed it was better not to draw attention to his sleuthing.

Rita would not approve.

She was still in shock. Shock that murder could occur right here in the remote countryside and in a peaceful village like Chortleford. What made her shake with fear in her shock was that the killer was still at large and that, as everyone knew, the killer was Michael Martyn.

Why, it had even made it difficult to concentrate on the latest Glynis Parham, all very annoying when it was proving one of her best romantic novels. Oh, how Rita loved them. And how she wished she knew the author, for Glynis must surely have suffered all the pains and passions of love that she wrote about.

The woman wrote with such depth, such anguish, such ecstasy, such warmth, so much soul. What a woman she must be! Rita envied Glynis her ability to write such moving prose, and to stir such feelings in the reader. Rita also envied Glynis for all the loving encounters she must've experienced to be able to write so openly and fervently.

Colin had never been the romantic sort and intimacy was almost a dirty word. Anything tenuously connected with marital intimacy was most definitely something to be done in the dark and done quickly, and never spoken of.

So poor Rita had spent her life engrossed in books about romance, dreaming, ever dreaming, of a lover to kiss her so tenderly, to whisper soft words of ardour, to hold her and caress her so gently, to make love to her in an exhilarating manner, to take her into orbit about the Earth while she experienced a cataclysmic explosion of wild, thunderous and extraordinary feelings.

All she had were her sad dreams.

And they were nothing like the reality about to overtake her.

* * *

Vaughan Pervis hated it. How he hated it.

His escape to the country had gone awry, not at all to plan.

Having married Mr and Mrs Pervis sold their less than humble abode in Sittingbourne and moved to a large yet lovely modern house in the heart of Chortleford. It had once been the rectory but had been tastefully extended by the previous owners who had now moved on to a far more glamorous location and an even bigger property.

Villagers had been repeatedly dismayed by the ease with which the owners managed to obtain planning consents given so many people objected to them. Some suspected corruption. Regardless of the truth the finished item sold for a pretty penny, but then Vaughan Pervis had many pretty pennies to spend.

He worked in large scale residential and commercial property development and commuted from Ashford to London on the high speed train every day.

The move had gone wrong for two good reasons:

Vaughan and Katie Pervis suffered from the same idyllic dream of a move to the country so beloved of all too many city and town dwellers. They saw a fairy-tale picture of rustic peace and charm in a land where the sun shines all the time, and everything is beautiful and serene. Thus were they divorced from reality.

Secondly, they were not prepared to adapt to country living and the ways of a village community.

They held noisy parties that usually ran on well into the wee hours, played loud music in their garden while they relaxed outdoors on summer days, and they complained bitterly about crowing cocks and the chimes of the church clock throughout the night.

They drove massive and expensive cars and it was not unusual for their visitors, arriving in their own massive and expensive cars, to 'burn rubber' on the country lane when departing. The noise of screeching tyres came as a nasty shock to villagers. Especially at 3 a.m.

If they detested the country, the country was far from enamoured with the Pervis pair.

However, nature rolled the dice once more and it came to pass that Katie Pervis fell pregnant and that looked like putting the kybosh on their merry existence. It positively put a damper on Mrs Pervis's social life, revolving, as it did, around trips to the gym, regional shopping centres and a bronzed and athletic Adonis-like gentleman in Alkham.

The latter abandoned her upon the instant having heard the news.

Her personal trainer lingered a week or two longer and then set off in pursuit of other ladies in his portfolio.

Vaughan had been ecstatic but then he wasn't the one who had to carry their creation for nine months. Katie's girlfriends gleefully suggested she go for a water birth but that was something with very limited appeal for a fun-loving free spirit who simply wanted to party, not be a mum.

She'd shown no interest in the death of Mr Kerbidge beyond often forgetting his name and cruelly advising Vaughan that was one villager less to hate them.

But Vaughan had taken a quiet interest.

He could see all too clearly Michael Martyn was responsible for the wicked act and, like everybody else, wondered why the police hadn't charged him. His view was that there was a piece of vital information not in the public domain that prevented the police dealing with him. And it was a barrier that might be overcome.

Money!

To a man like Vaughan Pervis money could buy information and solutions, and it was just a case of looking in the right places, asking the right people. But, as he was to discover, money used in such a way can also buy enemies.

Chapter Three

Michael Martyn was not doing well.

The death of his stepfather was an inconvenience in itself, but being the prime suspect was not at all satisfactory and an unhappy diversion from fully focusing his mind.

He recalled that afternoon too well and too often.

The book had been going well, very well. The words had poured through his fingers onto the screen in front of him.

His imagination had, as ever, run riot, and he found the text flowed and sang like sweet music as he wrote about Hilary's aching broken heart, the despair of loss, the emptiness of life, a world devoid of hopes and dreams that had been dashed and scattered hither and thither. The desperate sighs, the floods of tears, the squeals of torment, the wretchedness of the destruction of her soul.

He had encompassed it all as his fictional creation realised her great romance with Edward was ended, and she was broken, destroyed.

Martyn could suffer, and made himself suffer. He had taken on the role of Hilary and reduced himself to tears induced by emotional agony as he imagined himself as a woman torn apart, driven asunder, a woman cast out by the man she loves.

The words appeared on his screen. He created them, polished them, filled them with passion and allowed them to express Hilary's feelings in glorious colours, flaming crimson, fierce blues, stark orange, shrieking greys. He used words where a great artist would paint a picture, where a great composer would write a majestic symphony.

It was what his audience craved, and why his books sold so well.

On that fateful day and by late afternoon, exhausted by his emotional effort, he sat back, closed his eyes, and pulled himself back to reality.

He exhaled noisily, opened his eyes, clicked 'save' and decided he needed a cup of tea. And if he was going to make a cup he might as well ask the old codger. His stepfather was presumably still in the back garden. Michael acknowledged that William would never dream of putting the kettle on if it meant offering his stepson a drink. Heaven forbid.

And as he went into the back garden that warm afternoon his world fell to pieces.

Not because he found Mr Kerbidge dead, but because of all the trouble it caused.

He was taken away. His clothes subjected to forensic examination. All the innermost secrets of his computer were revealed. His home and property were searched top to bottom, and given the full forensic treatment.

Questioned for hours he ached only for sleep.

The memory of that day and the days that followed stayed with him and haunted him, and today, when he was trying so hard to get back to his novel, he couldn't concentrate. He momentarily thought about Hilary simply collapsing and dying of a broken heart, but knew he was barely a third of a way through the story. And, besides, his public wouldn't want that.

His heroines never died and always found true and lasting love by the last chapter.

He was struggling and he knew it.

Damn them all, and most of all damn the killer! But there was a silver lining to this cloud. The family home would be his, lock, stock and barrel, together with all the money the old man had amassed, and he was sure there was a few bob involved. Nothing to trouble the taxman with; comfortably below the inheritance tax threshold anyway, even with the value of the property.

He would be quids in.

And then these dreadful villagers could go to hell. The thought cheered him and a simple chuckle escaped from his lips.

He just had to hold his nerve. He would sort Hilary out, no worries there.

* * *

Drype and Penderfield were relaxing over pints of Spitfire in the Log and Weasel.

DC Emma Brouding sipped at her lemonade and lime. She was driving. What a woman's for, she decreed with sarcasm. Equality? Huh!

They were on their way back to base after another fruitless wander around Chortleford. An afternoon wasted seeking answers without actually knowing what the questions were. That was Emma's view.

Keeping her thoughts silent she pleaded with an unknown authority, possibly God, maybe the Chief Constable, to let the women sort this one out. Please, most of all, she argued, get these useless timewasters off the case.

"It has to be Martyn," implored Charlie Penderfield, "Let's just run with it, do him, and let the court decided. Win, draw or lose."

"Trouble is, Charlie, as all we have is circumstantial we have to demonstrate we have exhausted every other avenue of inquiry. What we're left with has to be the truth. Even Sherlock Holmes knew that." And Drype managed a wry grin to emphasise that the literary connection was meant almost light-heartedly. He continued.

"What do you make of his novels?"

DS Penderfield considered his answer.

"Rubbish, and that's being polite. How you getting on with the romantic stuff, Emma?"

She looked up.

"If you like that genre I suppose it's okay, like, but not my scene. Girls throwing themselves at unworthy men. Yuk. All goo and slobber. If you want my opinion they're written for frustrated women who can't think for themselves. Women should be taking the lead. These stories pander to those full of romantic notions who don't have a shred of romance in their lives. Not exactly empowering, like, for women, is it?"

She did not let on that she loved such tales, yearned for gentle romance that had always escaped her, and that the immediate object of her attentions, Charlie Penderfield, was sitting right opposite her. How she wanted him. Unlucky in love Emma could've been created by Glynis Parham. Too shy to make the first move, unsure about how to approach him.

Glynis Parham would've come up with the answer, but then Glynis was actually a man and that rankled with Emma Brouding. And that was before you considered that he was probably a ruthless killer too.

"What I don't get, sir, is how a bloke like that can write in two such diverse genres."

"Well, Emma, I expect there's a weird connection somewhere," concluded Drype, adding, "It's all about a vivid imagination, really. He's got a talent for the romantic and it's made him money, but I suspect his great love is his crime novels and he just can't believe he's so useless at it."

They all shared a tired chuckle before drinking up and moving on.

But Emma decided to research her theme. That 'weird connection' might just prove to be a lethal one, and in agreeing a course of action with herself Emma was letting her inner police officer rise to the surface, and point her (unwittingly at this stage) down the right road while her senior male colleagues wallowed in her wake.

* * *

Being late September the keen gardeners in the village were preparing their charges for winter with one eye on the summer beyond.

Gladys Frobisher was, as ever, guiding her sister-in-law, admonishing and criticising where necessary, advising and instructing, and occasionally, very occasionally, offering words of praise in the manner of one praising a dog for cleverly retrieving a thrown ball.

Edna Frobisher handled all of it with a meek smile of submission and compliance. Never one to complain, always one to accept Gladys's role of command. Not once had it ever hurt her, for if truth be told she preferred being led as it relieved her of any responsibility. In the same way she accepted a good telling off from time to time, believing that as she had obviously done something wrong she deserved to be chastised.

Gladys played on Edna's perceived weaknesses, and silently poured scorn on her for being such a weak woman. But it was the way she liked life. Incredibly the two women had formed a close relationship based on warm friendship, pleasurable companionship and the fact Gladys was in charge and Edna was there to do as she was told. It worked well for both of them.

'Mrs Holmes' Frobisher had been giving much thought and contemplation to the recent murder, and had bounced a few theories off the helpless, hopeless Edna. The result had merely confirmed Gladys's position of superiority as her sister-in-law lacked any medium by which anything at all might produce bounce.

Dealing with a particularly tricky buddleia, secateurs in gloved hand, while Edna trimmed the edges of the lawn and not always to Gladys's liking, 'Mrs Holmes' gave vent to her latest idea.

"That man must've been, what do they say? tooled up. Is that it? I don't know. Anyway, I think he put on old clothes, strangled poor Mr Kerbidge, then somehow, somehow, got rid of them before he dialled 999. Must've been wearing gloves. Now where could those clothes be? I have it on good authority the police did that forensic business on all the clothing they found.

"But there's a missing link here, Edna. No DNA, so I understand, at the scene of the crime, so just how did he do it? Tell me that?"

Edna, who rarely spoke without sounding timid, recklessly decided to choose this moment to propound a theory of her own.

"Nobody seems to have considered the possibility of suicide, do they? I mean, Mr Kerbidge had by all accounts been missing his late wife very much indeed, and he hated his stepson. He could've tied that string round and round his neck and pulled and pulled until he lost consciousness...."

Her voice trailed away. She had her back to Gladys but sensed the glare and realised she was shaking with fear. Had she gone too far? Again? It was a matter of seconds before she learned the sad truth.

"If you were a young gal I'd box your ears. Self-strangulation indeed! As you started to pass out you'd involuntarily ease the grip. Dearie me, Edna, dearie me."

Edna, who felt as if she had had her ears boxed anyway, apologised and carried on trimming, older and wiser, her mouth now sealed lest she should transgress further. But that didn't prevent her feeling that her sister-in-law might just be wrong.

* * *

Katie Pervis gave up on the article she was reading and tossed the expensive magazine on the floor.

She really didn't want a child; it hadn't been in the masterplan when they'd married.

And being pregnant would change her voluptuous figure, the birth probably condemning her to those awful stretch mark things, whatever.

Friends who had children had not left her with a picture that giving birth was one of life's joys. It sounded an excruciatingly ugly experience, painful and insufferable, not at all allied to her ideas of the enjoyment of life. Presumably you weren't allowed alcohol while undergoing this torture.

And as for Vaughan. Well, he'd never wanted kids, now he was like a dog with two tails, and was smothering her with far too much affection. What had gone wrong with the pill?

The other consideration was that she was not entirely convinced Vaughan was the father.

Would it matter? Would he be able to find out?

She just wanted to be unpregnant and return to her carefree lifestyle. Since announcing the news to her husband most of their social events, especially attending and throwing parties, had gone out of the window, for the baby's sake, he'd said. She could cheerfully kill him. And then terminate the pregnancy.

The latter thought gave her an idea.

Time to go online and make some enquiries.

At least, she mused with a wicked grin illuminating her expression, she wouldn't have to worry about murdering Vaughan, and he was, when all was said and done, her meal ticket and her bottomless cash machine.

However, in all these matters, some of the issues were about to be taken out of her hands.

* * *

Colin Nash-Perry weighed up his options.

His computerised analysis of the recent murder had fashioned three scenarios, one of which, upon close examination, looked heartily ridiculous as well as physically impossible. He dismissed the concept as computer error, whereas it was a fine example of a poor workman blaming his tools.

Perhaps strangely, he was left with two possibilities that were as close as could be to the two most recent theories expressed in the Frobisher household.

Self-strangulation or the clever and pre-planned apparent evaporation of clothing or at least anything in possession of the killer's DNA.

But Nash-Perry did not disregard the idea of self-strangulation, mainly because he Googled the notion and was horrified by the results. He clicked off the page with great alacrity, shaking with revulsion, sickened by what he saw. Nevertheless, it demonstrated that the one thing Gladys Frobisher had batted away could be achieved.

Of course, neither he nor Gladys had conferred on the subject.

In trying to put the terrifying issue out of his mind he concentrated on his other answer: clothing and the loss of DNA. One aspect of the safe removal of evidence was that it either had to be concealed where it wouldn't be found, even in an intense search, or left where it was all too obvious and thus accidently discounted by virtue of being overlooked.

There was really was no way Martyn could've destroyed it, such as by setting fire to it, as remains would've been found. So Colin decided he rather liked his clever idea that evidence, in this case probably clothing, had been discarded where the police had simply ignored it.

However, that gave him a headache in investigative terms, as he had not observed the crime scene and frustratingly had no idea where to turn now. It would sound daft explaining his theory to the police. Another amateur on the loose!

But had Kerbidge committed suicide? Well, there was clearly no note, so unlikely.

Which, in the broadest of terms, took him back to square one.

Happily Rita suggested coffee in the conservatory at this stage, so a welcome break beckoned.

"I wonder," she began, as she settled in her armchair and started munching a digestive, "if Mr Kerbidge really loved Maisie? I mean, he must've done, really, but it just seems a very odd match. And then, did she really love him, or was she truly just after his home and his wealth?"

"Something we'll probably never know, my pet," Colin replied in full patronising mode, "but from everything we've heard he certainly missed her once she'd gone, especially as he had to put up with that dozy, lazy stepson."

Rita's hand shot to her mouth. "Oh," she gasped, "and now he's killed him. But .... you see ... I was just wondering, if Michael loved his mother and held William in some way responsible for her death .... oh my ... it just doesn't bear thinking about, does it?"

"Mmm ... what was that dear?" a totally disinterested husband enquired, having tucked into the paper to the exclusion of conversation with his wife.

"Oh, nothing, dear," an exasperated Rita sighed. But the thoughts stayed with her. Could that possibly have been what drove Michael to kill? She looked at Colin and suddenly realised how easy it can be to contemplate murder, but thankfully drove such demons from her mind before she could dream of garden twine wrapped around her husband's throat.

Chapter Four

Corinne Drype was in many ways an ideal copper's wife.

Naturally nosey she wanted to know what all her neighbours and friends were up to, and in pursuing such quests often dug deeper than might be presumed polite.

Needless to say she followed this precise calling where her two teenage children were concerned and most definitely in the case of her husband. Had Henry Drype wished to divert from the straight and narrow and enjoy a brief dalliance with another woman Corinne would've been on his case from the outset.

Since she would also have formed the triumvirate of prosecuting counsel, judge and jury, and allowing for the fact Henry would not have been granted legal aid, let alone any defence, conviction and retribution would've been swift and painful and prolonged.

It did not follow that Mrs Drype was herself above suspicion.

On the contrary, her mantra was do-as-I-say, not-as-I-do, and had, by sheer coincidence, marked each of her husband's promotions by indulging in another affair. He had been a uniformed sergeant when they married and was now a Detective Chief Inspector so it will be understood that she had appreciable history in extra-marital arrangements.

So, on the one hand, she would've made a good detective and, on the other, an excellent criminal, well versed in concealing crime.

She also possessed the wisdom, and the stamina, to ensure her husband was happy, content and satisfied in their relationship as that was some guarantee that he would remain without doubts. Whether he knew or had any sort of inkling was another matter, but it appeared Corinne's efforts to make him a happy man at home were successful.

Having brought up their two offspring (the eldest was at university, the youngest had started her first job) she continued in her dutiful role as a housewife without having to worry too much about being a mother. Her time was her own. Henry provided the money, and he was earning her sort of money as a DCI. No need for her to rock the boat.

He foolishly regarded her as discreet and so often ran puzzling cases past her, revealing information the police would not normally disclose, in the hope she might come up with an angle they hadn't considered, or better still provide a plausible solution.

Generally speaking she rarely came up with the goods, but it made him feel better and allayed any doubts he might have had about her playing away. In his opinion not clever enough to hide an illicit romance.

Tonight he discussed Mr Kerbidge's fate with her.

All he gleaned from the ever eager Corinne was that of *course* Michael Martyn did it. She showed a keen interest in the knowledge that Martyn was a novelist but was unable to extract from her husband his pen name or the type of books he wrote. In her desperate thirst for information she even carted Henry Drype to bed and attempted to seduce the data from him.

It was unsuccessful as a medium for intelligence gathering, but highly successful in satisfying his lust, so, for the time being, that had to do. One objective achieved.

DS Charlie Penderfield was single and unambitious in employment, love and life. He had surprised himself rising as far as he had done, but didn't relish the responsibility of high office. He lived at home with his parents and showed no signs of wanting to fly the nest.

This distressed his mother on two counts. He was in the way, and she was longing for him to settle down with a nice girl and present her with grandchildren.

His idea of a riotous evening was to settle down with a book (his current choice was the Charles Dickens novel Little Dorrit) and listen to some Brahms or Mendelssohn or Beethoven or whatever.

Not at all how one of today's young men should behave.

She almost found herself longing for him to crawl home drunk one night.

He was blissfully unaware that DC Emma Brouding had lit a light for him, and would've been embarrassed to learn that she had rampant desires that, in her eyes, only he could satisfy.

Tonight Dickens lay undisturbed. Dvorak's 6th Symphony filled the air in a peaceable fashion as Charlie liked musical accompaniment to be in the background, particularly when he was assessing a problematic subject, and not loud enough to be a nuisance, never mind a head-vibrating row.

His was just another name on a long list of people trying to solve the tragedy at Chortleford.

His conclusions wafted around in his mind. The answer's in front of us, it's probably more obvious than we can grasp. Martyn *must* be the killer. It can't just be circumstantial. And all Drype thinks we have to do is eliminate all other possibilities – what possibilities? – and we're home and dry.

Martyn's computer records show what exactly? That he was at work in his study most of the afternoon. So what? There were gaps between the info the computer recorded, some of several minutes duration, plenty enough time to dash into the garden and slay an old man. Yet Drype thinks we can't arrest him.

If Martyn had been clever enough he'd have undone the side gate or something like that to suggest a possible means of entry for an intruder. There were no footprints other than those belonging to victim and assailant. Was Kerbidge taken out by a drone? No, it's not funny, and Martyn's getting away with it.

Charlie mused quietly on the sum of his comprehension of all things relevant to the case.

And while it all made sense – Martyn *must* be the man – it also made no sense at all.

We've missed ..... *something*, his final thought on the topic.

Corinne Drype was of the same opinion.

"You've missed something Harry. If you're asking me, DCI Henry Drype, you're missing something. What do you always say to me? When you can't find the answer you go back to the start with a blank sheet of paper and begin afresh. That's what you need to do Harry. Have a fresh start.

"I take it you can't arrest him and torture him down at the station?"

For a split second Drype thought she might be serious but a glance at her gleaming, smiling face revealed the truth, and only served to make him want her more.

DC Emma Brouding was also giving it some thought.

Unlike Charlie she was awash with the music being played at brain-damaging decibels in her local and, as she was no longer driving, was demolishing vodka and orange as if there was a forthcoming shortage and panic buying was demanded. Her friend Jackie was tackling a pint of Doombar with equal determination and the third person at their table, Kailee, wasn't going to be left behind in this drinking marathon. She was downing single malts.

Emma wasn't on duty the next day so was taking this opportunity to enjoy a girls' night out.

They knew how far they could go, each girl's maximum intake being a target rather than a limit.

A young man, known to all three, swaggered over.

"Rutting season's about to start, girls," commented Jackie, seeing him nearing their table.

"Why, it's Ms Brooding and her attendants," he exclaimed, as if revealing some hitherto well hidden secret, "and which one of you would like to decorate my bedroom tonight?"

"You're drunk or stupid or both," Emma observed, "and as you well know my name is *Brow*-ding, you animal. Now clear off." Jackie and Kailee giggled raucously and both gave the young man a few splendid if repulsive words to help him on his way. He took the hint and promptly fell over, his glass shattering and his beer soaking other drinkers.

"Drunk," bellowed Jackie with a hearty laugh to match, "You were right, Em. 'ere, did you know, 'e likes dressing up in womens' clothes." It was intended as a joke, as a means of shrivelling up any self respect the man might have left, and as the girls roared fit to bust at his misfortune a little idea locked itself away in Emma's mind. Not that she knew it then.

Not then, but later.

* * *

Gladys Frobisher was expounding her views on so-called gardening experts who, she claimed, knew little or nothing, but earned a sizeable fortune spouting nonsense.

Edna listened without comment.

They had planned to watch a DVD featuring wildlife cameraman Gordon Buchanan after their modest tea, but Gladys had been holding sway for so long it was now getting too late. The subject matter had proceeded from the murder to the government, back to the murder, on to local transport, back to the murder, and now forward to gardening expertise.

Along the way Gladys had discussed (mainly with herself) the state of the NHS, Brexit and the shocking price of vegetables, and the way products increased in price whilst decreasing in size.

Edna nodded or shook her head at various points in the lengthy discourse. Her sister-in-law didn't really want Edna to discuss anything as her opinion was of so little value, and her comments might just conceivably be at odds with Gladys's viewpoints and therefore the basis for argument.

You didn't argue with Gladys, Edna had learned that years ago, so now didn't bother.

Inevitably the one-sided conversation returned, for the umpteenth time, to the murder.

By now Edna had had enough and dared to speak.

"Well, say what you like, my dear, but my money's on suicide whether you like it or not."

Gladys didn't like it but was initially so far taken aback that her sister-in-law had uttered such words that speech deserted her completely. Her mouth moved up and down, rather like a goldfish in a bowl, but no response came.

It was as if Edna had announced that the world was about to come to an end, and should they put the lights out?

She waited patiently for the thunderclap she knew was coming, a verbal equivalent of a damn good hiding, but discovered she was in for a disappointment.

Rather than a metaphoric thrashing she was sent to her bed, or at least that was the sum total of Gladys's condemnation and resultant punishment. So the pair of them retired, Mrs Frobisher with steam escaping from every orifice, Edna with her tail between her legs.

"Still reckon it's suicide," her parting shot, but voiced only once she knew Gladys was safely out of earshot.

* * *

Rita Nash-Perry was now thoroughly enjoying the latest Glynis Parham.

The aftermath of the killing had left her with little appetite for such pleasure but now she found she could sit back and lap up the story.

She lounged on her sofa and immersed herself in the emotions of the tale unaware her husband was working his brain to a standstill trying to solve Chortleford's great murder mystery.

    Katie Pervis was also relaxing.

    She'd decided how she was going to act. No way would she let a child be a barrier to her immediate happiness and fun. Life was too good, and Vaughan could once again work his socks off to fund her lifestyle.

    Recalling the murder she did allow herself a rueful smirk, for she would inherit the property, the cars and the money should something so equally unthinkable befall her husband.

    So while Rita and Katie unwound, Emma constructed a hangover, Drype and Penderfield were pronounced to be missing something, and Edna suffered an early night for her folly, the county of Kent went on to approach midnight and the coming of a another day. And the coming of another murder.

Chapter Five

It wasn't so much that he was dead or that he'd been murdered.

It was where his body was found, and who found him that raised interest levels right off the chart.

She instinctively threw a hand across her mouth and her eyes bulged as she slumped into an armchair when the police officer gently, and as kindly as she could manage, informed her that her husband had died.

But then something curious happened.

Rita Nash-Perry thought she should be weeping and wailing and yet didn't want to. When her daughter arrived, to be followed by Dr Monroe (who had generously offered to call), the general impression was that it was delayed shock.

Tea was periodically suggested but politely refused, Rita stating that she understood brandy was particularly effective for shock. Eventually, a neighbour who had been in attendance when the police arrived, and who seemed determined to stay, was given appropriate funds and despatched to the village shop.

She returned with a litre bottle, an occurrence that briefly put a smile on the new widow's face.

Colin Nash-Perry firmly believed women should not drink and consequently his wife took very little in his presence, and a great deal more when she knew the chances of discovery were slender. Now she could have just what she wanted, when she wanted, *and* in her own lounge.

This is what they must mean by empowering women, she decided, but kept her words unspoken.

Dr Monroe tried, in vain, to intervene and supplied what he hoped would be seen as good medical advice against consuming too much alcohol. Rita's daughter, Vanessa, appealed along the lines that it would all be far worse when the physical shock took hold. Dr Monroe nodded as did the well-meaning neighbour.

Rita poured another glass in defiance. Dr Monroe, Vanessa and the neighbour shook their heads in unison, and the woman police officer joined in for good measure. Rita *sank* a good measure. And burped. Then laughed. Then was serious again, solely because she thought she ought to be.

She was far more concerned that she had no feelings whatsoever apart from a lovely warm glow induced by the spirit and having the freedom to drink it at her own leisure. Vanessa shed tears in short little spells of misery, and otherwise took tea by the gallon, hugged her mother and proffered words of comfort, and embarked on brief discourses about how wonderful dad had been.

Eventually Dr Monroe took his leave and the well-meaning neighbour remained, much to Rita's chagrin as she had never cared for her much and she was now becoming overpowering. She tried comforting her daughter as Vanessa was very upset but Vanessa was equally determined to comfort her mother, and the two became quite entangled on the sofa.

Rita suddenly arose, announced she needed some fresh air and wanted to be alone for a while, and marched into the back garden where she closed her eyes, threw her head back, and inhaled deeply and slowly.

She realised she hadn't been given the chance to talk to the police officer who had brought the news and therefore knew very little of what had happened, beyond the fact Colin's body had been found on the doorstep of Mr Kerbidge's home, and by that Michael Martyn of all people.

Then she recalled that Colin had flung himself down the stairs and bounded out of the house earlier in the day muttering something about confronting 'that killer face to face'.

God, she wondered, is that what took place?

She'd taken no notice as Colin was renowned for similar explosions. It was a commonplace occurrence in their household. When he didn't return at once she merely assumed that he'd found something else to do other than blow a gasket all over Michael Martyn.

He suffered from, and was being treated for, high blood pressure, and he had a nasty habit of locating a temper over even the most trivial of things. Choosing those moments to quietly tell him his face was beetroot red only ever served to make things infinitely worse, and the thought brought a broad grin to her own visage.

Did he have a rant and rave at Martyn and was overtaken by a heart attack?

No, the police officer said he'd been murdered. She didn't know how. It was time to find out, and she stormed back indoors where Vanessa inevitably offered her a cup of tea.

"How did he die?" she called out to the officer as she approached the lounge.

"Rita ... look, I'm sorry ... I didn't really want to..." but her reply was cut short.

"Just tell me. Simple plain English, if you please. Cold and clinical will do nicely, I'm okay, so there's no need to dress it up."

The officer, who had leaped to her feet, promptly sat down again and suggested Rita do the same.

The widow folded her arms, tried to look as threatening as she knew how, and actually tapped her foot in annoyance.

"The facts," she snarled, thinking it prudent and polite to add in a softer voice, "Just please tell me the facts."

"Well, it appears your husband called on Mr Martyn and was, apparently, according to Mr Martyn, in something of a rage. So Mr Martin told him he wouldn't have an argument with him on the front doorstep and closed the door.

He thought, so he said, Colin had gone away. Later, as he had some letters to post, he opened the front door and Colin fell in. He'd been propped up against it, so it would seem. His tie had been ... well ... well ... Rita, he may have been strangled with his own tie." Her voice betrayed her nervousness.

"Thank you," Rita responded, and poured a decent quantity of brandy.

The officer, Vanessa and the neighbour had been dreading Rita's reaction, and there was none to observe beyond the imbibing of more spirit. It was Vanessa who went to pieces over the news and everybody else got in a muddle trying to rush to console her.

Once again, Michael Martyn was in the position of having to proclaim his innocence after stumbling upon a dead body. And once again there would be no evidence to suggest anything but his guilt.

* * *

Michael Martyn was no longer a murderer, he was a serial-killer, and what were the police doing to protect them all?

Gladys uttered the old chestnut "We'll all be murdered in our beds" and Edna couldn't help feeling she might just be right.

Katie Pervis, in a particularly evil moment, wondered whether she could hire Martyn as a hit man to take out her own husband.

DCI Drype started to have doubts. Either they had a lethal maniac, Martyn, in their midst or he might possibly be innocent of both crimes. But then again perhaps he was guilty of one but not the other? Right now he needed to talk to the grieving widow, sooner rather than later, and was dreading it.

He needn't have worried. His officer called in to inform him that Rita was anything but distressed although the medical view was delayed shock. Drype felt that, knowing his luck, the shock would manifest itself all over him.

DS Penderfield was miffed because Drype was taking Emma Brouding instead of him, for the feminine touch the DCI explained.

Local reporter, Olivia Handest, was sent post-haste to Chortleford. She'd filed a story on Mr Kerbidge's murder that her editor thought noticeably pleasing and she'd published it almost without alteration, it was that good. She knew the girl was destined for greater things and she had a nose for a front page story. Olivia would not tarry long at local level, that was for sure.

Olivia had the ability to root around where angels, or at least the police, might fear to tread and had a happy knack of being in the right place at the right time. She could also extract matters some would prefer to remain hidden and by that medium had unearthed an important clue for the police to successfully follow up relating to an armed raid last year.

Ms Handest could get people to talk especially if they were reluctant to talk to the authorities, and was able to prise out information that would be denied to most, information that often had enormous value to her as a journalist.

Drype had encountered her on a number of occasions and had an open admiration for her skills which pleased her no end, not least because Drype could also be a victim of her craftsmanship. He had been encouraged to let slip small confidential snippets that he would most definitely have kept from the rest of the media. She recognised that he also appreciated her as a young woman and was able to turn that to her advantage.

There was that day, back in March, when a seemingly accidental display of her stocking tops, complete with bright red suspenders, had earned her a tidbit that gave her a headstart over the other hacks. Joy!

She might not be the loveliest flower in the garden but she knew how to show her blooms in the best light.

And right now Olivia Handest was heading for Rita Nash-Perry. As was DCI Drype.

Mrs Nash-Perry was actually pleased to see the detective as it gave her an excuse to banish the neighbour whose attentions were beginning to get on her nerves. And frankly, if Vanessa offered her another cup of tea and another lecture on the perils of drink there might well be another murder done!

She settled down, looking remarkably comfortable and pleased with herself, glass of brandy in hand, crossed legs to display how relaxed she was, and told Drype to proceed. He had hardly begun when Rita changed colour from light pink to dark red, leaped to her feet and dashed into the downstairs toilet to be sick.

Her daughter went with her to coax her, admonish her, soothe her and look after her general well-being. None of this was welcome. Drype looked at Brouding who returned his glance and did so with added despair and resignation. This was looking like being a long interview.

* * *

Olivia Handest pulled up outside Rita's to find a police presence and no chance of admission.

On to the *Log and Weasel*.

One or two of the ranks of local reporters and photographers were standing in the car park, so she drove back out and along to the crime scene, this being taped off. No joy there. There were signs of the police operating door-to-door enquiries and likewise ladies and gentlemen of the press trying to talk to whoever would speak.

Villagers generally tolerated these intrusions as there was always the chance they might appear on television or at least get their pictures in the paper. The 'fifteen minutes of fame' syndrome.

There didn't seem to be anyone in the village stores so she went in, bought a fizzy and unhealthy drink, and casually asked about Colin Nash-Perry and Michael Martyn, the latter not having been arrested this time. She collected no additional intelligence above that which she already knew. Part of that knowledge was the fact the villagers detested Martyn, especially after Kerbidge's demise, and that there was certainty about his guilt in the latest murder.

Although there was a church there was no priest. St Michael's was tended by a vicar who had three parishes under his wing and services here were held on every third Sunday in the month.

She tried the church door on the off chance but it was locked. Now she sat in her car with the engine running, tapping the steering wheel and screwing her mouth into a wide range of unlovely poses as she contemplated her next move.

Originality. That's what was required. An innovative move. But what?

A few yards from the church was the war memorial, and to the names of a handful of village men who laid down their lives in the first world war was an equally small collection of names from the second world war. None of the names was inspirational as far as the present mystery was concerned.

She looked at the church notice board. Under the name 'St Michael' some wit had scribbled the words 'patron saint of underwear' and she allowed herself a girlish giggle. Normally she didn't do 'girlish' and never in public or in any sort of company.

Leaving the car again Olivia walked round and studied some of the notices, but they lacked inspiration. Realistically, they lacked any kind of inspiration even for parishioners who might be interested in the contents.

"What you doin'?" a youngish voice intoned from behind her.

She looked round and saw a small girl, maybe ten or eleven or so, staring at her with her head tilted to one side in an enquiring manner.

"I got a cold," she announced, "that's why I ain't bin to school."

"Shouldn't you be indoors if you've got a cold?"

"Nah. Bin 'elpin' me mum, ain't I? Better than goin' school, like."

Olivia thought that the gaps in her education were showing. And if she wasn't actually diseased and laid up in bed a day at school would prove most beneficial.

"Anyways, what you doin'?" the little creature persisted. Olivia exhaled and looked purposefully at the young girl with a cold. There was surely nothing she could tell her, but the reporter's nose was already sniffing and finding a potentially interesting lead. The girl was also sniffing, as if to emphasise her ill-health.

Not sure how to start her probe Ms Handest elected to commence conversation and then simply go with the flow, follow wherever chat might take them. You never know, something extraordinary may arise.

"I'm sick too," she lied, "and I'm getting some fresh air. Good job my boss doesn't know I'm not lying in bed too ill to move. You won't tell her, will you?"

"You got a lady boss, then?" the little creature queried, eyes now aglow as if to illustrate she was impressed. Olivia nodded. "Wow, that's good for us girls, ain't it? What me mum always says, like."

"Why aren't you helping your mum right now?"

"Oh, she's got this man in, like, and he helps her do somefink in the bedroom, an' I have to go out and play for ages an' ages, like."

Perhaps it was as well the little creature's education was somewhat lacking. Olivia wanted to ask her name but wasn't sure she should.

"I'm Natasha," the little creature volunteered, thus removing a tricky problem from the reporter's mind. "At school, when I get asked me name, and I say Natasha, they say 'bless you' and I'm fed up with it."

"I'm Olivia and when I was at school they used to make fun of my big nose." As a hack she had become used to fibbing.

"You ain't got a big nose."

"No, but that didn't stop them saying nasty things about it."

"Man with mum, he's got a big nose. And I heard 'im telling mum he knows who killed the old man down the road." Yes, thought Olivia, everyone knows it was Michael Martyn.

"Mr Kerbidge at White Cottage?" she asked, growing bored with a conversation going nowhere.

"Nah, old man with two names. Says everyone's already got it all wrong 'bout someone called Martin somebody, cos 'e didn't kill nobody."

Approaching boredom reversed, Ms Handest's journalistic nose was starting to twitch.

"Where do you live, Natasha?"

"Just down that road over there."

"And where exactly?"

"Dunno. Fink it's called the Bitches or somefink. Summing to do with trees, mum says."

"Possibly the Birches, Natasha?"

"Yeah, that's it. 'ere, ain't you clever, Olivia?"

Yes, thought Olivia, and your mum won't be clever enough when I ask her about her caller, especially if Natasha has a father! Ways and means, ways and means...

"I'll come and see you and your mum sometime soon, if that's alright with you?"

"Yeah, whatever." Natasha's interest was waning in direct opposition to the increase in Olivia's.

The two parted.

Probably a dead end, Olivia considered, but worth a follow up. Worth a follow up.

* * *

Drype and Brouding sat quietly, side by side, rarely glancing at each other. The DCI was tapping his fingers on his legs.

"Excuse me, sir, I wouldn't do that; looks like impatience." Drype turned his head slowly towards the DC who had just dared, just *dared* to correct him. He spoke almost in a whisper.

"That's because I'm impatient. If the wretched woman hadn't knocked back an immoderate amount of brandy we'd be talking to her now." But Emma Brouding was clearly on a roll.

"Losing a loved one is one thing, having him killed in cold blood is another. She's terribly shocked." As an afterthought she added, "Sir." Neither party looked at the other. Drype spoke again.

"Well, thank you, Constable, for pointing out my shortcomings and admonishing me for my insensitivity. I appreciate your efforts to make me a better person," and raising his voice to accentuate his sarcasm, "and a better police officer but perhaps you'd now like to hold your *tongue*." They still hadn't looked at each other.

"Sorry .... sir," came the meek response. At that juncture Rita and Vanessa emerged, the former looking worse for wear, and her mood was not improved when her daughter said she'd go and make some tea. Through gritted teeth, and speaking one word at a time, Rita replied:

"No .. thank .. you .. but .. please .. ask .. our .. guests." Exasperation was clearly her companion. Quickly Drype rose and declined the offer on behalf of himself and Emma and then sat down again. Vanessa went off to make herself a drink and Rita took her lead from Drype and sat opposite him, reclining in the armchair trying to focus blurred eyes.

She swayed slightly seeing two Drypes and three Broudings. Gradually, and with much effort, she managed to resolve the picture into one Drype and a slight shadow, and two Broudings. That would have to do.

"Mrs Nash-Perry, Rita, I know this is a bad time for you, but we really do need to know about your husband's movements prior to his untimely ... his untimely ..."

"Death," said Rita. "Untimely death, Chief Inspector. There, it's easy to say. Now, repeat after me, death." There were now three Drypes in her field of vision, a situation she found faintly amusing, and allowed a twisted smile to decorate her face. Three Drypes and one unclear Brouding, or perhaps that should be one Brouding with rough edges. And with that observation she laughed out loud. Drype pressed on regardless.

"I'd like to know what his mood was, what he was doing before going out, if he mentioned going to White Cottage, that sort of thing. And if you know it, roughly what time he departed."

Vanessa walked in with two cups of tea.

"Made you one anyway, mum..." And that only served to increase Rita's mirth but her laughter subsided rapidly as she leaped from the chair, hand across her mouth, and dashed into the toilet.

Her daughter stood with a cup of tea in each hand and apologised. Drype rose.

"I fully understand, Vanessa ... I may call you Vanessa?" Vanessa nodded. "We'll pop back in a bit if we may. I have other enquiries to make in the village and it will give your mother time to recover."

She put the cups down and showed them out.

"Here's my card," he said, "My mobile is on there. Please feel free to call anytime, and once again our condolences on your sad loss. I am so sorry the police have had to bring you and your mother such awful news."

"Was that sensitive enough?" barked the Chief Inspector loudly once they were back in the car.

"I've apologised, sir," admitted the Detective Constable, but she realised her boss was going to let the incident fester from now to eternity, and there would be further references to it throughout her career. Damn, she thought, why are men so stupid?

Chapter Six

DCI Drype and Ms Handest arrived at the Nash-Perry household at the same time.

Despite undoing the top two buttons on her blouse and leaning forward so that he might enjoy a greater vision of the treasures lying not-so-hidden therein, and using her eyes and lips in a most suggestive style, her request to sit-in on the interview was denied. But she knew it would be.

Handing him her card she winked seductively and said "Call me." He took the card, smiled knowingly, and slipped it into his inside jacket pocket. "And here's one for Mrs Nash-Perry."

He even took that card and placed it in the same pocket without any intention of passing it on.

Vanessa, having offered her mother and Drype the now traditional greeting of an easily refused cup of tea, took herself upstairs and out of their immediate environs. He hadn't brought Emma this time so they had the lounge to themselves.

Rita was now quite different, but showing no signs of distress or shock.

She'd changed her clothes, smartened up her curly hair, put on a little enhancing make-up, and now sat cross-legged opposite Drype who was, if truth be told, admiring the view.

"I have made some notes, Chief Inspector ..."

"Please call me Harry."

"As I was saying, er ... Harry, I've made some notes based on the questions you tried to ask me so that I don't forget anything. So please ask away, and you can take these notes with you if that's any help."

"Thank you, Rita, that would be excellent and I am very, very grateful for the time you've taken to do all this. It really is appreciated."

He felt wonderfully relaxed in her company. There was nothing to suggest an overdose of brandy had badly affected her (although he hoped she had no intention of driving), and equally she had overcome the sickness that had, at least temporarily, brought an end to the drinking.

Henry Drype was warmed with her presence. His whole body was stirring and he knew he shouldn't let it. Unbeknown to him Rita was also experiencing stirrings as she found him a most handsome man.

"Are you married, er ... Harry?" she blurted out. Taken aback he swiftly assumed that her question related to bereavement, whereas she sought the knowledge for a completely different reason.

"Well, yes I am," he replied, trying to sound utterly sympathetic.

"Is your wife understanding about your job? I mean, you have to keep long hours sometimes, don't you? Oh .. oh .. I'm sorry, Harry, I shouldn't be asking questions like that. Where are my manners? I'm so sorry..."

"No, no, no, please don't apologise, that's perfectly alright. In fact I believe my wife, Corinne, is very understanding. At least she knows I'm not straying from the matrimonial straight and narrow." He followed this with a nervous little laugh, extinguished at once.

He had no idea whatsoever why he added the last line, but somehow it seemed important so he had no regrets, especially when Rita chuckled mischievously, and did so for only a second or two, then looked down at her lap, almost embarrassed.

Moving on, Drype asked questions about Colin, received pleasant, succinct and largely accurate answers, and made some notes of his own to accompany Rita's handiwork.

"I think he was obsessed with Mr Kerbidge's death, y'know," she added, "and it might be worth your while to look at his computer. I'll take you upstairs to his study if you like?"

"Yes, please, Rita, but what exactly did you mean by obsessed?"

"Well, he was always getting bees in his bonnet. He had high blood pressure and he allowed things to niggle and upset him and make him very, very annoyed. When he was angry he was angry, if you follow me, er, Harry." Harry did. And then he followed her upstairs.

Seated at the terminal he located and opened a file named 'Kerbidge Murder' and he and Rita were amazed by what they found. Such detailed information, so many workings out and cross-referencing.

"See, Harry, see what I mean? A bee in his bonnet, an obsession. I used to ignore him as much as I could." Harry saw alright. Colin had an unusual hobby, that was for sure! And he saw the conclusions, first relating to self-strangulation and then to 'hiding' clothing where it could be easily seen! He also made a mental note of the words 'how on earth would I explain this to the police?'

Rita had something in her hand.

"If you want, Harry, copy anything you like onto this memory stick." Harry copied the file, and they returned downstairs. Vanessa came down primarily to offer them cups of tea. Refused politely as usual.

"You've been very helpful, Rita, and I truly appreciate what you've done given the most dreadful shock you've had, and, of course, in knowledge of your terrible loss...."

"It was a pleasure, Harry, and I don't think I loved Colin, y'know." This revelation came as an absolute surprise to Drype. Rita continued:

"I may have loved him once, but I haven't loved him for a long time, not true love, y'know, not that deep, gloriously binding love that grows so beautifully over the years. Far from it, Harry.

"In the end he was just there, with his aggressive moods. Oh, you should've heard him going on about those who opposed Brexit. Wore me out, it did. So I just started completely ignoring him."

"Not a man for intimacy. I read a lot of romantic fiction, Harry, and I love it because of the release it gives me from my humdrum existence with Colin. I'm reading the latest Glynis Parham; it moves me because it's so full of passion, so full of pain, and I can't help but feel that woman, a brilliant story-teller, a quite exceptional author, who can describe all those innermost feelings with such eloquence, must've suffered the agony and the ecstasy herself...."

"Oh God, Harry, listen to me rabbiting, I'm so sorry...."

"No apologies, Rita, I was quite moved by your own words if you don't mind me saying so." Rita blushed quite pink and looked everywhere except at his face.

Knowing the truth about Glynis Parham he couldn't resist asking if Rita was confident about Mr Kerbidge's murderer, just like the other villagers.

"I've no idea, Harry, and if he's done for my Colin then even putting him away forever won't bring anyone back, will it?"

"No Rita, that's true, but as a copper I have to catch 'em and justice has to deal with 'em as appropriate, and that's the truth. Still, better be on my way. Thanks again, Rita. By the way, the media will be after you. You don't have to talk to them, of course, and do let me know directly if any of them annoy you or pester you.

"And I'd appreciate you not mentioning anything we've spoken about in any case." Rita nodded and rose and led the way to the door.

"Would you like a cuppa before you go?" Vanessa called from upstairs.

"No he wouldn't," bellowed her mother, bursting into spontaneous laughter that spread automatically to Drype.

The laughter subsided and they looked into each others' eyes. Rita wanted to kiss him and Drype wanted to kiss her. But naturally wanting was as far as it got, and he took his leave and marched away from the house.

Rita watched him go. Sad, but resigned. Glynis Parham would've had them embracing and enjoying a fabulous awe-inspiring, red hot steaming kiss, but he was married and she knew nothing would ever happen like that. Only in books, only in books she thought as she slowly closed the door.

Henry Drype sat in his car thinking many things. One of these was 'you cannot seduce a newly widowed lady'. He sighed and started the engine. As he pulled away he saw Olivia Handest draw up and he knew she'd been awaiting his departure.

* * *

DS Penderfield looked back over the transcript of the interview with Michael Martyn.

Once again, innocent until proved guilty. His story tied up right down the line as they say in TV detective series, he mused. The problem this time was that the victim was technically outside the property, up the front garden path, to which all and sundry had access, and had met his end on the front doorstep.

The photos confirmed what he already knew.

Once through the gate a visitor would be lost to view from the country lane outside the cottage. It therefore also followed that a killer could advance upon said visitor by the same path and also be invisible once on the property.

Trees, shrubs, hedges, all prevented observation. Indeed, only by standing at the gate would anyone on the lane be able to see the front door and all that might happen there.

And that's where it was so entirely different to William Kerbidge's death.

This time they hoped the killer, if not Martyn of course, would have been seen either going in or coming out of the front garden, or at least in the lane. Once they established a more accurate time of death they might be able to nail a witness.

That is where all their hopes lay. If Martyn had murdered Colin Nash-Perry it might be as close to the perfect crime as you could get. There were no hopes attached to forensics. Where it all became nasty, from the police point of view, was that the soon-to-be enriched Michael Martyn had now hired what Penderfield called a 'smart-arse lawyer'.

Or in better terms a solicitor who knew all the ropes and was skilled in making life difficult for the police.

* * *

Gladys and Edna Frobisher went in fear of their lives.

Why on earth hadn't those lousy policemen arrested Martyn and put him away?

A madman, a lunatic, a merciless serial killer was living right in their village waiting, just biding his time, before committing another heinous murder. And Gladys or Edna or both could be victims.

It wouldn't do, it just would not do. Whatever were the police up to?

Dave, the local taxi driver, had always liked Colin. They talked the same language, or rather they grumbled the same language. There was always something to be grumbled about and at extreme length, and the only mystery was how each managed to get a word in edgeways, so vociferous were the pair of them. Dave had an opinion on everything including matters he knew absolutely nothing about.

So he grumbled about Martyn as he grumbled about the police. Bad as each other.

Martha, who played the church organ and did so with little regard to the music and the composer's intentions, was beginning to have doubts about Martyn's guilt, but kept her misgivings to herself. It wouldn't do to let on that you weren't convinced about Michael Martyn.

Steve, the butcher, was often asked for his views, and was usually garrulous in reply. Now he claimed to have reached the conclusion that the police had their reasons for taking the course they were, and everybody ought to wait and see. But his words on the subject were brief, not at all the fluent Steve they knew and loved.

It was also noted that he wasn't wearing his straw boater, an essential feature of his appearance as a butcher. He normally went out of his way to look the part, being pleasantly portly and bedecked with his apron at all times, but right now he was, for some reason, shorn of his mischievous grin and hatless.

Not the Steve they knew and loved.

Keith, the newsagent, had been worried by the way Martyn was condemned out of hand for the death of his stepfather, although he gave his concerns a low profile, and he was indubitably not in favour of rushing him to the gallows now.

In due course the time of Colin's death was moved from approximate to definite and an appeal for witnesses went out. Police officers carried out a further house-to-house. Very little traffic used the country lane where White Cottage resided but there was always a chance a passing motorist, tradesman or delivery driver might have seen someone, anyone, and it was thus very important to spread the word.

The police contacted companies, such as Royal Mail, who might've had employees in the area.

Attention didn't just focus on the lane. Fifty yards to the west it junctioned with the main street which in its turn led north into the village itself. Anybody abroad on this section might have seen the killer and not, of course, appreciated the fact.

As is the way of so many of our villages the main street in Chortleford meandered and went in any direction that pleased it at the time. It twisted back and forth and rose and fell so determined was it to appear anything but straight.

Properties of varying ages and sizes and designs either clung to the roadside or lay a safe distance from it. Every now and then the presence of a narrow pavement arose but was quickly extinguished.

The village struck Drype as being as convoluted as the case.

He phoned Olivia Handest to plead for help. This was offered freely in exchange for information. Once again the DCI was not led astray, but he had no data to bargain with in any event. Happily Olivia's paper played ball and the issue was given high status on the publishing group's website and in all subsequent editions throughout the county.

"You owe me," was Olivia's closing comment to Henry Drype, and he wasn't at all convinced he wouldn't have to pay up at some future stage.

Katie Pervis was too busy making her own arrangements. Being thoughtful and considerate was not in her nature. Being arrogant and unfeeling was. She didn't care about William Kerbidge and Colin Nash-Perry, confused their names with consummate ease, and only then when she could remember any part of them.

She wasn't bothered about her husband, but was wise enough to know that she needed to nurture their marriage to ensure that he continued to love and worship her, emotionally, physically and financially. Especially financially.

A lovely dream home, a magnificent and extensive wardrobe, flash motor, expensive and exotic holidays, parties and all the social life she could wish for. No, she wasn't going to jeopardise that. And she wasn't going to curtail parts of it as a result of pregnancy. Vaughan had surprised her. She had never, for one moment, suspected he held any family designs, and had assumed he was the same free spirit as her.

But he had changed.

He was so looking forward to being a father. Damn him, she thought. He hasn't got to carry this burden and then go through giving birth. And God, neither am I, she resolved. Since he had already ruled out a full-time nanny for junior, saying Katie could rear their infant, she was quite positive that all this pregnancy nonsense had to stop.

And she'd found ways of handling that.

Meanwhile, during his leisure hours at home, Vaughan had been giving his own unique attention to the other killings. But his brain was not wired for what was basically police work and he soon acknowledged he was wasting his time. But he thought he'd go and have a chat with Michael Martyn just the same, making out he didn't believe the rumours and supported the fellow. Yes, that might do the trick very nicely.

But he was overlooking the fact that such a course of action had recently been undertaken by Colin Nash-Perry with tragic results. Happily, lightning doesn't strike twice in the same place.

Does it?

Chapter Seven

With autumn well and truly approaching it was about the time Gladys and Edna usually made their seasonal visit to nearby gardens that were open to the public. Chortleford's part of Kent was awash with such venues.

They adored Doddington Place Gardens where Gladys particularly admired the mighty yew hedges. But Edna could never wait to skirt round the outside of the house to the sunk garden and its overwhelming profusion of colour, fragrance and variety where she would undergo what could only be described as a horticultural orgasm.

The cosmos and alliums were her favourites; but it was the astonishing atmosphere conjured up by the surroundings, an exhilarating paradise of plants producing unbelievable sensations, that excited her beyond reason whatever the season.

In contrast both ladies found the gardens at Belmont emotionally peaceful places that exuded calm and led the visitor to a serene state of mind. Utterly captivating, yet simple and delightful. The kitchen garden was a must and Gladys always spoke enthusiastically about the quality of the rhubarb she purchased earlier in the year.

Both ladies gazed in awe at the prodigious trees in the Pinetum.

Gladys marvelled at the fabulous wisteria and wished she could have something so expansive and gorgeous at home, whereas Edna did not like climbers, creepers or indeed anything creepy, and that chiefly included men.

And then there was Mount Ephraim, a restored Edwardian garden that Edna loved if primarily because it hinted at a bygone and sadly long-lost era. Gladys invariably photographed the fine examples of topiary while Edna looked on is disbelief; her sister in law must by now have a library of such pictures!

They always took sandwiches and enjoyed them on a bench by the lake, a notably beautiful part of the garden, down the hill from the house.

At Godinton the herbaceous borders and wild garden were the main attractions, the latter especially in spring when the daffodils were out. And they visited the gardens they worshipped at least once in each season, spring, summer and autumn, for all four destinations presented an ever changing scene of glorious beauty and loveliness.

They gave Gladys the chance to exercise her knowledge and bestow it upon Edna who was rarely able to absorb it. This may have been just as well as Gladys was not always accurate in her plant identification, nor in her observations about their care.

All had proceeded quite well on their spring and summer visits, but the fly in the ointment right now was the Chortleford mystery, and the pair of them seemed loathe to depart the village lest they should miss some major occurrence or other.

* * *

"Sir."

Drype looked up from his morning paper and saw the ever-willing face of Emma Brouding, bursting as usual with an overdose of enthusiasm, and itching, positively itching to speak. He held back the flood for a few moments and then with a nod released the torrent he knew would follow.

"Sir, just a thought. Martyn writes very eloquently as Glynis Parham, almost as if was suffering the agony and the ecstasy, like, y'know, going through all the emotions he writes about. Just a thought, like, but supposing he's more in touch with his feminine side than we think. Supposing he wanted to get closer to being a woman than we realise.

"Supposing, y'know, all those right-on womens clothes didn't belong to his mum at all, p'raps they're his ..... sir."

Drype achieved a look of boredom and patronisation all in one effort.

"And how, pray, does that help us? How does it explain the death of his stepfather?"

"Well, sir," Emma proceeded tentatively, "maybe Mr Kerbidge, being old fashioned, couldn't come to terms with it, and it drove him crazy seeing Michael dolled up as a woman, especially if he was, well, wearing provocative clothing." Drype went to interrupt but was cut short.

"Always a possibility Martyn sometimes reminded him of his late wife .... sir. Could've unleashed all kinds of things, all kinds of demons." Emma stood in front of Drype's desk looking like a crestfallen pupil awaiting whatever punishment the headmaster might choose following her twilight of the gods style revelation.

The Chief Inspector screwed his face up as some of the possibilities travelled unchecked through his mind, not least the concept of William Kerbidge actually fancying Martyn parading as Glynis, the image of the late Mrs Kerbidge. But then wouldn't the most likely scenario have been Kerbidge killing Martyn?

Then again, there was the chance the man taunted 'Glynis' for the similarity and that drove his son-in-law to murder.

"Good point, Brouding," he announced, managing to show his annoyance at not having thought of it first.

He had developed a sound career based on the detectives' manual of motive-means-opportunity and always preferred his cases to be black and white, whereas Emma had introduced various shades of grey (so to speak) to the whole matter. But, he had to admit, she had a good point.

Well, several actually.

All that was needed now was a confession, and route one might be a full, sharp confrontation on the subject. Yet he was nervous. Martyn now had a legal eagle and if he took offence the lawyer might have the same effect on Drype as a ton bricks submerging the police officer from a great height.

Not good.

He now had two dilemmas. Confront Martyn and effectively put his job on the line or try and convince DC Brouding the concept was not a good idea.

The former was straight-forward. The latter would mean explaining himself to Emma in an acceptable manner and winning her over, and neither result seemed very likely.

He mustn't appear indecisive either so an immediate response was called for, and therefore, faced by such a conundrum, his mind was in danger of overload and a fuse was rapidly approaching.

"Would you like me to just go and have another word with him, sir? See if I can get the conversation round to where I want it to go?" Emma had saved the day. What a good idea, and if it all went nastily wrong Drype could duck most of the responsibility, saying she had acted on her own initiative.

"Well, I think talking to him, especially if you told him you were a fan of his romantic books, and gave the impression of being, shall we say, on his side, it might work, but I can't sanction a confrontation. If you pursue that course, Emma, then you're on your own if you follow me."

Emma followed him only too well.

Man of power and authority avoiding accountability: the prerogative of the male of the species.

"Thank you, sir, leave it to me. Your message received and understood..." and she was through the door before he could compose let alone deliver any reply.

* * *

Martha, who, it will be recalled, played the church organ and not to everyone's satisfaction and appreciation, was visiting the butcher's with a view to making a purchase.

Steve was now revived and in full flow cheeking Mrs Knatchbull and doing so in a saucy vein. All perfectly acceptable banter and only to be expected in the shop.

It was widely thought that customers went to the village's meat emporium for the express purpose of being belittled in that manner. Certainly Steve's wit was as cutting as any implement he had in the shop, often dry and usually funny, and clients were normally at the butt end. Occasionally a visitor would hit back with a humorous retort which would only add to the mirth.

Mrs Knatchbull was duly packed off and Martha approached the counter.

"Good morning, Steve. Do you have any ham?"

"Ham? *Ham*? What do you think this is, a butcher's?"

Martha dissolved into little squeals and giggles.

"Oh, Steve, come on, do you have any ham?"

"None of your business what I've got." More chuckles from the church organist.

Eventually a transaction was executed and ham was purveyed. It was then that Martha chanced her arm in relation to the latest murder and asked Steve for his views.

"Well, Martha, me old duck, I reckon that Martyn fella would be real daft to do someone else in when the hand of suspicion was heavy on his shoulder already over William Kerbidge. Don't see it, meself. On the other hand, *on .. the .. other .. hand*," he added, bringing a hint of conspiratorial suspiciousness into his dialogue, which he further endorsed by leaning forward and looking from side to side as if to make sure nobody else was listening, "he might just be the clever one, mightn't he? You know, gettin' away with two planned killings an' all."

And he winked.

Martha wasn't at all sure whether or not to take him seriously. But it was a thought. Was Martyn in fact a very clever murderer who could cover his tracks superbly and, having got clean away with one slaughter, found he had developed a taste and performed the trick again?

The thought sent a shudder down her spine as she left the shop.

Good heavens! If he really had a taste for it then it might take him only a matter of months to wipe out the entire village. Was that what he wanted? Chortleford all to himself?

And her shuddered spine suddenly felt icy cold.

* * *

Recently widowed Rita Nash-Perry was warming to her role as a grief stricken woman, especially where the media was concerned, and found she could produce tears to order and an assortment of stories about her relationship with her late husband that could be turned into heart melting newspaper accounts.

None of these tales was true.

Rita relied heavily on what she had gleaned from the romantic novels she'd loved, especially those by Glynis Parham, and expressed her loss in words of searing pain and excruciating emotional anguish. The actress in her rose magnificently to the surface.

Oh, how she'd wailed in agony when the police told her of Colin's brutal demise. Never again would they share those spectacular nights of passion, the tender and the furious intimacy that drove them remorselessly to greater love-making achievements.

Never again would they revel in quiet, romantic candlelit dinners, sharing love and humour and fine wines. Never again would she be able to giggle at Colin's charming little asides and risqué comments, the gentle times that warmed them and made their hearts sizzle.

How she wished it was all true. Colin didn't have a romantic bone in his body and she'd never located anything approaching a sense of humour and a desire for fun within him.

But today she was going to be interviewed by Olivia Handest and there was the chance that exclusive and detailed revelations might be rewarded with a financial compensation. So she had been busy dreaming up juicy tidbits not yet revealed to media representatives, and making sure her eyes looked red, her cheeks tear-stained. Perfect.

However, when she opened the door she was mildly taken aback to see not Ms Handest but Chief Inspector Drype on her step, and it was he who spoke first.

"Mrs Nash-Perry, Rita, I'm so sorry to turn up unannounced, but I wondered if you could spare me a moment, if it's convenient of course."

Rita's heart fluttered. What a handsome brute! She had so engulfed herself in fantasies straight from the pages of her beloved romantic novels, ready for Olivia's visit, that it was an easy transition to move into romantic mode with a tasty dish of a man wanting to enter her domain.

But, but, but, ... she quickly admonished herself, I am a grieving widow so I must play this very carefully.

For his part Drype saw the ravishes of sadness in Rita's careworn face and instantly regretted making such a call realising he was intruding at a bad time. In a senior police officer it was worrying that he could not see past the facade, recognise it for what it was, or for that matter read the signals that a hungry woman was before him.

And she wanted a meal of several courses.

"Chief Inspector ... I mean Harry .... I'm fine and you are most welcome at any time. It's not inconvenient, and besides," she added, her acting career gathering momentum, "I'm keen for you to catch the awful villain who ... who ... who ..." The words stuck in her throat as they were replaced by tears in her eyes.

Surely an 'Oscar' must be beckoning?

Her audience lapped it all up. Drype slipped through the door, closed it behind him, and took Rita in his arms and cuddled her in a most un-policeman like way, all the time muttering very concerned but patronising 'there-theres'. A listener might have assumed a small child had fallen over and was being reassured by a parent in the soothing way many parents have.

Had they but known it, they were throbbing for each other, neither having the knowledge or experience of how to move to the next stage. She was recently widowed. Drype knew it was 'bad form' and a case of no touchee-

touchee. Rita's mind was a whirl, caught up in a morass of similar incidents in her romantic novels, each having a different progress and outcome, all very confusing.

He was a married man, good heavens! And a professional officer of the law. It was out of the question.

So they settled for a sit-down in the lounge, pleased that there was no Vanessa to offer them tea.

"Rita," Drype began, allowing his passions to subside as his brain re-engaged business status, "it's just that we may have a bit of a clue and, as you're a local yourself, I thought I'd put it to you first. Y'never know, might ring a bell somewhere." He noticed the look of curiosity on the woman's face, a look that, in different circumstances, might've been mistaken for fear.

"Go on, Harry, anything I can do to help I will." Her eagerness was just a trifle too strong for a lady bereaved in such an unpleasant situation as murder, and the DCI observed the fact thinking it rather strange, but perhaps excusable.

"Well, we've had an anonymous 'phone call. Since we publicised the times we're interested in we've basically drawn a blank, and then this 'phone call. The caller appeared to be male, our experts reckon early middle age, and he said he saw a woman in a black coat in the area of White Cottage. Naturally, he didn't take much notice as it never occurred to him it might be important to do so. Well, none of us ever does, do we?

"Anyway, all he could recall was medium build, curly hair he thinks, but not sure, and he didn't see her face at all, so not much for us to go on. But the time's right. Sadly could be just a coincidence. He rang off before he could be asked any questions. Number was an untraceable mobile. We checked with the phone company. Not been used to make any other calls whatsoever and the line's dead suggesting the sim's been discarded.

"Or, of course, it could be the killer trying to put us off the scent. Now Rita, does that very, very vague description mean anything?" Rita looked puzzled or at least made a good fist of looking as if she was trying to unfathom a major mystery.

"No, Harry, it doesn't. Could be anyone really. After all, I've got curly hair, I'm what you might call medium build. But then I haven't got a black coat." And she sniggered and put her hand to her mouth by way of achieving both apology and regret for her short outburst of laughter. "But then I wouldn't want to kill the man I adored and worshipped, would I?"

No, thought Drype, what any good murderer might say, but he disposed of the indiscreet if professional thought as swiftly as it had flashed through his mind.

"Aaahh," he sighed, "but thanks anyway, Rita, and thanks for your time. I'll be on my way now. Sorry to have bothered you at this time." He rose and made for the door pausing in the hall.

"Oh, one last thing, Rita," he said as he turned to face the woman who was now close on his heels, and realising he had just uttered a line to be found frequently spoken in crime fiction from Colombo to Rebus, from Morse to Poirot. One-last-thing, and usually a deadly matter of serious consequence if crime fiction was to be believed.

"You said you didn't love Colin, hadn't done for years, and now you describe him quite differently, as a man you adored and worshipped." He watched her face betray the truth she now sought to hide.

She blushed, looked everywhere except at Drype, stuttered, babbled a few meaningless words and desperately fought to regain her composure and reach the appropriate words. A few tears were called for and, of course, she managed those with ease. A well practised woman.

"Um, Harry, well, I-er ... I was so shocked that it just hadn't struck me. I-I-I-I thought I knew I didn't love him," the words now tumbling out at a speed that would not have been out of place at Brands Hatch. "It's only now that I've come to realise I loved him so dearly, and I really did, Harry. He was my soul mate, and we shared so many precious times together.

"But, y'know how it is, what with time and all that, we just got a bit kind of stale, I suppose, and that was my first reaction to hearing my man had been brutally slain.

"It was such a shock, Harry, you must understand that. And only now do I know that I'm missing him like nobody's business. He was my rock, oh, Harry, Harry, whatever shall I do ... now?" And the tears flooded down her cheeks and soaked her blouse as Drype once more offered comfort by the medium of a snuggle.

But this was now a different Drype.

For example he now had his doubts about Rita Nash-Perry. Real doubts.

Love Colin or loathe him? He suspected she loathed him and was now presenting an act. But why?

Or *could* there be something more sinister?

One-last-thing. Gets 'em every time, he concluded, pleased with his ability to mimic the fictional master detectives. One other thing occurred to him. He wasn't sure he fancied her any more.

And Rita was no longer sure she wanted to get any closer to the officer.

He took his leave requesting she did not discuss any detailed matters with the media, one representative of which was waiting patiently in her car outside.

His request would be largely ignored.

* * *

DC Emma Brouding had not met any expected resistance from Michael Martyn and he had readily agreed to entertain a visit for a 'quick chat'. Emma had turned on the sympathetic charm and, without actually saying so (that would not have done) managed to suggest she believed his version of events.

As she walked through the now overgrowing front garden of White Cottage nerves got the better of her and she started to shake, and she was aware she was unsure of herself and how she was going to handle the situation. This was not the real Emma and she couldn't make head or tail of the way she was feeling.

And it wasn't good enough.

Here was a Chief Constable in the making; she mustn't fluff her lines and mess this up or they'd be no promotion and in all probability the sack. Was getting the sack from the police force some kind of ritual, she mused? Did they break your sword over the knee and rip your epaulettes off?

She laughed. Of course not. She didn't even have a ceremonial sword....

Too many films, she scolded herself, and permitted the thought to help pull herself together. What dislodged further progress in the direction of self re-assembly was Martyn's sudden appearance at the front door and his cheery 'hello there'.

Twenty minutes and an ice cold Diet Coke later (Michael Martyn was an attentive host) she decided on the first roll of the dice, one that required all the knowledge she had acquired from her previous night's homework.

"I very much like your romantic books, Michael, but, well, you know, being a police officer I thoroughly enjoy your crime books and wish you'd written more. They're really my scene, like, and you're such a good story teller, I can't put them down. My favourite is 'The Murder of the Kentish Maid' ... brilliantly thought out, surprise ending. Even as a copper I couldn't work it out right!

"But I suppose you prefer the romantic stuff as you've penned so much and maybe you're not, like, all that keen on crime writing." Both aspects of this approach were fabrications for she knew his real interest and by the same token considered the crime fiction rubbish, especially if the only book she'd read, the one referred to, was anything to go by. Utter tosh.

Nevertheless the ruse worked. Martyn was taken in.

"Thanks for that, Emma. I'm surprised though. I don't usually get praise for the murder mysteries and I wouldn't have expected it from a copper. But then maybe you're a special sort of detective, one who appreciates how well constructed and realistic my efforts are. It may surprise you in turn but my great love lies in that direction. I could take or leave the romantic fiction."

"But," Emma interjected quickly, lest he should run the train off her rails, "you also write in that genre quite brilliantly. I wonder, just how much do you put yourself, like, in the position of the main character. For example, in

'The Murder of the Kentish Maid' did you really want to sort of *feel* the part of Inspector Godwin? Did you allow your imagination to put you in his shoes?"

"Yes, that's right Emma. I almost play the part. I get so involved, so engrossed. I conduct the interviews in my study! Sounds daft, doesn't it, but you're right. I have to *be* the character to write the part accurately."

So far, so good. We're heading in the right direction, she thought. The next part was going to be tricky and she had to get it spot on.

"But tell me, Michael, how does that work with the romances? Do you have to adopt the mantle of your heroines?" Michael Martyn was in his stride and marching along Emma's well laid path right into her trap. She hoped.

"Yes, I have to confess that's true, Emma, and that's actually what I do. Kind of live the part, y'know. I have to psyche myself up and it's not easy. But once I'm on a roll then the words come easily....."

"Does that mean that you have to, well, pretend you're a woman, that sort of thing?" Emma interrupted nervously. Now was the moment it could all go wrong. She needn't have worried for Martyn could barely contain his zeal for explaining and doing so to what he thought was a sympathetic and appreciative audience.

Timing was essential. She had to get this right. Wrong word, wrong place and bong, she'd be out of a job. She listened intently as he described just how wrapped up he became when playing the part of one of his heroines. And then she dived in like a sparrowhawk snatching an unaware bird for its dinner.

"And do you ever dress up as a girl to get a better feel for the part?"

"Oh, yes, and .... I mean .... well, what I mean is no I don't. Of course I don't."

"I think you mean yes. And those clothes upstairs, they're yours, aren't they? You said your stepfather kept them as a memento of your mother, but you could've disposed of them after he died. They're yours, Michael, aren't they? And are they relevant to William Kerbidge's death?"

Chapter Eight

Meandering around country lanes for the most part, negotiating the inevitable obstruction of a main road now and then, it was possible to have an otherwise pleasant country drive within a reasonable radius of Chortleford.

Atop the North Downs and south of Faversham the traveller from Chortleford might easily bump into small settlements such as Eastling, Stalisfield Green, Tong, Milstead and Frinsted whilst enjoying extraordinary views of pleasant lands. Thus would they remain happily ensconced in their world of bygone rural Kent, and peacefully removed from the pains of today.

Glimpses of fruit trees, hops and oast houses would be an accompaniment to the general feeling that yes, this indeed was the Garden of England.

Keith the newsagent, and his wife, both keen walkers, took advantage of any time off they could manage to take a short drive and enjoy a stroll in Kent's unspoilt countryside, of which a great deal lay within their immediate compass.

Neither were drinkers so pubs never figured in their plans.

Marion usually made up a delicious picnic that they could easily carry in their back-packs and, armed with an Ordnance Survey map, they would thus proceed on each simple adventure.

Conversation was wide-ranging. They spoke quietly because that was their nature and they never argued, even if they held different points of view on a subject, as sometimes happened.

Having ventured to the other side of the A28 they made their way up the hill to Crundale church and parked outside. This was well-trodden territory for them. In some respects the church looked isolated and lonely yet Keith, who was by no means religious, thought it was impossible to feel lonely in this most picturesque of spots.

If he had ever wanted to believe in God he knew this was just the sort of place he might come to do so, for he sensed a warm, comforting presence about the location.

From the seat beside the car park you could look across the farmed valley below and find yourself revelling in the glories of rustic Kent.

And so they strolled hand in hand along the footpath and presently came to the woods.

They had discussed the state of the country, Brexit, rampant housebuilding in Kent, the cost of gas and electric, the joyousness of being in love (as they were), the marvels of nature, anything in fact other than the one topic they both eagerly wished to talk about.

It was as if to mention the vile crime of murder would be to sully and despoil this outstanding scenery, and to wreck their enjoyment of being alone together in this heavenly vista while sharing their own special feelings for each other.

Keith knew that if the police hadn't nabbed Martyn they had very good reason, and that reason might just be that possibly someone else was responsible. Marion felt that Martyn was probably the killer but the police lacked the damning evidence.

And whereas they might have debated the issue at home, or just about anywhere else, to raise the subject here where nature reigned supreme and where they felt so blissfully in love, would be an anathema. So Keith paused, kissed Marion gently on the lips, as if he sensed that they were both experiencing the same wariness, and they proceeded on their way through the woods without allowing murder to infiltrate a place and a situation where it didn't belong.

* * *

Vaughan Pervis believed money could open doors, as indeed it had done for him down the years as wealth mounted before his very eyes. An ace entrepreneur, his business empire had flourished and blossomed and the rewards had increased seemingly by the hour.

His business methods were not above scrutiny, however, and there had been all too many 'dodgy-dealings' and underhand arrangements that bordered on the illegal. He had taken the expression 'cash-in-hand' to the next level and found a pocketful of readies all too handy for oiling the works, for circumnavigating difficult and immovable barriers, and for obtaining information he was not necessarily legally entitled to.

He possessed (in his words) a fabulous young woman who let him take whatever pleasures he wished, and who now was going to be mother to his child. *His* child. He hoped it would be a son, yes, *his* son.

Meanwhile the visit to Michael Martyn to offer a sympathetic ear had proved a waste of time. The man wasn't interested, but had thanked him politely and not allowed him over the threshold. Right, decided Vaughan Pervis, time to dig around and see what money could buy. Somebody, somewhere must know something more and be willing to earn some dosh. Time to start asking.

He made some initial enquiries around the village but those he engaged with had nothing worth buying.

Then he thought he'd return to White Cottage for a scout round, take a really good look at the lie of the land at the house as well as in its immediate environs, and to his surprise found another man probably doing much the same. Both had crept round to the rear of the property where they quite literally bumped into each other. The man spoke.

"Funny goings on 'ere, mate, funny going ons, if you get me drift. Gor, the tales I could tell yer."

"Tell me some," ventured Pervis, simultaneously producing a thick wad of twenty pound notes which he made a pretence of studying. The other man's eyes were on stalks.

"How much you be paying for them tales, then?"

"Well," said Pervis, "I pay for the truth and truth alone, sunshine, and only for tales, as you call them, that have a value. If you want some of this, pal, the tales had better be good and true. Because, if I find they're not, I'll find you and I won't want just a refund, if you get MY drift."

The man got Vaughan Pervis's drift and related a 'tale' that he hoped would earn a financial appreciation. It did, but he was disappointed with the sole twenty that came his way and was foolish enough to remark on his disappointment. Vaughan grabbed the front of his jacket in both hands, hauled the man forward until their faces were less than an inch apart.

His face afire with menace and his speech sizzling with barely controlled rage Vaughan hissed in a quiet but vicious manner that he only paid more for goods and services that had a higher merit. He let go and walked away leaving a distressed and frightened wreck of a man to contemplate his folly of upsetting Mr Vaughan Pervis.

And resolving to get his hands on more of the cash by acquiring verifiable data that qualified as top notch in Pervis's eyes.

Armed with his newly purchased information Pervis himself headed back round to the front of the cottage and another try with Michael Martyn.

* * *

Olivia Handest was stifling a yawn.

She was only too aware Rita Nash-Perry was embroidering her stories on the scale of the Bayeux Tapestry, and fantasising about X-rated matters in a way that demonstrated beyond reasonable doubt that she had no first hand knowledge and personal experience of such blissful pursuits.

For a few seconds she actually felt sorry for Rita. Olivia had tasted the fruits of passion and found them to be much to her liking, so much so that tastings had often developed into feasts and banquets, and she was saddened that Mrs Nash-Perry had clearly been deprived of all she was describing.

But what did interest Ms Handest was the revelation about the woman in a black coat.

Now what was DCI Drype doing keeping that to himself, particularly when Olivia's paper had probably prompted the anonymous call?

Unfortunately, Rita was unable to avoid embellishing even that story and, believing nothing would come of it, gave forth 'exclusive' data that were far removed from the truth.

"According to Drype," she explained, "the woman was wearing black patterned tights. Well, a man would notice things like that, wouldn't he? Now bright red shoes ... bit of a colour drama there, I would say, but perhaps I'm old fashioned. High heels. Was walking very elegantly, apparently, y'know, very erect. Small black handbag tucked under her left arm. The caller said she appeared quite shapely, but not sure how he knew that, y'know, as she had a coat on.

"All grace and sophistication. Bound to turn a man on. Small wonder he remembered so much! But that's all the Chief Inspector could tell me. Oh no, that's not true. The caller said her short, curly hair had a way of bouncing on her shoulders as she walked. I think that's another man thing, isn't it? Colin always liked the way my hair bounced like that."

Olivia made copious notes.

Her editor would be well pleased. Yet happier still if Olivia could find a 'suspect'.

Then break the story ahead of the rest of the field and before the police announced it! Pure magic.

But first how to keep her 'exclusive' exclusive. Money was going to have to change hands, that was for sure.

"Have you told anyone else, Rita?" she enquired and received a shake of the head in reply followed by a more detailed verbal response.

"Drype had only just left here when you arrived, Olivia, so no, you're the first person I've told." Ideal, thought the journalist, now let's try my hand at negotiations.

She found Rita extremely canny when it came to negotiations, despite being pretty cute about such issues herself. In fact, Rita showed all the signs of forgetting her role as a heartbroken widow so enthusiastically did she tackle discussions.

It was a fair while before agreement was reached by which time Mrs Nash-Perry was acting anything but a distressed recently bereaved woman.

Olivia Handest noted the coldness and reflected on the woman's behaviour, which had become positively ruthless in the pursuit of gain, and, being a wise young owl, concluded that her interviewee had probably been economic with the truth possibly to the extent of making some of it up.

Nevertheless, she'd make a good story out of it, stitching the widow up at the same time by making her look like a brazen hussy, bearing in mind she now possessed one piece of intelligence the police had not released.

With the latter in mind Olivia decided her next port of call would be Natasha's mum.

* * *

Gladys and Edna were getting on with their lives feeling those lives were exceedingly precious given a serial killer was on the loose, or at any rate too close for comfort at White Cottage.

Otherwise it was business as usual.

Edna was trying hard to follow instructions as Gladys embarked on a little DIY. She was moving a kitchen cupboard from one wall to another and thus far had successfully removed said object ready for repositioning. Edna couldn't do a thing right, as Gladys explained to her over and over.

Finally, she wasn't supporting the weight of the cupboard correctly as Gladys undid the last screw and the cupboard freed itself from the wall and overpowered her sister-in-law.

There was a little squeal, a cry of 'help me' and Edna toppled backwards onto the floor with the cupboard on top of her chest.

Without thought or consideration for Miss Frobisher's plight Gladys set about delivering a verbal barrage of condemnation, listing all the tasks Edna had failed in that morning, from incorrectly plumping up the pillows on her bed to her inability to execute the most simple orders in this latest exercise.

"Help me …. *please*" a little voice whimpered, and at last Gladys relented and extricated a relieved Edna who further blotted her copybook by saying she wasn't going to help any more.

"Edna," Gladys began, hands on hips, eyes piercing into those facing her, "when you were a little girl were you not spanked for being stupid?" At long last Edna decided to fight back.

"You silly woman, Gladys. Do you think I really wanted to end up on my back covered by a cupboard just to annoy you? The trouble is I don't think you could ever have been spanked at all. You must have got away with murder as a child….."

The words shocked both of them.

Got away with murder. Yes, just like Michael Martyn was doing.

Once again fear united them and they enjoyed a tearful reunion in the middle of the floor, hugging, weeping, apologising, wailing and professing undying love for each other.

A nice cup of tea sealed their togetherness and provided the basis for bonhomie which didn't last.

As soon as Gladys started drilling the wall Edna was in trouble again and it was all her fault Gladys was drilling in the wrong place, despite the fact her sister-in-law had said and done nothing at all.

Business as usual.

But still the threat of a serial killer hanging over them. *Whatever* were the police doing?

One police officer was doing rather well and about to unravel one mystery, or at least make more sense of it.

Emma Brouding was in Martyn's lounge and unaware two men, one of whom was Vaughan Pervis, were lurking outside. In any case she had a more important matter to attend to right now.

* * *

Emma was sitting on an armchair, feeling awkward but determined to see this through.

She watched the wreck of the man opposite, curled into a ball, sobbing and making a dreadful noise, suffering all kinds of anguish that she couldn't imagine, suffering pain that could be neither extinguished nor relieved, and she felt sorry for him.

Sorry for him as a fellow human being, for she never doubted what she was seeing was genuine, but keeping a professional aloofness that would be necessary to maintain her status as an upholder of the law.

The kind, caring woman in her wanted to help ease the pain, perhaps with a hug, but the police officer in her had to stand to one side and somehow be separate from all this.

It was a long time before either spoke, and then it was Emma. And as quiet as a church mouse.

"Michael, tell me what happened. Please." He looked up and his reddened eyes pleaded for an end to his torment and his endless nightmare. Emma saw this and seized the moment.

"Please tell me. You have no idea how much better you will feel. All this terrible pressure gone. This enormous burden you've been carrying; release it, Michael, release it, be free." He slowly nodded as tears continued to swamp his face, his chin and his breast.

"Do I need my solicitor," he whispered. Oh God no, thought Emma, not that.

"No Michael. This isn't a formal interview or anything. Just a chat. I'm here to help. Please let me help, Michael. Tell me your story and just take your time. You will feel so much better I promise you. Please trust me." She now felt awful knowing that not all her words could be true, but that was how the police got things done, wasn't it?

"If we have to go to the police station then you may want your solicitor, and that'll be fine." She tried to sound reassuring but thought she might have failed.

"Okay," he said, his voice steadying. "I'll tell you everything."

And he uncurled his form, sat back on the sofa, and began, slowly, carefully, quietly.

"I loved my mother. It was she who encouraged me to write. I was getting nowhere in life, one dead end job after the other. For a hobby, I suppose, I started writing in my spare time, but I sent a short story to a womens magazine, writing as Glynis Parham, and they bit my arm off.

"So I had no trouble getting my first book published. Mum was over the moon. There's no Dad, by the way. Ran off soon after I was born. I seem to have that effect on people." And he managed a weak laugh, Emma a weak smile.

"Mum had a job and we just about got by. Lived in a flat in Strood. Nothing much. And then she met William and our lives changed. I knew it wasn't a good idea but, do you know, she told me she did it for me. I told her she was stupid, deserved a life of her own and all that kind of thing, but she hugged me, told me how much she loved me, and that we'd be okay if we stuck together.

"Eventually, then, they got married and we came to live here. A lovely cottage in the country. He was batty for her. Well, she made sure he was. Turned it on for him and, do y'know Emma, she never stopped her act long after they were wed. She kept it all up for me.

"I think William realised what was going on but he loved her beyond words and eventually agreed to reflect the situation in his will. I would inherit either way. If mum died first, which she did of course, I would get her half share, and if he died, even if mum was still alive, it would all come to me.

"For the love of mum and mum's memory he never sought to change his will when she passed away. That's to his credit, poor old devil. We never hit it off, y'know, he never really came to terms with me writing romantic nonsense and under a feminine nom-de-plume, did you ever.

"At first I used to annoy him by putting on some of mum's clothes and strutting around the house pretending to be overly effeminate, if you know what I mean. Drove him wild, absolutely crackers, but mum just laughed at him and that made matters worse.

"But gradually I found that I liked dressing up, liked being a woman. So on the quiet I got myself clothes that I wanted and dressed in those when I was writing as Glynis. Really turned me on.

"Mum found out and told me it was alright, and it was she who helped me with make-up and that sort of thing. Then she died. William and I shared heartbreak but had nothing else in common. In a funny sort of way I blamed him for her death.

"But now I was co-owner of White Cottage and he couldn't throw me out. It wasn't even one of those uneasy truces. I kept a few of mum's clothes which I put on to irritate him. He'd go blood red in the face with rage and order me to take them off.

"I used to tease him then. Say things like, oh alright then, give us a kiss, saucy. Made him worse.

"The afternoon he died I fancied a cuppa, like I said, and thought I'd offer him one. Of course, I was still dressed as Glynis. He got in a rant, suddenly wrapped the twine round his throat and threatened to kill himself. I didn't believe he'd do it, so told him to do whatever he wanted and came back indoors to finish making the tea.

"I happened to look out the kitchen window and there he was, lying there. I dashed out and knew he was dead and I panicked. I knew if I touched him or anything it would look as if I'd killed him, and there'd be evidence, DNA or whatever. I never killed him. Nobody did. He did himself in.

"Maybe he didn't intend to but perhaps he lost consciousness before he could loosen the twine. I don't know. But I just panicked, that's all Emma.

"I'm so sorry, I'm so sorry...." and his weakened voice trailed away as the sobs returned, his head sinking into his heaving chest.

In due course he murmured something about Nash-Perry which she didn't quite catch, but he did then emphasise that he hadn't killed him either, reiterating that Colin arrived on the doorstep for an argument and he closed the door on him.

"He was alive when I shut the door. I thought he'd gone away, honest to God, and I had nothing to do with his death. Didn't see or hear a thing."

Later, much later, and after Emma had phoned in, they gathered up their things ready to go to the station. Nothing could've prepared either of them for what happened next.

* * *

The Birches.
That's the one, thought Olivia Handest.
There was a man working in the front garden and Olivia hoped he wasn't the gardener. Natasha's father would be much better for Ms Handest's purpose.

"Hi there," she called out, waving her press card loosely in the direction of the man. "Olivia Handest, from your local rag. Can I have a word, please?" The man was sick and tired of the media coming round asking questions, but he needn't have worried.

The cunning reporter had only one objective in mind and that was to establish that Natasha's mother either had a husband or a significant other. She merely commented on how friendly and lovely the girl was and how Olivia just happened to be passing and thought she'd see where Natasha lived, and duly received the confirmation she sought. The gardener was dad.

She went swiftly on her way. No need to arouse suspicions. Call back when dad's out. Now let's see about finding a woman who fits Rita's description. Although she had seen through Rita's deceit when it came to affairs matrimonial strangely enough it did not occur to the intrepid journo that the woman had similarly misled her with the information about the curly-haired lady she now hunted.

So Olivia Handest was immediately at a disadvantage and it was no surprise that chatting to locals produced a zero output. Nobody matching her plentiful notes came close in the memories of those she spoke to. Steve the butcher jokingly remarked, much to the amusement of customers in his shop, that the description actually fitted Mrs Nash-Perry herself, not that he or any of his clients then present could recall seeing her dressed like that.

A frustrated reporter left the shop having declined to purchase today's special offer, rib-eye steak at an incredibly low price. Even for a well paid hack the 'low' price was anything but. She sat in her car, once again screwing up her face in a wide variety of poses as she pondered the enigma and tapped the steering wheel with her fingertips at frequent intervals.

Brain, brain, brain, come on, work, damn you, she pleaded in silence.

There was a tap at the window.

Natasha!

"Hello Natasha, still off sick?"

"Yeah, now dad's gone to work and the bloke's come round to help mum in the bedroom, and I'm fed up. I get shoved out when I'm not well. It ain't fair."

Perfect time for a visit, reasoned Ms Handest, but the fly in the ointment was Natasha wandering the streets in possession of a cold, real or imagined. Then she had a bright idea. Give her some money, point her in the direction of the shop and from there in the opposite direction to home.

Chapter Nine

DC Emma Brouding let out a short scream and allowed her professionalism to stifle it before it could vibrate the windows of White Cottage.

As she opened Michael Martyn's front door a body, which had been propped up against it in the sitting position, fell into the hall.

Instinctively she felt for a pulse (there was none) and placed her cheek close to his face in the hope of detecting breath. In that moment she saw the livid red and purple marks on the man's neck and realised she was checking out a corpse.

She phoned in. An ambulance was on its way, no doubt hotly pursued by DCI Drype. She performed CPR on the body but it was an act executed without hope and equally without response, and she abandoned her efforts. Besides, she didn't want to disturb a crime scene.

Slowly her own body lay back against the door jamb and she felt as if she wasn't aware of anything, not part of life at all, not even on planet Earth.

Overhead some starlings flew past seemingly on some urgent mission and she wished she could join them, just for an hour or two maybe. Perhaps manifest herself as a starling merely to find out what it was all about and to experience that freedom, that ability to take wing and fly, and fly, and fly for hours if need be.

She could hear emergency sirens in the distance and she wanted to fly away right now.

Looking at the creature in front of her, presumably strangled to death, she knew she was part of a world she wished didn't exist in such a form. A world where death could be meted out so easily, where a precious life could be taken by someone who had no right, no right at all to do so. She was suddenly conscious of Martyn behind her.

"Can't pin this one on me, can they, Emma?" he said softly and quietly.

"No," she said with great resignation. "Any idea who it is .... was?"

"Yes," replied Martyn, then adding a lengthy pause for dramatic effect, "...... it's Pervis, Vaughan Pervis."

* * *

"I'd like to speak to the man, please, the one you keep in your bedroom."

Olivia Handest looked and sounded hoity-toity, exactly the effect she wanted to produce.

"What?" bellowed Natasha's astounded mum.

"The bloke who comes to service you in your bedroom"

"What?" came a replica bellow.

"Look, don't let's mess about. There's two ways we can handle this. Let me talk to him and I'll hush it all up, like, no words to anyone from me. Or I can go to the police right now and spill more beans than your husband can ever hope to eat at one sitting."

"Okay, okay," Natasha's mum responded after carefully considering the situation and more particularly the position she now found herself in.

"No names, no pack drill, Mrs doo-dah. Don't want your names. Just a chat with the bedroom man and then I'm on my way, out of your lives forever."

Convinced, because that was all she could be, Natasha's mum led the way to the lounge and said she'd send the 'bloke' down.

He arrived in an ill-fitting dressing gown which Olivia assumed belonged to Natasha's dad.

Cutting to the chase Olivia asked what she hoped would be her one and only question.

"Natasha led me to believe you may have seen Colin Nash-Perry's killer. Even if you don't know who it is, just give me all the clues, right?"

Bedroom man sank into an armchair.

"I was driving here and I saw Colin on his way to White Cottage, not that I knew where he was going then. We're friends from way back when. I tooted and waved but he ignored me. Not far behind him, well, maybe a hundred yards, was his missus. Rita.

"Going back from here, I saw her alone coming back. Just a bit of coincidence, that's all. What I said that Natasha overheard was just a bit of gossip, that's all. Just coincidence, but put my own slant on it, if you like. I wanted to suggest, light-heartedly, that I thought I might know who the real killer was. I wasn't being serious. It doesn't prove anything, does it?"

"How was she dressed?"

"Black coat, as I remember it, that's it."

"Thank you, Mr Bedroom man, that'll do nicely. Now I'll be off. Don't worry. You secrets are safe with me. I'll let myself out, no need to disturb Natasha's mum. I expect she's waiting upstairs for you to disturb her in another way...." And she was gone.

* * *

Edna Frobisher was in trouble.

That was her normal and accepted status.

She hadn't actually done anything wrong, it was simply that Gladys kept her in her place largely by the expedient of letting her know most of the things she was doing were wrong, even if they weren't. Praise was a rarely bestowed gift, and always delivered in a patronising fashion designed to belittle.

On this occasion Edna had once again put her head on the block and suggested, nay insisted, that there was always the possibility Mr Kerbidge had taken his own life, and Gladys was beside herself in damning her sister-in-law in a very wordy and vigorously conveyed tirade.

Here was a prime example of Edna being absolutely correct but in Gladys's eyes totally wrong and therefore worthy of a savaging. It was just that neither of them knew the truth that Michael Martyn had revealed to DC Brouding, and, naturally, there would always be an element of doubt. The confession didn't clear the man completely, but he was right that he couldn't possibly be in the frame for Vaughan Pervis.

That just left the murder of Nash-Perry.

Did Bedroom man possess a positive clue or was it pure coincidence?

Drype looked along the path to White Cottage. Gravel, not a good home for DNA and footprints, and beyond that a tarmac road complete with some fine examples the now infamous car wrecking Kentish potholes.

He'd found one himself.

He spotted a large crater at the last moment, managed to pull to the left of it where he located another one lying in ambush, and felt as it all his internal organs had been utterly re-arranged so shuddering was the impact and effect on his car. He looked in the mirror to see if any of his teeth required re-siting back in his mouth, concluded none did, and drove on at a vastly reduced speed to the crime scene.

Via one more bone jarring pothole.

He noted that at some point in ancient history someone had painted white lines around this one preparatory to repair. The lines were almost totally faded from view so presumably the people sent to mend the defect hadn't arrived.

Maybe they had been lost many years ago and now, like the Flying Dutchman, were condemned to forever roam the lanes of Kent with no hope of returning home. Or filling in a pothole.

As far as Michael Martyn was concerned his version of events might have to be good enough and acceptable as there was no way of proving he murdered Kerbidge. He couldn't have strangled Pervis while he was talking to a police officer, and that left the death of Colin Nash-Perry which even now Olivia Handest was trying to clear up with the merry widow, armed, as she was, with crucial information.

Martyn was on his way to the station to be interviewed by DS Penderfield in the presence of Ms Smart-Arse lawyer. So there was going to be little point trying to pin much on him at all other than wasting police time, and maybe trying to pervert the course of justice. Ms S-A-L might do her best to persuade the police not to proceed with the latter.

He was still firmly in the picture for Nash-Perry, but Drype was only too clear there was now at least one other murderer to be apprehended. Emma was on her way to visit yet another widow who was blissfully oblivious to the way the hand of fate had now struck.

* * *

"Just wanted to double-check a couple of details, Rita. Could've phoned but at my paper we like the personal touch, and after all you've been through we appreciate you would probably prefer a visit." Rita nodded and thought of the money and nodded again.

Olivia was softening up her victim but she still couldn't prevent herself diving in at the deep end.

It was her nature. No time for sensitivity or charm, no time for small talk, no time for a gentle and mellow approach to further put the unsuspecting person off their guard.

"When you followed Colin to White Cottage did you intend to kill him or was it spontaneous? You were seen going and coming back, Rita, so no need for pretence."

Rita sat open mouthed and for once wished her daughter was on hand, even with a nice cup of tea. But she regained her composure, gave herself time to think straight and came to an important conclusion.

The reporter could not have the sort of information she was implying so was probably trying it on, ready to observe and assess the reaction, ready to jump on any dubious aspects in Rita's retort. And surely she would've taken positive intelligence to the police? Perhaps she still would. No matter. Brazen it out.

"I loved my husband dearly, his loss is unbearable, and your comments are, quite frankly, intolerable. We may have an arrangement, Olivia, but how dare you now accuse me of this horrible, horrible crime." And the tears, summoned to order, saturated her eyes and her face and made their way southwards.

"Just wanted to see your reaction, Rita. Thank you. I'll leave it at that. Sorry to have upset you. I'll be on my way. Sorry again."

But she wasn't sorry at all. She was now convinced by Rita's reaction that the widow was guilty. Now, how to prove it and land a scoop for the paper, especially while the police were treading water and getting nowhere.

"Oh, there was one other thing, Rita. Is your name an abbreviation?" Mrs Nash-Perry made a dramatic show of drying her eyes, blowing her nose and trying to compose herself, and the experienced Ms Handest recognised it for what it was.

"Yes, it's Margareta, and that's an e at the end, not an i."

"Thanks again, Rita, and I am so sorry, but I had to ask as someone told me they saw you not far behind your husband going in the direction of White Cottage and then later apparently coming back."

"Well, it wasn't me. I didn't go out. And, as I told DCI Drype, I don't have a black coat."

"No, well I understand that now. Sorry love."

Margareta, with an e at the end, not an i, wondered how Olivia could've acquired such knowledge and not reported it to the police unless, of course, she was deliberately making it up. It had been such an unsavoury meeting and Rita had the first pangs of regret at entering into a compact with the paper merely for financial gain.

* * *

"It is important to my client's career and his livelihood that details of the names he writes under are not made public. How can we avoid that, Sergeant?"

Ms Gorling-Parter was sitting next to the snivelling Michael Martyn and had been busy making DS Charlie Penderfield's life especially difficult.

"It won't be up to me....." he began, only to suffer an immediate interruption.

"Who then?" barked Ms Gorling-Parter. Charlie looked at her. An attractive young woman, not that such pleasant aspects were of much interest to the Detective Sergeant. A nice figure, dazzling brown eyes that were boring into his, but black lipstick! Black lipstick, black liner right round her eyes, and a ring through one side of her nose. An odd combination for a man like Charlie Penderfield to come to terms with, although he assumed it was simply fashion.

"Not me, and that's as far as we can go on the subject in this interview, I'm afraid." He felt afraid alright, and not as confident as his words and their blunt delivery suggested. Happily the solicitor let the matter rest with a straightforward statement.

"I'd like it noted, if you please, that my client wishes, in the strongest possible terms, to protect his pen names as his livelihood is at stake. His livelihood, Sergeant." And once more her eyes flashed and sank their gaze deep into Charlie's brain and penetrated every barrier his soul might have. Some woman, he mused.

She's ripping me apart just by looking at me! It's as if she knows everything I'm thinking, can see my mind working, and thinks she can influence me by taking me over. I'm in danger of becoming a robot, a zombie, and I'll not let it happen.

"Noted, Ms Gorling-Parter," was all he could say, but he felt that in all probability she knew all the things he might have said, and it made his blood run cold.

"Now, can we move on to the death of Colin Nash-Perry, please?"

"If you must. So start by providing all the evidence you have that my client committed said murder."

Charlie sighed inwardly, knowing this was going to be far from easy, and even further from enjoyable. *What I joined the police for*, he reminded himself in a sarcastic and wearied vein.

Another police officer feeling weary was Henry Drype.

This time no murder weapon. What had Pervis been strangled with? Colin Nash-Perry had perished by the medium of his own tie which had been left wrapped tightly around his neck. William Kerbidge might have died by his own hand, but the garden twine was still in situ. This time there was no sign of a killing device although it looked as if it might have been another tie, or rope of course.

The doctor wasn't sure and it was going to be up to forensics and the post mortem to produce a more positive suggestion. Meanwhile officers had started a fine-tooth search of the garden and the areas beyond. Just in case.

His phone rang.

"Yes?" he snapped, believing it to be nobody important.

"Harry, is that you? It's Rita. I wondered if there's any chance you could pop round sometime soon. I need to speak to you urgently." Drype's attitude changed upon the instant and a smile appeared on his worried face, supported by a warm glow inside.

"Hello Rita. By marvellous coincidence I'm in Chortleford right now and will be able to call later, if that's convenient. I'm really tied up right now."

"Harry, that'd be great. I'll be in all day so just show up when you can. Be pleased to see you."

The call ended with the usual shared pleasantries and Drype set about his work with energy anew.

In the meantime Emma Brouding had been progressing a far less pleasant task but with what proved to be a curious and surprising outcome.

* * *

Interview over, DS Charlie Penderfield was escorting Ms Gorling-Parter from the premises.

"Tell me," she said, "do you have a girlfriend, Sergeant?" It took him completely by surprise. He was at once suspicious of her motives in enquiring.

"Sorry to sound rude but it's none of your business." He was bristling and ready to fight.

"No, sorry, that was a little blunt. I was going to say this. If you haven't, and it would be most imprudent and improper to ask before this business is over, I'd like to take you out. Perhaps we could share a romantic meal somewhere, or I could always take you home and prepare something very special to your liking.

"I have cosy accommodation in Chatham docks, y'know; overlooking the water. A very romantic setting."

To begin with Charlie had never thought of any part of Chatham as being in the least romantic, although he was aware there had been some excellent new developments, and there was always St Marys Island beyond. The town had presumably improved since the days of its naval associations.

Secondly he was now confronted by a solicitor who wanted to date him, a solicitor who, until just a few minutes ago, had been happy to bait him. Now she was soliciting he thought, and allowed his amusement at his own humour to display itself in a slight grin which Ms Gorling-Parter noticed and believed to be a show of interest.

"My name's Angelique, by the way, and yours is Charlie, is that correct?"

Charlie was stunned. Shocked. Surprised. Astonished. Amazed. He spluttered in response.

"Y-y-y-yes, Charlie it is … er … Angelique. That's a nice name … er … Angelique."

"Yes, and there's much, much more to discover about me, if you've the mind. But after the case, eh? Bye for now." And she swept away leaving the Sergeant open-mouthed and rooted to the spot.

It was some time before he recovered his senses, well, to any realistic degree, and then found he couldn't dislodge Angelique from his mind.

He also felt rather strange.

Which was exactly how DCI Drype was going to feel any time now.

* * *

Drype was wary of Rita Nash-Perry.

He was unconvinced by her explanation regarding her feelings for her late husband, but in itself that was no real matter.

But being a policeman he was suspicious about anything that didn't ring true, and was therefore disinclined to take Rita's words at face value. At this moment he was concerned about the woman in black seen near White Cottage at the time of Colin's passing, and not at all happy about the prospect of believing Rita had never had such a coat.

Could she be the woman in black?

Was it relevant anyway? It didn't necessarily make her a killer. And that was the only reason he was still entertaining thoughts of a particularly masculine nature where Mrs Nash-Perry was involved.

In short he fancied her despite, or in spite of, his scepticism.

He was strongly of the view she detested her husband and, even in bereavement, might appreciate the attentions of a well meaning man.

However, he was first and foremost a senior police officer and it just wouldn't do to get carried away with a lady who might yet be a suspect. The thought cooled his ardour, but marginally so.

She was immersed in grief when he arrived, having worked herself into the appropriate style in anticipation. Naturally comforting hugs followed which were precisely what both wanted. He was led into the lounge where more comforting was enjoyed.

Rita worked herself into a majestic lather explaining about Olivia Handest's visit, aggrandizing even the most trivial detail, inserting dialogue that had never occurred between the two of them and was purely the product of her imagination, and such accounts raised the need for more comforting.

Henry Drype obliged.

They were tight in each other's arms when he offered to have words with the journalist. Rita turned her head upwards in that minute so that their lips were no more than a couple of inches apart. The irresistible kiss that followed smothered their emotions, exploded in their minds, set their hearts ablaze, and ripped through every sensation their bodies could produce.

The throbbing continued for several moments after their lips had disengaged and that gave Drype enough time to recover some degree of sense and decorum, and it was he who prised them apart, an action that was much to Rita's distress.

"This can't happen, Rita, much as we both wish it could. And I think that now confirms the sad truth that you had no love for Colin. The grieving widow is an act." She went to protest but he silenced her by putting a finger to her lips. "No words Rita, no words. They're not necessary. So please cut out the suffering for my benefit. It's wasted. Keep it for the village, keep it for Olivia, that's all fine. Don't do it for me anymore.

"I want you as much as you want me. And I do want you, Rita. But I don't need your act any longer. If we're going to get anything together we are going to have to be a mite cleverer than everyone else. So no more acting."

Rita understood and the excitement returned to her face to replace the look of disappointment and sadness Drype's earlier words had conjured up.

Another heart-melting kiss was enjoyed.

"I must go now, but I'll be in touch, and I'll put Ms Handest in her place, that you may rely on."

Before Rita could make any reply they were sharing a parting kiss, a kiss of passion, a kiss of promise, a kiss that foretold of a fabulous future.

Except that it didn't.

Drype was turning the tables and was now the one acting. And he was dying for a chat with Olivia Handest.

It was just that his methods clearly hadn't been part of his police training programme and his career was now on the line and in someone else's hands.

After Drype's departure Rita made an urgent visit to cloud nine.

She waltzed around the lounge singing '*I could've danced all night*' and '*Shall we dance?*' all the time imagining herself in a ballgown and Harry in tails as well as in her arms.

The waltz became a polka and her lounge had not been designed or furnished for such adventure as her leg discovered when it came into violent contact with the footstool.

Squealing with pain and grasping the wounded limb she rolled around on the floor in the manner of a footballer trying to win a free kick after a noticeably vicious tackle. As the agony eased she found her eyes closing and her mind wandering into fantasy-land. She was rolling around with Drype in the long grass just as a heroine of one of Glynis Parham's novels had done.

Agony transformed itself to ecstasy.

For the next few minutes Rita relived the scene from the book, smothering her lover with desperate wee kisses, her fingers running amok over every part of his body she could get her hands on, wildly, excitedly, urgently, persuasively.

And Harry eventually responded, just as Jed had done in the book.

He seized her, held her firmly on the grassy bank that was to be their lovers' cot, and stifled her own pitiful kisses with magical, utterly devouring kisses of his own. She recalled the words from the book as she lived through every sensation that followed.

'Jed's strong, firm, manly arms prevented any movement she might want to make. Alison was surrendering to her dreams, her passions, her desires and she wanted him now, oh how she wanted him! And he was all hers. Neither of them was capable of halting that which must now overtake them.

'His kisses and caresses swamped her whole being and she knew she was powerless. And she knew how much she craved his love, and her capitulation became complete as the glowing summer sun slid slowly beneath the horizon.'

"Oh Harry, Harry, please, please, please..." cried Rita as she lived out the part of Alison on the floor of her lounge. Then the tears came, the tears of truth.

Rita had never enjoyed such passion. Never, ever. Was it truly within her grasp? But with a married man? It was reality not passion that now overtook poor, lonely Rita, and left her a sobbing wreck on the carpet.

Chapter Ten

Chortleford's summer seemed destined to end with all the drama it could possibly want had it ever felt the need to expand into a centre of spectacle, which it didn't, of course.

Had Martyn explained at the outset how his step-father died, and accidental death been accepted as the verdict, Nash-Perry would not have been anywhere near White Cottage on the day he perished, and presumably the same applied to Vaughan Pervis.

There would've been one sad death and the end of the story. Probably no national media coverage, and Chortleford would've remained under life's radar, well away from the limelight. Yes, no doubt the village gossipers would've made merry and still condemned Michael Martyn out of hand, especially if the circumstances had come into the public domain, as appeared likely.

But otherwise a village cloaked in anonymity, much to residents' liking, cast back into the shadows before the sun could get a grip.

However, it had not worked out like that.

Martyn chose to conceal the truth and it could therefore be argued that he indirectly led Colin Nash-Perry to his doom. It certainly led Chortleford to a place it didn't relish or court.

There again, the inhabitants made a show of loathing it, whereas most were lapping it up, at the same time hoping they weren't earmarked as the next victim. Or victims.

The biggest shock most faced was learning the identity of Glynis Parham, and that was a scenario now appearing over the horizon despite the best efforts of Angelique Gorling-Parter. For some people other shocks were just around the corner.

Rita was about to learn the cruel lesson of entering into an exclusive arrangement with a newspaper, and Katie Pervis was about to discover her funding channel had been permanently blocked and that her husband was not as solvent as she thought he was.

Charlie Penderfield was struggling with the concept that a woman, any woman, wanted to date him, that he might be of interest to anyone of the opposite sex, and that quite clearly eating a meal with her was going to be the least of his worries.

Supposing she wanted to kiss him, and she surely would, how would he cope with black lipstick?

To a man with limited knowledge of girls, and an even greater lack of experience, the whole affair was frightening. Maybe he would turn her down, but deep down inside he knew he wouldn't. He still had no notion that his colleague Emma wanted to get to know him better.

Emma had her work cut out trying to handle an alarmed, distressed and heartbroken Katie Pervis, who was stomping around her home, the Detective Constable in tow, ranting and raving about her future, about her financial status, and what on earth was the world coming to when a two-bit village like Chortleford wasn't safe.

Inevitably, the police came in for more than their fair share of criticism, and Emma was growing tired of being shouted at. Thankfully, from her point of view, Katie eventually collapsed in a heap in the kitchen, crying profusely and banging the floor with her fists calling out 'Why? Why? *Why?*'

For the umpteenth time Emma quietly asked about any relatives or friends that could come and stay for the time being, and this time was rewarded with a whimpered response.

"Look in my phone book, by the phone, call Hayley or Jackie W or Simone, I don't care. See if they'll come. Mum's in Streatham and doesn't drive. I'll call her later. Now let me suffer."

The words were screeched amidst squeals of discomfort and agony, and Emma was far from convinced the heartrending pain being worn on Katie's sleeve was solely for the loss of her husband. She went to the book, called the three ladies, explained to each in turn what had occurred, and listened to each girl in turn say why she was too busy right now.

She relayed the responses to Katie who just wailed all the more and set off on another trek around the house, shouting and crying and blaming the police.

"God Almighty," she roared, "try Stevie, that's a girl, or Mandy or Carla, or go through the whole bloody book, I don't care." With that she threw herself into the downstairs toilet and locked the door.

This time there was success.

Mandy came up trumps and living in the next village was there in minutes. A lovely lass, Emma decided, someone who genuinely cared, and she found herself wondering why she had become friends with someone so shallow as Katie.

It was most definitely not the time to ask Katie questions. She'd leave that to Drype and serve him right!

Drype was about to be served right having all but insisted on meeting Ms Handest now, not later, and agreed to her suggestion of a country pub rejoicing in the name of *The Pig and Tree Stump*.

* * *

The scene of crime brigade were impressed with a number of impressions.

Recent footmarks around the outside of the grounds of White Cottage.

At first sight one set might well belong to the shoes worn by the deceased. The soil and fields that surrounded the cottage were pretty dry but a few signs of two people walking there very recently were clear enough, and good enough to get impressions from.

Were these two people together? Were their visits actually some way apart?

It was more than the police had ever had here before. There was no obvious evidence that any sort of DNA might be found on the gravel path, and certainly no imprints from shoes. But it was all being checked. That Pervis had called on Martyn was not in debate, but there was no way the latter could've committed the crime and propped the former against his front door.

Not during the time Emma Brouding was there.

Back at base Charlie Penderfield was going through Pervis's possession, precious few though they were. Keys, diary and mobile phone. Nothing to learn from the diary although Charlie would look through again. No wallet? Odd, he thought. No means of identification, and that meant they couldn't be one hundred per cent sure until Mrs Pervis carried out the ID. The team was checking out the mobile but there had been no calls for almost two hours before his body was found. It was painstaking work but they had to check every call, every text, in and out, and probably go back days, maybe even further.

Apart from his wife Vaughan Pervis made or received calls from business associates, clients and others he wished to do business with. Each person had to be contacted and relevant details recorded.

The diary had occasional notes in it, nearly all relating to meetings in connection with business deals, and that was it. No personal matters whatsoever. No names and addresses therein, with all his contacts stored on his phone; but perhaps his computer would yield more data when examined.

Back at his home Mandy had proved a calming influence on the over-dramatic Katie and Emma believed she could temporarily desert the scene, leaving the way clear for a formal visit from the DCI later. She sat in her car and phoned Drype to pave the way and sensed from his attitude that anguished widows were not his flavour of the month.

Shouldn't have joined, she thought, and giggled naughtily as she ended the call.

In the adjacent garden Harry the gardener watched the comings and goings and realised all was not well at Pervis Towers.

Since retiring he'd been working as a gardener in the village and had achieved an appreciable portfolio of patrons, mainly comprised of elderly widows, who appreciated his green-fingered touch. In common with most of his customers he held Michael Martyn guilty of the murder of William Kerbidge, a dear old friend, sadly missed, and was as yet unaware Martyn had been all but cleared.

He used to enjoy his occasional voluntary work in the churchyard when he worked with Mr Kerbidge who was similarly engaged. The two were ancient members of Chortleford's community, though neither had been born or bred there, and were regarded as village elders, men of outstanding breeding, culture and bearing.

In short, they were the village's gentleman, and loved for it.

Harry had not been successful applying for work in the Pervis garden, this employment being carried out by landscape gardeners who, to Harry's mind, were incapable, incompetent, and easily led (so it seemed) by equally dozy TV presenters. Oh, how he hated TV gardening shows!

And how he hated incomers, forgetting he had been one once.

Harold Dunsburn, to give him his correct name, epitomised Chortleford in the sad circumstances in which it found itself.

He dreaded the village being centre stage, loathed the publicity, detested the intrusions visited upon the place, hated the murdering Martyn with a vengeance, exchanged tittle-tattle with other residents who had the same mind, and secretly loved the whole affair.

And that, generally speaking, was a Chortlefordian's lot.

Not publicly liking it for one moment, privately adoring the situation.

"Funny goings on 'ere," Harry muttered to himself under his breath, "funny going ons. Things I could tell people, things I could tell....." and he returned to forking the border.

*　*　*

Church organist Martha was not far away and returning from the shop with a few groceries. She employed Harry Dunsburn for a once-a-week tidy-up in her small garden, an event which was now a once-a-week resume of murder and the dastardly deeds of Michael Martyn.

As she strolled back home, taking the time to enjoy the flight of birds of different feathers in the blue skies above, she realised that, in an odd way, she didn't feel safe, not safe at all. Why, oh why, didn't the police lock that madman up so they could all sleep peacefully in their beds, and Chortleford return to its blissful, untroubled nothingness?

A coldness ran through her, a coldness she could not explain, least of all on this hot late summer's day. She drew close to where Harry was working and called out a merry 'hello'. Straightaway he dropped his fork and strode over the lawn to the boundary of the garden he'd been working in.

"Martha, my dear, something's afoot. Funny goings on, Funny going ons, I must tell yer."

Always keen to lap up some gossip and with a view to spreading it further, usually with flowery additives to spice it up, she leaned forward so as not to miss a word. Of course, Harry only knew a police officer had called on that nasty Mrs Pervis but he and Martha managed to make an entire saga out of it.

It was irrelevant anyway as the truth was going to be all over the village in double-quick time very, very shortly. But for now developing some scandal and rumour relating to Mrs Pervis and her unpleasant activities occupied the organist and the gardener in full.

DCI Drype was fully occupied.

Having been prepared by DC Brouding he found Katie Pervis lived right down to his worst expectations. Her first concern took him aback.

"No wallet? Your lot pinched it, have they? No wallet? Of course he had his wallet. Always had his wallet and I want it back. He kept loads of dosh .... I mean money in it...." Drype interrupted as politely as he could, which in truth lacked the politeness a recent bereavement might necessitate.

He wasn't impressed, least of all by his colleagues being called thieves, and so his interruption had a tone of exasperation and annoyance about it.

"Mrs Pervis, if he carried a wallet stuffed with cash then that might well be a motive. I am so very sorry, I truly am, but any help you can give us may prove vital. And I'm afraid we need someone, such as yourself, to identify him." He stood still waiting for the eruption that he knew would follow as surely as night follows day. But nothing happened. Eventually she spoke, and in a much softer way than she had previously demonstrated.

"Inspector, I'll do anything I can assure you. Anything. And I'll do the identification as soon as you want, no problem. But please don't try telling me my husband was killed for the contents of his wallet. If he had to die I hope he'd have been murdered for something much more than that."

So, he concluded, she would've been 'happy' if Vaughan had been slain for some major headline grabbing reason, but was 'unhappy' he might have been done in for something so mundane as his wallet! Her Vaughan, a victim of a mugging. No way. She would've preferred it if a multi-million pound business transaction had resulted in 'afters', which, she probably knew, did happen in the world of underhand dealings.

It also occurred to the Detective that she was more disappointed that ready money had gone missing than by the loss of her loved one.

Obviously she felt let down by the fact there might be a great deal less publicity in a mugging than being taken out by a syndicate-hired hit man. She needn't have worried; the location of the death ensured an appreciable amount of publicity would be forthcoming and the opportunity to further her own career, if it could be called a career.

Katie Pervis was already dreaming of exclusives in expensive magazines and pictures of herself, scantily-clad, adorning not just the mags but the national papers too. What a terrible picture of loss she could paint. What appalling pain she could describe. What unimaginable suffering she could relate.

And in furtherance of these matters she was already turning out the wedding photos and any other memorabilia that might be of interest to the world's media. Katie was determined to launch herself on the back of Vaughan's demise, little realising she was going to be plunged into dire and desperate financial straits very swiftly indeed.

* * *

Earlier Henry Drype had enjoyed a brief meeting with Olivia Handest.

He was astonished at how much nonsense Rita Nash-Perry had off-loaded onto the reporter, and even more amazed that Olivia believed it. She hadn't swallowed it but didn't want Drype to know.

Besides the Chief Inspector was busy regaling her with the truth, and she didn't believe that either.

So it was an unusual kind of stalemate. The meeting was not going to last long.

He warned her that she'd look stupid if she printed a description of the woman in black that the police could deny, and would do so vigorously. Rita's woman in black simply didn't exist.

Olivia thought he was deliberately trying to put her off the scent and resolved to run an even better story. The one Bedroom man had told.

And on that basis they parted company, Drype remaining in ignorance of a vital piece of information, the later revelation of which would be most likely to cause a breach of the peace between police and the media.

With undue alacrity the news of Mr Pervis's end spread around Chortleford rather like the aroma of fresh manure from the surrounding fields. It was all engulfing and reached into every nook and cranny.

Steve the butcher had a whole new line in banter as customers queued up to discuss the topic rather than purchase meat, or so it might have seemed to an onlooker. Martha dashed out to find Harry and Harry was making haste in her direction for the same purpose. Dr Monroe heard the latest from his receptionist and then every patient following which caused him to run well behind schedule.

Keith the newsagent was startled. The story flooded through the village like a tsunami, and Keith was pleased that Martyn was in the clear, at least over this one. He'd always had his doubts and never voiced them, and although he didn't yet know it, he was about to be proved right in his reservations.

Being a small community where chitchat and scandal were in the ascendency the tale, in the style of Chinese whispers, gained and lost much in translation as it travelled and it arrived almost unrecognised when it reached Gillian's ears.

She noticed a police presence as she drove her bus past the church, but dismissed it as it had become an all too regular occurrence. Mrs Lacey boarded at the next stop and was so busy trying to tell Gillian what had happened that she got in a right muddle with her bus pass, twice dropping it on the floor, twice removing it before it registered on the pad, and then delivered the coup-de-grace by dropping it under Gillian's feet.

Both ladies tried to recover it resulting in a bang of heads, and Mrs Lacey never stopped to draw breath, apologise, or venture away from the account of this new murder. Gillian located that which was lost, operated the pad on Mrs Lacey's behalf, returned the bus pass to its owner, thanked her for relating the news, and thankfully drove on, leaving Mrs Lacey to bend the ear of another passenger. Relief for the driver.

She couldn't afford to let details fill her mind and distract her, she must concentrate on what she was doing. But it sounded so awful.

Mrs Lacey, at full gabble, had told her there must've been a fight and Mr Pervis had died from multiple injuries, being strangled at the end just to make sure. There were blood stains everywhere and the other person must surely be badly hurt. Mrs Pervis was, so it was said, quite distraught, but if it meant her selling up and moving away, well, wouldn't that be fine. Good might yet come of evil if she moved on. Don't want their kind in the village, never have.

Blah-blah-blah....

Gillian's mind was wearied, but being a good professional she'd listened politely and tucked it away while she drove. But she was just dying to tell them all when she got back to the depot.

In the *Log and Weasel* there was only one theme to conversation.

By now the saga had gained sufficient ground and superfluities that certain drinkers were convinced that monster Martyn had snuffed out Pervis's life, despite the knowledge her was being interviewed by a police officer at the time. In fact, one or two didn't believe that to be the case, and were confident he was alone when Pervis called.

Ample opportunity to kill his visitor.

Mrs Lacey was not alone in hoping that Mrs Pervis might move away.

Gladys and Edna hoped that would be the upshot. Edna tried in vain to defend Martyn, knowing him to be innocent of this crime, but Gladys wouldn't hear a word of it.

"Rumour, Edna, rumour. Don't you go listening to rumours. He, that Martyn man, he's killed Pervis, mark my words. Had a policeman with him, indeed. That's just a rumour, my gal, and not for you to be spreading nonsense like that." Edna wanted to protest but knew it was not only hopeless, not only undesirable, but also likely to lead to a fractious scenario in which she would be buried underfoot and not allowed to speak again for a long time.

So she held her tongue and contented herself with knowing the truth.

* * *

And so it was that Chortleford and the police awaited a bombshell they had no idea was heading their way.

Chapter Eleven

The newspaper lying on Drype's desk had all the appearance of a hand grenade with the pin pulled out. He was not the only person entering a state of shock.

Rita Nash-Perry's shock had all the signs of becoming long term trauma. Keith, the newsagent, had stared in disbelief as he opened his delivery of the local papers. He then sat on the floor where he was and read on with eyes wide open.

Gradually copies of the paper found their way to a variety of destinations. In Chortleford residents started ringing each other and in a few cases people left their homes to pop next door or across the road to engage in dissecting, analysing and being utterly scandalised by what they had read.

Dr Monroe tutted over breakfast and was so engrossed reading that he inadvertently dipped his tie in his boiled egg, and actually munched on the end of his tie before realising, much to the amusement of Mrs Monroe. Dave the taxi driver filled his head full of theories and conclusions ready for the day's conversations with his passengers.

Martha finished up in Harry's as they both studied the same newspaper copy despite having one each.

Steve and his assistant had halted preparing the day's choicest cuts in order to thoroughly comprehend the words before them.

Emma Brouding concluded the story would probably make Drype's day, if not his entire year, but she did not mean it in the pleasant way normally associated with the expression. And a wry grin shone on her lips.

Chortleford was not the only place awaking to a delicious front page story.

A retired vicar living near Canterbury read his local's scoop and was shocked and excited all at the same time. A motor mechanic in Faversham attempting to service an old Ford Fiesta paused, mug of coffee in hand, to revel in the details. A man litter-picking in Dover also stopped what he was doing in order to peruse the account and found himself quite jealous of the X-rated activities of Mr and Mrs Nash-Perry, especially when looking at the photo of the seemingly desirable lady in question.

A young mother in Folkestone, having dropped her children at school, sat in her 4x4 and concluded it was all very disgusting and people of that age should know better. The receptionist at a factory on the outskirts of Maidstone, finding herself with nothing to do, scanned the news and declared the whole thing was vulgar particularly if Mrs N-P then killed her husband.

Two male friends, waiting for a bus in Gillingham, spoke of the couple as a 'right randy pair' with one adding Mrs N-P was like a black widow spider, killing her mate after pleasures had been taken. Sitting on the bench overlooking the seafront at Tankerton a middle age lady glanced through the paper and returned to the main story, deciding it was too 'juicy' as she would've put it not to read again.

Olivia and her editor were well pleased.

Approaches were arriving urgently from the nationals. Trying to by-pass this queue and with an even greater sense of urgency was DCI Drype.

Rita was too overcome to take any action at all despite the desire to wring Ms Handest's neck, and there had been all too much neck-wringing of late.

It wasn't one of the better photos the newspaper cameraman had taken, Rita was sure of that, for he had shown her the ones he preferred, the ones that made her look like a poor, sad, careworn woman, heartbroken and crushed. She'd put on her best act for those.

It was before they got down to business. He said he'd take a few general shots just to make certain of the best angles and that he'd got the lighting right, all that sort of thing. And one of those made her look like a glamorous tart, if there ever was such a thing.

He'd asked her to remove her jumper for these warm-up pictures.

He'd made her giggle and laugh.

She never intended to take her top off. She had a flimsy blouse underneath. At one point he'd stood over her and, unbeknown to her, managed to take this wretched photo in such a way that it enhanced her well-displayed bosom. All those pictures were not shown to her. Damn.

It was back on with the jumper and time to look sad. She conjured up a few tears and rubbed her eyes. It was the shots he took now that she was able to see.

They had done the dirty on her. Yet the photo was the least of her worries.

What took her breath away was that the paper was hinting she might be a killer.

They included a report from a witness who had seen her following her husband towards White Cottage and then returning a short while later. The nameless witness claimed to know her.

Rita was ridiculed as a shameless woman who probably took her pleasures where she could find them, and not always with Colin who, quite obviously, was unable to satisfy her on the grand scale she sought. Where did they get all this from?

At this point she shrieked in anger, bitterness and frustration. A piercing shriek.

Not only had they painted her as, well, a painted lady, the paper had as good as suggested she was a murderer, and a cold-blooded one to boot. She screamed again and heard hammering at her front door. It was her well-meaning neighbour concerned for her welfare.

And for once Rita was pleased to see her.

* * *

Gladys Frobisher was suffering from shock, so much so that her sister-in-law, Edna, was actually fanning her with a copy of the local paper as she swooned in her armchair, slowly shaking her head. Edna considered telling her to pull herself together, or perhaps even to grow up, but dismissed both possibilities knowing full well she would never, ever utter either.

"I'm going to have palpitations, Edna," announced Gladys.

"I don't think that's a good idea, if you don't mind me saying so."

"Please don't interfere, Edna, there's a dear. My palpitations are mine to have as I see fit, and I'm going to have some."

"Wouldn't you prefer a nice cup of tea?"

"No I would not, for heaven's sake woman. Don't you understand? Are you too stupid? Goodness me, it's small wonder you never married. We now have, in case you hadn't noticed, two, yes *two* murderers in our village, *right* in our midst. You or I could be next. Oh God, I think I'm going to faint..."

Edna flapped faster and reflected on these latest appraisals and comments. Yes, she understood. No, she wasn't stupid at all and that was precisely why she had never saddled herself with a husband. Unquestionably ensured that I never needed to kill him, she mused, and stifled a snigger that might have given the game away.

"We don't know for sure Mrs Nash-Perry killed her husband," she ventured timidly.

"Oh, God save us all, Edna. There's no smoke without fire. Of course she did. It says so in the paper." Actually it didn't and Edna recognised that, but also recognised that to mention it might lead to the outbreak of domestic war in which there would be only one loser. She tried a different tack.

"But I do agree, we must feel unsafe all the time the police don't appear to be doing anything. And, yes, there may be two killers on the loose, Gladys." She hoped and prayed that would suffice and was blessed with success. Her sister-in-law sighed a-plenty, enjoyed what Edna assumed might be her own personal palpitations, and ordered a cup of tea anyway.

Relieved, Edna stopped flapping and went to the kitchen.

However, Edna was not the only person in a flap.

* * *

Bedroom man was in a flap. Katie Pervis was in a flap. DCI Drype was in a flap.

Olivia Handest and her editor were in a state of high excitement and firing on all cylinders.

They had even managed to hint that the Chortleford Minx as they termed her, might, *might* have had something to do with the killing of Vaughan Pervis. Was Rita the Chortleford Choker perchance? That was the nickname that appeared on the paper's website.

So Rita was definitely in a flap.

Michael Martyn was becalmed, a fine state to be in for one whose life had been in turmoil for a long time now. Well, well, well, he thought, what a rascal you are, Rita! And he pondered the possibility that she might want the services of a solicitor. More business for Ms Gorling-Parter, maybe. Perhaps I should recommend her, he considered.

Better still, and to add to village gossip and send it right over the top, why not pay the lady a visit?

And he set off to do exactly that, a wicked grin decorating his countenance.

Drype was all for visiting Ms Handest and doing her a mischief, little realising he might have to get in a queue behind Rita Nash-Perry and the Bedroom man.

The national media was on the scent. Things were looking ugly. And getting hot.

The Kent countryside braced itself for a September invasion, and little Chortleford, tucked neatly away where nobody need find it, was in danger of being suffocated with attention. Chortlefordians, old and young alike, made a show of not liking this one tiny bit, whereas they privately harboured a desire to milk the occasion and revel in the publicity.

After all, poor Mr Kerbidge was one thing. Rita Nash-Perry, murderess, seducer, sex-maniac, husband-slayer was quite another. And Katie Pervis was now in a lather, a self-induced rage brought about by the loss of limelight at the very moment she was to step centre stage.

For a brief second she could've cheerfully strangled Mrs Nash-Perry. That would surely promise her publicity! Suddenly nobody seemed particularly interested in Vaughan's passing; he was almost just a footnote to the Nash-Perry affair. And she was marginalised! How very dare they!

Histrionics flew unbounded in the Pervis household as once again the woman pranced around, throwing herself from one room to the other, ranting, crying, squealing, and with Mandy in tow desperately trying to say the right thing at the right time and be a calming influence. Katie didn't deserve a friend like that.

Mrs Pervis was letting fly in all directions and in addition to the newspapers, Rita Nash-Perry, the police and Chief Inspector Drype, all the other villagers, and many more besides, fired broadsides at numerous other parties including the government, Southeastern Trains and the Russians.

Nobody escaped unscathed.

Eventually she exhausted herself having exhausted her list of recipients of her umbrage, and demanded Mandy pour a glass of Bollinger.

"It's in the fridge, it's in the fridge, oh do hurry yourself, there's a sweetie." Mandy hurried herself but had never opened champagne before and therefore caused a delay that was not much appreciated.

"Oh, give it to me, give it to me, here, here," Katie demanded. Mandy handed the bottle over on request and stood well clear, glass in hand. Out flew the cork, hammering into the ceiling, to be followed by escaping drink.

Quick as thought Katie had the bottle to her mouth, had upended the bottom and was drinking in heavy glugs as further drink missed the target and trickled over her face and chin and down her front.

Mandy watched in amazement.

Katie collapsed in a chair, clutching the bottle to her chest and wiping the froth from her mouth.

"Get y'self a glass, babes, let's get plastered." Her friend gave her the glass and went to fetch another resolving that she might as well take a drink. It wasn't every day she got to imbibe Bollinger, after all, and she'd reached the stage where she was ready for alcohol herself.

* * *

"Thought I'd come and say hi."

Martyn was on Mrs Nash-Perry's doorstep.

"I know what it's like to be accused of murder you haven't committed, so I thought I'd pop round and see if you'd like a chat. I also have an excellent solicitor just in case you feel the need to sue someone." Sarcasm laced every word.

She looked at him as the distaste overwhelmed every part of her. She swayed slightly, weighed up the situation and decided she was in just the mood to take revenge. Wasn't this the man who strangled Colin and left her, unintentionally of course, to take the blame, as it had now been suggested in the newspapers?

"I want to kill you, Mr Martyn, so why don't you leave now while you're still intact?"

"I haven't killed anyone, Mrs Nash-Perry. Nobody at all. It's important you *understand* and *remember* that." There was simmering menace in every word. He emphasised *understand* and *remember*, saying them slowly and with intimidatory threat. "I'll tell you what I've told the police about my stepfather, a story they accept, and so must you."

She felt the coldness as if an icy blast had torn through her clothes and seized her body. Making up her mind Rita decided on her course of action.

"Come in and keep your distance. I am going to get a carving knife from the kitchen and as soon as I decide to use it I will make such a terrible mess of you. Might as well be hung for a lamb as a sheep, or whatever the phrase is."

She indicated the lounge and told him to sit while she repaired to the kitchen cutlery drawer to claim the aforementioned weapon. He felt he detected a hint of drink, possibly brandy, about Rita's presence. There was no sign of the well-meaning neighbour.

When she returned he related his story, in full, leaving his hostess open-mouthed and with the knife dropped on the floor. In front of her was Glynis Parham! No, no, it could not be so.

The best he could do in the circumstances was ask Rita what her favourite Glynis Parham was, and upon receiving an answer proceed to tell her all about the novel together with background information normally denied to readers. She was all but convinced, he could see that.

Meanwhile Drype had tasked himself with a confrontation with Olivia's editor.

"Now look, Mrs Cundy..." he began, only to find himself cut off midstream.

"It's *Ms* Cundy, *Chief* Inspector," she chided.

"Well, Ms Cundy," he continued, unabashed but annoyed, "your reporter has information vital to police enquiries relating to a murder and has not only decided to withhold it from the authorities but to make a hideous and, I might say, libellous article out of it."

"Do you realise that this article could jeopardise our investigations and have serious repercussions in any trial? You have also denigrated an innocent lady who is having to deal with the trauma of a husband being killed in a particularly vicious manner." Ms Cundy was ready for this.

"As far as *that* is concerned my reporter has merely taken all that Mrs Nash-Perry told her and built a readable item around it." Drype was now at a slight disadvantage, for he knew Rita was capable of exaggeration and of imagining a loving relationship she had never known. It was fifteen-love to Ms Cundy and Drype realised he needed to serve an ace to even the score.

"Do you not realise, Ms Cundy, that your witness might well be the killer diverting attention?"

Fifteen-all.

Sidestepping a valid point the editor served a volley of her own.

"We verified the witness's presence in the village and do not believe he went anywhere near White Cottage, a collaborated fact, Chief Inspector."

Thirty-fifteen.

"And therefore you do not know, Ms Cundy, that Mrs Nash-Perry was anywhere near White Cottage either, and you may have maligned an innocent woman in pursuit of sales figures."

Thirty-all.

"My legal team assures me we have printed nothing libellous. We had an exclusive arrangement with Mrs Nash-Perry in which we have paid handsomely for anything she wished to tell us, and we have faithfully recorded it in print. Surely she cannot argue about that? If the readers *choose* to believe she murdered her husband that is up to them. We do not say that, not at all."

Forty-thirty.

"Nonetheless we need to speak to your witness urgently. And I mean right now. We are talking about cold-blooded murder, Ms Cundy. Contact him and tell him to get in touch pronto if you're unwilling to present me with his details."

Deuce.

But frankly Drype was beginning to wonder if new balls please was more the order of the day. However, he wasn't prepared for the editor's next line.

"Chief Inspector, okay, I hold my hands up. Olivia met someone by chance. She didn't get his name as he wouldn't have told us what he did otherwise. He was having a regular assignation with a married woman in Chortleford, and he knows the Nash-Perrys from way back when.

"The deal was no names. That way we got the info. Look, Chief Inspector, we're a local rag and we have to come up with scoops like this to stay in business. Its a jungle out there....."

It was Drype's turn to interrupt.

"I need to speak to him, full stop."

After a moment's hesitation she said she'd get Olivia to give him the address of the woman, and he breathed a sigh of relief.

It wasn't the only meeting that started badly and was now running more smoothly.

* * *

Rita was still sceptical and approaching inebriation having produced the brandy. At this juncture, and for reasons that eluded her, she offered him a can of beer. He was amazed to see her tackling the brandy neat, but put it down to shock, and despatched his own drink becoming increasing comfortable with his surroundings. He was duly offered a second.

"It was Colin's and he rarely had any, so there's plenty of beer, er ... Michael."

"Thank you Mrs Nash-Perry, I mean, Rita." And they smiled across the safe distance between them, he one side of the lounge, she the other. Both were warming to this most unlikely of friendships.

"All that stuff in the paper, er ... Michael, I made it all up. My husband and I did not share a close relationship at all and I simply remembered all the beautifully romantic things that happened in your books, so I suppose if I'm guilty of anything it's plagiarism!" And they both laughed.

"They were all the things I wished I'd experienced but had missed out on, and that's the sad truth." She hung her head, the brandy intake adding to the dramatic emphasis. "I thought some money, now Colin was gone, some money might be useful and made a pact with the paper. A pact with the devil it turned out. And look what they've done to me."

"I know, I know," said Michael softly, "just as they did with me, just as *everyone* did with me. We're both victims, Rita. You all thought I'd done

William in, but it wasn't true, and I didn't touch Colin, anymore than you did. Both sad victims, you and me. *Understand* and *remember* that.

Those words again. Understand and remember. It was like being brainwashed and in her tipsy state Rita repeated those words quietly to herself twice over.

"I'm so sorry this has happened to you, Rita, I really am.

"The police can't prove you killed Colin, so Rita I think it will all blow over and I think it will be for the best if it does. They can't prove it was me either, so let us both allow this horrible thing to pass away, and let us be friends accordingly.

Now of necessity, in a village environment, one alleged killer visiting another is bound to cause unrest to say nothing of rumour and fear.

"They'll kill each other," was Gladys Frobisher's conclusion, "and maybe that will be for the best. But I can't say I like it. I don't like it at all. They could be plotting their next murder. And to think he slaughtered poor Mr Nash-Perry just to get his hands on his lover, that dreadful, dreadful woman.

"Imagine that, Edna, a crime of passion, right here in Chortleford, a woman cavorting with someone behind her husband's back. Why, it's disgusting, not just immoral. Whatever is happening to life's standards, I may ask you, whatever is this world coming to."

Sister-in-law Edna, used to these one-sided conversations, knew no answers or comments were required and, as normal, held her tongue. Gladys had the floor, as ever, and was lecturing Edna when Edna didn't want to be tutored. That was of small concern and Edna never questioned Gladys's right to hold sway and give vocal appreciation of any matter that fell within their compass.

It was assumed (by Gladys) that Edna's opinion would always be the same as hers and if it wasn't, well, it damn well ought to be.

Back at Rita's Michael Martyn was saying that the fact he had two nom-de-plumes was about to be broadcast and she was asking about the second one.

"Peter Quendon, Rita. Extraordinarily I write, of all things, crime novels as Peter Quendon. Can you believe that? Apparently I'm not very good at it. However, I shall certainly be giving that up as I don't feel I could ever write about fictional crime ever again.

"Now love stories, yes, I shall always be able to write about love and romance."

"Oh, I do hope so, Michael, I do hope so. I adore your work with a passion, and I appreciate it all the more now I know how you get in the mood, so to speak, to write with such immense feeling."

She re-filled her glass and passed him another can. It never occurred to her to offer him a glass and he didn't ask. They were totally engrossed in their discussion and in each other.

By now Rita had moved across the room to sit close to her visitor, the carving knife lying forgotten a safe distance away. She started to ask him about the ecstasies and agonies he wrote about so movingly, so beautifully, and wasn't even aware that he was unconsciously arousing her.

It was not his intention to create such an effect, nor was it his intention to be aroused by the Chortleford Minx in return. But the truth was that, fuelled by alcohol, rapt in company they found so exciting and stimulating, they were in danger of surrendering to urges rising within them.

* * *

Drype had been trying to suppress the *anger* rising within him.

Emma Brouding offered to visit Natasha's mum believing she might be able to head off a difficult situation at the pass. Drype's proposal was a full-frontal assault with all guns blazing and Emma realised that risked ruining the lives of innocent people. Tact and diplomacy was needed and the Chief Inspector was not renowned for possessing, let alone displaying either.

He thought he'd better go and see Rita as well, so accepted Emma's suggestion that she drive and drop him off on the way to Natasha's. She exhaled extensively when he agreed. Phew, a dicey and delicate situation loaded with explosive content defused. And they were on their way.

Katie Pervis and her friend Mandy, knocking back champagne and feeling all the merrier for it, were starting to talk about the future. Mandy was pleased if only to get Katie away from the crazy behaviour, the bellowing, the flouncing, the false tears, and the vocal condemnation of everyone else.

"Wad I do, Mand? I mean, really, what *do* I do? Who do I need to see about money, Vaughan's money, all that sort of thing? The will, like. Tell me babes, how do I get it sorted?"

Mandy explained and offered to assist hoping that would further calm things.

"Stay with me, babes, help me through, babes, please. Do all those things for me, well, *with* me. Let's do 'em together, like, eh babes?" Mandy nodded, not quite sure what she was letting herself in for, but determined to help.

The champagne was taking its grip. Elsewhere brandy and beer were also having an unseemly effect so early in the day, and Rita and Michael were now sharing the sofa and gazing into each other's glazed eyes as they talked fervently about love, romance, passion, desire and need.

And bearing down on them was one fiery Chief Inspector.

DC Brouding was driving and thinking about how she was going to tackle Natasha's mum and knowing the man sitting next to her would be expecting an immediate outcome. Failing that he would probably set about the poor woman himself for he was certainly in the mood.

She had to make it work, and she had a plan. The alternative was an exploding DCI.

Drype leaped from the car at Rita's and made a dash for the front door, and Emma put her foot down and sped off before he could change his mind.

It was all set to become a most interesting day.

Chapter Twelve

Fortunately Natasha's father was at work and, having assured her mother that they were speaking in strict confidence, Emma extracted the name and address of Bedroom man.

He lived in the village of Selling, twixt Faversham and Canterbury, and was currently unemployed, other than as a bedroom serviceman of course. Having checked with the DCI who, she had to admit, sounded rather flustered and preoccupied, she set off post-haste.

No doubt Natasha's mum would call him and warn him but Emma had stressed that he was a vital witness and was needed quite urgently. The reason for his visits to Chortleford would be kept quiet if he co-operated, and if it was within the power of the police to do so. DC Brouding wasn't sure on that point but did not relay her thoughts.

Happily, from her point of view, Glen Bardrew stayed put. His wife, thankfully as it happened, was at work so he was not going to be made uncomfortable by her presence.

He related all that he'd seen that fateful day, namely his old friend Colin Nash-Perry walking purposefully towards where he now knew White Cottage was situated, and that Rita was no more than a hundred yards behind him.

"I tooted and waved to both, but no acknowledgement. Then, coming back I saw her again, going the other way, that is, away from White Cottage. Again, no response to my toot and wave. It's as if both were in a trance, y'know, wrapped up in what they were doing."

She asked for and obtained a description of both, a rough idea of timings, and advised Mr Bardrew that he would be needed for a formal statement.

Driving back to Chortleford she realised something at the back of her mind was bothering her but couldn't put her finger on it. But she knew it was relevant. What the devil was it?

She was not alone in puzzling.

Drype had found himself at the heart of a real mystery.

He was astonished that he was unable to gain admittance to Chez Nash-Perry, Rita resolutely and almost aggressively standing firm on the doorstep and refusing to let him in.

Yes, she was fine, thank you. Yes, she had the name of a good solicitor, thank you.

No, she didn't need to talk to him.

This was the woman he had taken in his arms, risked his career and marriage for, and all in the line of duty. The woman he had caressed and kissed in pursuit of his enquiries. Finally he asked her bluntly.

"Second thoughts, Rita? I can't blame you after the newspaper article."

"Harry, seriously, you're a policeman. The village is like a reality TV show at the moment. Do you really think your visit hasn't been noticed? In all probability you've been photographed. Most people have cameras on their mobiles and anyway there might be a press photographer stationed out there now, taking pictures."

"Rita, I understand that fully, but I am the investigating officer and there is nothing unusual about me calling upon you." He was starting to raise his voice and it had already climbed a complete octave since the start of the conversation. And he was getting ratty and red in the face.

"Fine. You've called. Now be off with you."

"I need to speak to you, ostensibly about the newspaper story. Did you or did you not follow your husband to White Cottage, or follow him at all that day?" His voice had fallen just short of contralto, the words had flown from his mouth at rat-a-tat-tat speed, and he sounded a frustrated and desperate man.

"I've told you, no I didn't and I don't have, and never have had, well not in recent memory, a black coat. It was a hot day. Why would I wear a coat at all?"

"You might've worn a coat to sort of disguise yourself." His voice had reached shriek level and Rita, spurred on by an unwise intake of brandy, burst out laughing. And took the opportunity to close the door.

"Rita, Rita, open the bloody door," he screamed as he hammered on the framework.

"Chief Inspector, what an *angry* man you are, and its Rita is it, not Mrs Nash-Perry? Getting friendly with the suspects now are we? Fancy your chances with the Chortleford Minx?"

Hearing the sarcastic tones of a female voice he turned to see a grinning Olivia Handest and standing beside her was a very good example of a press photographer.

"Tell him to put that camera away, Olivia, or he'll be wearing it where it causes maximum pain," he bawled.

"Now, now, Mr Drype, hardly the language befitting a senior police officer." But before he could react, and from the look on his face his reaction was going to be nuclear, she spoke again.

"Michael Martyn. He's in there. That's why you can't get in. Simples. I don't know what the collective noun for murderers is. A Serial perhaps. A Coffin maybe. How about an Abattoir? An abattoir of murderers. Yes, and that's what you've got in there, pal, an abattoir of murderers."

And she laughed out loud.

Drype stood stock still with eyes bulging, blood pressure rising, nostrils flaring, hands shaking and Olivia considered calling the ambulance she was sure he'd need any moment now.

* * *

Martha and Harry were totally absorbed in scandal and gossip and were enlarging every aspect of developments as they saw them, and adding their own ideas to the whole picture. And that picture now bore little resemblance to what they actually knew and what had actually happened.

"Funny goin' ons" Harry intoned for the umpteenth time, "I could tell 'e some stories 'bout that White Cottage, y'know. I could tell some tales." And he tapped the side of his nose and ignored his companion's implorations for details.

"Oh do tell, Harry, please do," Martha pleaded and obtained silence in reply. Harry wasn't saying.

Martha, having a reasonable degree of intelligence, came to the conclusion Harry had nothing of worth to tell and whatever he was keeping to himself, if it existed at all, was the invention of his imagination.

Equally absorbed in scandal and gossip were Gladys and Edna, the former delivering an essay of appreciable length that the latter was not required to comment upon, let alone question in any way. Just for good measure Edna was occasionally berated for her lack of gardening skill and knowledge as a further means of keeping her underfoot.

"This village, Edna, is not going to be worth living in soon if things carry on the way they are, and thanks to that awful police force we are permanently unsafe and afeared for our lives. I don't know about you, Edna, but I don't want to be strangled. Now, what's this one called?"

"Er ... osteoporosis, Gladys?"

"That's a disease of the bones, brittle bones, Edna, my goodness me. It's an osteospermum you *stupid* woman. I think those police officers are mere jobsworths, we tax payers are paying them a fortune to swan around asking people, oh I don't know, *hundreds* of questions simply to justify their existence and incredible salaries. And this bush, Edna. Name please"

"Mmmm ... I think it's a Buddha ..."

"Oh, you're impossible, you really are. It's a buddleia, numbskull, a *buddleia*."

"Yes, Gladys, thank you." And Edna watched Gladys's retreating figure with a sense of relief, knowing relief would be short-lived and with that in mind began to envisage her sister-in-law being strangled. What made it worse was that in Edna's dream it was she doing the strangling.

What would she strangle her with? William Kerbidge had been throttled with garden twine, also appropriate for Gladys of course, but it had already been done. Edna wanted to be original but before she could apply her mind further in its evil pursuit her reverie ended as Gladys reappeared and was noticeably in possession of a reproof for something or other ready to be delivered to Edna's ears.

As the hapless woman was taken to task she found the words went in one ear and out the other.

She was thinking.

The belt off her beloved silk dressing gown, Edna resolved. I think the going rate is four times round the neck and pull tight! A fitting end for one being put to sleep for good.

* * *

Emma Brouding had unravelled her enigma.

She phoned Glen Bardrew.

"Glen, very important. You said Colin was wearing an open neck shirt. So no tie. Just how sure are you?"

"Positive. Swear to it. In fact, I don't think it was the kind of shirt you'd wear a tie with. Colin was very precise about things. He always, always wore a tie when it was right and proper to do so, but he wouldn't have worn a tie with a smart, casual shirt. No way. Why d'you ask?"

"He was strangled with a tie, Glen, and Rita identified it as his. Might he have gone out wearing it then realised how hot it was ..."

"Not the Colin I know. Well, not from way back, if you know what I mean. If he'd decided it was right to wear a tie a bloody sauna wouldn't have changed his mind; he'd have stuck with it even if it had made him feel ill."

She ended the call. She didn't want to find herself going into greater detail. Besides, she now had what she hoped would be interesting information for Drype. Time to find out what her DCI was up to and pick him up if he's ready.

Her DCI was up to his eyeballs.

He'd tried to send Olivia Handest away with a flea in her ear and a warning to stay clear of Mrs Nash-Perry, but the reporter had a fly-swatter capable of dealing with impudent fleas and gave Drype the rough end of her tongue to be going on with. The couple did not part as the best of friends.

Given the knowledge Olivia had imparted he was finally able to get past checkpoint-Charlie and into Rita's abode where, unsurprisingly, he found Michael Martyn lying in wait.

The three of them now sat quietly in the lounge occupying the corners of a triangle, Drype on the sofa by the window, Martyn in an armchair a safe distance away, and Rita on the pouffe to the side of the fireplace from where she could observe both men easily.

She had offered Drype 'something from the drinks cabinet' which he turned down, poured herself another brandy and gave Martyn a further can. The officer not only noticed the aroma of alcohol, he felt the eyes of the other two were decidedly glazed, and Rita was rocking very slightly, but smiling at him beguilingly.

There was a brief recital of 'Sheep May Safely Graze' which Drype realised was coming from his mobile. Behind his back Corinne must've changed his ring tone. She often did that. He hated her for it, and loved her for it. It was something that often resulted in his embarrassment, like now, and he recalled her words the previous evening.

"Way things are going in Chortleford only the sheep are safe at the mo!"

The call was Emma relating her news and it produced a hard stare at Mrs Nash-Perry who just smiled all the more alluringly, leaned one way then the other and finally completed her manoeuvres by toppling right off the pouffe. Martyn to the rescue. Two angles of the triangle convulsed with laughter.

"Yes, come to the house please, Emma. If that Handest girl's still out there see if *you* can make her go away. Don't be long, if you please." The DC smiled as she drove on, thinking there was every chance Drype was facing a difficult situation. He needs a woman's support, she knew, and her smile widened into a broad, toothy grin of pleasure and satisfaction.

* * *

In a village like Chortleford juicy news will spread like wildfire without any outside interference or input. But add an incident, the police and the media, and a fireball of gossip will tear through the community at a rate of knots.

The police were in possession of new information that meant Michael Martyn was unlikely to be charged with murder and everyone wanted to know why. Rita Nash-Perry was a suspect in the death of her husband and both she and Martyn were holed-up together with the investigating officer.

Olivia Handest was a catalyst for the dissemination of information and mis-information alike, and a focal point for other media representatives heading into the Kent countryside and the previously quiet, unspoilt and undistinguished village.

Right now, having ignored Drype's suggestion to leave the area, and posted herself within yards of Rita's front door, she was pleased to see the three occupants emerge together led by the DCI.

"No comment, nothing to say," he announced boldly.

"Wish I had a fiver for every time someone's said that to me," Ms Handest shouted. Cameras clicked. "Why aren't you being charged, Mr Martyn?" she tried.

Rita interrupted proceedings by slipping and tumbling down her steps, once again to be rescued by Martyn.

"We're off to the station," cried Drype while the rescue was effected, "contact PR there through the usual channels."

"Are they under arrest, Chief Inspector?"

"No. They are helping us with their enquiries."

"See. So much for no comment. There, that wasn't difficult was it? Might've well have told us that right at the start." Olivia's statement did nothing to improve Drype's temper.

Emma came flying to a halt narrowly avoiding the reporter and her photographer who both looked askance at the unsafe intrusion.

"Stay in the car, we'll get in," advised Drype. A small crowd of villagers and other reporters and their professional entourage had assembled, and Emma had to pick her way through the throng with rather more care than the manner of her arrival. Then they were on their way.

The villagers now scattered to the four corners with their red hot news.

* * *

DS Penderfield had been tasked with examining the murder of Vaughan Pervis and he was busy with some of the team looking into the man's background.

There was a great deal of darkness. To describe Pervis's business life as shadowy was an understatement of elephantine proportions. Some connections, alerted to his demise, simply vanished, mobile phones 'no longer in use' and, of course, not registered. It just made life more of a drudgery for the police, a labour with little outcome by and large.

But one thing was becoming so clear it was almost as if a spotlight was being shone upon it so that the police might not miss it in the gloom that otherwise hid so much.

Vaughan Pervis was not exactly rolling in money. Quite the reverse.

His home in Chortleford appeared to be owned by a consortium of business people, Pervis holding a stake of less than fifteen per cent, and enquiries of other stakeholders revealed that, in the event of his demise, the remaining 'owners' could sell the property to regain their investment.

Interesting.

Probably a tax fiddle, Penderfield surmised. The deceased had two personal bank accounts, one jointly with his wife, and that was in credit by about two thousand pounds. Whereas the other was running an overdraft in excess of five thousand. He had a ten thousand pound overdraft limit.

He ran five businesses, all private companies, and all seemed to be running at small losses.

Again, a tax fiddle was the most likely situation.

Six credit cards. The one he shared with his wife was cleared every month without accruing interest. The limit was ten thousand pounds and often four or five thousand would be racked up in a month. It didn't require any research to show most purchases would've been made by Mrs Pervis and mainly through upmarket outlets.

The other five cards had outstanding balances of over twenty five thousand in total, not including a considerable amount of interest.

Investigation showed that being a property developer was little more than a thin cover. That business was a partnership with two other men and was undoubtedly where the money came from. His partners confirmed Pervis took a handsome sum, as they also did, business being exceedingly successful. Penderfield could believe that.

Gradually he pieced together where the earnings went.

The money went into Vaughan's solo personal account. Some was transferred to the joint account, some went into each of the private companies to help prop them up, some paid off all or some of the credit card bills, and a large quantity was withdrawn as cash.

Slowly it started to make sense.

So did the killer lurk in the undergrowth of his commercial empire and unpleasant dealings, some of which were obviously discharged by cash, no questions asked?

His wife? No, she had most to lose. Or, more to the point, she had almost everything to lose now he was dead. Definitely not her, the Detective Sergeant decided.

The partners in property development? No, nothing for them to gain especially as they said they would be seeking another partner in view of their workload.

The answer, he felt, lay in the black economy.

The dodgy dealings, the cash transactions. A quick look through the bank statements showed that Vaughan Pervis had withdrawn over a hundred and fifty thousand pounds in the last three months.

Where had that lot gone?

Time to ask the widow.

Chapter Thirteen

It was mid-evening when he arrived home.

He looked exhausted or at least his mother thought so. She had his dinner ready, so as soon as he'd washed and changed he settled down to a piece of lemon sole with a little salad and mashed potato. He hadn't wanted anything heavier.

Mr Penderfield senior was out for the evening and Charlie felt guilty about abandoning his mother but he wanted to study his case notes and do so in his own room, in his own world. She was understanding and told him not to give it another thought, although her facial expression, had he been awake to it, presented a different story.

She longed for him to find a girl and settle down, yet at the same time knew she would regret it once he left home.

Having furnished her only son with a cup of coffee she accepted his proffered kiss and watched him leave the lounge, then listened to his light footsteps as he climbed the stairs, and she sighed in a sad and forlorn way.

Utterly methodical, he laid out his notes and other paperwork with meticulous care.

Schumann's third symphony emerged as the slightest of background material as his pen hovered over a pad of blank paper and his computer screen flickered into life. The volume of the music was so low as to make it a very soft and almost unnoticeable intrusion, and indeed intrusion was really quite the wrong word anyway.

Early reports suggested Vaughan Pervis had been strangled with a belt. Apart from the footprints in the fields around White Cottage, one set belonging to the deceased, there was precious little evidence of any nature whatsoever, never mind vital forensic data.

The other footprints were probably male, probably size ten, probably a popular make of shoe or boot. Was any of this relevant? Knowing the way these investigations had been going he thought possibly not.

Then a strange thought wandered into the currently open spaces between his ears and he made his first notes accordingly.

Three corpses at White Cottage and we're certain to accept Martyn's story relating to the first: accidental death, he wrote.

Yet here's a thing. Three corpses and no close relative grieving. Mrs Nash-Perry's initial outbursts of sorrow and despair were laid waste for the lies they were. Mrs Pervis more concerned about her future and her money. Michael Martyn virtually delighted that Kerbidge had perished as he blamed the old man for his beloved mother's early demise.

Let's set aside William Kerbidge. Separate issue. Done and dusted if we accept the explanation.

I'll concentrate on the other two, he decided, and made a note to that effect.

Colin Nash-Perry. Strangled with his own tie. Rita identified the tie but a witness says he wasn't wearing one and almost certainly didn't have one with him. No DNA or any forensic evidence at the scene.

So did Martyn perhaps lose his temper and strangle him? That was what we believed although once again it was going to be difficult to prove, and a good Counsel would rip it all to shreds in a court.

Then there's the oddity of Rita being seen in the vicinity. She denies she was there, and that she has or had a black coat. Is the witness lying and if so why?

More and more notes appeared. Every now and then he would check his facts, such as against witness statements, and progressively a picture was formed in his fertile mind.

Now, Vaughan Pervis. Hard for Martyn to strangle him while he was being interviewed by our own Emma Brouding! He penned the word 'Mysteries' as a heading and underlined it, adding the number one immediately below and to the left.

Next to this he wrote: big man, nearly six feet tall, strong and powerful, with a now known history of settling business disputes with violence, or so the stories went. Of course, the tellers may have felt they had nothing to fear now Pervis was gone and no threat.

Number Two: Even if he was taken by surprise he would surely have tried to fight back. Would there have been a scuffle? Would there have been a brief cry or other noise?

And in the far margin he put a comment to test this out. Emma and Martyn were in the lounge close to the front door. It was warm. Were windows open? Alright, they were both engrossed in what they were doing, but neither could've heard a sound. Must ask Emma.

Number Three: Gravel path. The assailant might have been lying in wait or found some way to creep up on Pervis, but surely Pervis walked straight up the drive? Yet no sound?

Number Four: Killed elsewhere and dragged to the door. And again he remarked in the far margin that this theory needed more testing. Sadly, as he could see, there was no forensic evidence to support any such kind of action.

Number Five: Vaughan Pervis, according to Katie Pervis, never wore a belt. Did the killer?

And then a conclusion: This murder needed someone as mighty as the victim himself or even bigger and stronger, and that might indeed support Charlie's own feeling that this was almost an underworld slaughter, nothing to do with Chortleford as such. A hit man, maybe?

By now his eyes were sore and aching and he longed for sleep, so he was almost grateful when mum appeared to say dad was home and she was making tea for him, would Charlie like a cup?

He agreed, closed down the computer, took one last look at his notes and folded them all away preparatory to going downstairs.

Later, lying quietly in bed in the dark, he found the words 'hit man' raked around in his mind and briefly kept him awake. What did the damage was that he couldn't for the life of him align the words 'underworld' and 'hit man' in this particular case, and he just could *not* understand why.

Somehow, just somehow, he knew an underworld hit man wasn't involved.

And then sleep overtook him.

But his scrutiny, attention to detail and policeman's instinct had combined to plant a seed that might yet grow and solve at least one of the murders.

* * *

Rita had reminisced about the 'old days' and had almost been absorbed into a trance-like state as she remembered former friendships. At one point Drype thought she might have dozed off.

The reason for this piece of theatre (as Drype later described it) was his question about Glen Bardrew. Yes, he and Colin had been mates since their school years but the friendship had drifted into nothingness in recent years. And no, neither she nor Colin had seen him for a long time.

The DCI had felt the need to get them all away from the media circus in Chortleford, but was aroused by the possible reasons behind Martyn's impromptu visit to the widow, and also wanted to question Rita closely about her husband's death. And he wanted to get his hands on Mr Bardrew, suspecting now that he might be making some of his eye-witness statement up.

Did he bear Rita a grudge, perhaps?

Clearly not averse to playing away, had he tampered with Mrs Nash-Perry with her agreement when an opportunity presented itself and at a later date been spurned? Was this a case of revenge?

Maybe Rita matched the newspaper report as a woman free with her affections rather better than she'd care to admit.

One thing led to another as is often the case in a policeman's mind. Did she know Martyn before Kerbidge died, that is, did she know him intimately? Was he filling the sizeable gap in the limited range of services provided by her husband?

Martyn was still in the frame for Colin Nash-Perry.

If he and Rita were, to put it politely, fluttering eyelids at each other, bumping off her husband would remove a barrier to their continued and free happiness together. It was another possibility and Drype found he particularly liked the idea of nailing Martyn for the murder, especially after the run-around over his step-father. And there would always be an element of doubt over that.

Just no forensic support of any kind for the killing of Nash-Perry, nothing to put their evidence beyond the meagre circumstantial.

Rita claimed she did not see her husband go out on the fateful day but did agree he was always right and proper about dress. If he wore a shirt designed to be used in conjunction with a tie, and a tie matched the occasion, he would put one on regardless of the weather conditions. It was the way he was brought up. He lived life, she stressed, in 'right and proper' mode.

She argued that the shirt he was found in could be worn with a tie and, from experience, a visit to someone like Martyn would warrant correct attire, i.e. a tie. Drype looked at the photos and felt compelled to acquiesce on the point of the shirt itself as it had a collar and was not a sweatshirt or T-shirt. An ordinary cotton garment like the one he was wearing himself.

Both Michael Martyn and Rita Nash-Perry denied any friendship prior to the day's events.

He claimed he saw himself as a kind of victim and that he felt sorry for Rita being horribly exposed in the local paper, and condemned as a killer and man-eater. He wanted to tell her his story so that she might believe he had nothing to do with Colin's death.

For her part Rita told Drype that she cautiously invited Martyn in at knifepoint but was now confident his call was an innocent act of friendship in a hostile village where tittle-tattle ruled supreme. She said she believed him equally innocent of the violent crime.

To a police officer, a senior detective into the bargain, something didn't sound right in Drype's mind. Experience was kicking in. Could they have been in it together? Was that the solution?

Glen Bardrew was next on his list.

In the meantime Martyn instructed his solicitor to broadcast information about Glynis Parham and Peter Quendon, and they agreed a media release which they hoped might set the story right and counterbalance bad publicity. Both reckoned without journalists such as Olivia Handest.

The search of Chortleford and its immediate environs was widening and with it the need for more resources, that is, more police officers. It occurred to Drype that Pervis's killer may have simply put the belt back on his trousers and walked off, so the murder weapon might never be found.

There was still the question about why the village's victims invariably ended up at White Cottage, often propped up against the front door!

The whole business, in a village probably most residents of Kent had never heard of, reeked of one of those much maligned London bus routes: you wait half your lifetime and three murders come along at once.

The demon in Drype found some black humour to entertain him. Queue here, please, ladies and gentleman, and we'll strangle you at this picturesque cottage in the middle of nowhere as quickly as we can. An orderly queue, if you please. Just let us know what you'd like to be throttled with and if you require souvenir photos taken.

He decided being a long-serving officer made you like that, hardened you to the most awful criminal deeds and then allowed you to satirise such events to preserve your sanity and your ability to do the job. Perhaps it was an essential barricade between the harsher aspects of the work and being able to enjoy your own life, divorced from the horrors man could inflict on man.

Sergeant Ballford sprang to mind.

A very promising, very clever officer, an enthusiastic detective with a bright analytical mind and a focused determination to succeed. Drype had been convinced he'd go far. The furthest he got was the Job Centre, unable to cope with the terrible cases he had to deal with.

Finished up as a cashier in a petrol station. Still there to the best of the DCI's knowledge. A great loss to Kent Police and the Kent public.

Charlie would be alright. A plodder, needed igniting from time to time, but a copper's copper through and through. Never make it to the top, Drype knew, but then maybe he didn't want to rise through the ranks. A career sergeant but a damn good one.

Emma wanted to break through the glass ceiling, the glass rafters and the glass roof tiles after that, and there was nothing to stop her, Drype realised, if she proved herself a success.

He did not fear a junior being a better officer than him and was only too keen to ensure he did not in any way stand in her passage to seniority. If she was good enough, so be it. He'd known too many officers, especially in days gone by, who resented the fact a more lowly officer was actually better than them.

Particularly a male policeman threatened by the female of the species!

He knew those days were far from over.

Encouraging Emma and supporting her were core to his role as her boss, and if she was promoted over him, fairly and on ability, that was all well and good.

Emma had returned Mrs Nash-Perry and Mr Martyn to their respective homes, referred the ladies and gentlemen of the press to the police PR department, and did so firmly and politely, before doing something on her own initiative.

We've made enquiries, done the usual house-to-house more than once, but all we've done is ask questions relative to the murders. We are scratching the surface, she thought, and we need to get deep into village life. And what, she queried in her mind, do these villagers privately like whilst confessing their aversion?

Why, gossip and scandal of course! Chit-chat, tittle-tattle, rumour, hearsay.

We need to join in. What we need to do is to get people talking about what *they* think, what *they* believe. We discourage it as we make it clear we are dealing in facts. No! Let's find out what they're really, really thinking, and off the record, naturally! Now, where to start?

* * *

The next day the wheels finally came off Michael Martyn's nightmare express.

If it had been bad up to now it was about to get a whole lot worse.

Media websites, national papers .... the story of Glynis Parham was thrust upon an eager population, a revelation to surpass all surprise disclosures, a shock to the collective system, a startling expose.

Peter Quendon passed by almost unnoticed, much to Martyn's regret and annoyance.

It was Glynis Parham the public wanted.

At this stage the police had made no comment besides saying the matter of William Kerbidge was closed. The old man had died by his own hand following an argument with his son-in-law.

If Glynis Parham was just short of being regarded as a national treasure, particularly by avid lovers of her romantic tales, the astonishing news that she was in fact a man and had been implicated in a suspicious death only seemed to add to her/his acclaim and attraction.

It was as if readers exalted their beloved author because she/he had the very human flaws she/he wrote about in such graphic and spell-binding manners. And they supported her and worshipped her all the more for it.

Television appearances, exclusives for newspapers and magazines beckoned.

And once again Katie Pervis's friend Mandy had to contend with the widow stomping violently around the property, shouting, swearing, screaming and, at long last, throwing things and breaking things.

Eventually she wore herself out and collapsed in a chair demanding more champagne.

She hated Martyn with a vengeance. He had stolen her limelight. *He* was getting offers of TV and magazine stories, the very offers she had hoped for and was ready for. How dare he?

Didn't anyone care that her wonderful husband had been wiped out? Wasn't his killing of any importance? Didn't the world want to see the photos of the pair of them in happier days, photos in which she appeared almost naked and in seductive poses?

What she didn't realise was that DS Penderfield would shortly be visiting with an array of financial news that was going to blow the bottom out anything she might have left to be clinging on to. At this point she thought that she was at least a very wealthy woman, set up for life, and just a mite miffed on missing out on personal promotional activities.

Starved of the publicity she sought was one thing, but she could always fall back on piles and piles of money by way of compensation.

Except there were no piles. Just troubles.

* * *

What astonished Drype and his colleagues was that in a relatively small village, where everyone knew everyone's business and everyone's movements and were prepared to discuss such knowledge adding their own interpretations and assessments, there appeared to be no witnesses to anything very much.

It didn't make sense.

Fair enough, William Kerbidge died in his tree and shrub surrounded back garden, and the other two finished up on the doorstep of Kerbidge's White Cottage, a doorstep you could only see from the front gate. But the road outside? The road through the village? And the only witness a man who claimed to have seen Colin and Rita Nash-Perry as he was driving to and from extra-marital gratification.

This wasn't adding up.

That being the case something was being hidden. Maybe lots of somethings. Glen Bardrew had kept his information a secret until forced to reveal it, and even then he could be lying, or perhaps bending the truth.

Were others up to naughty activities, of one sort another, which they preferred kept quiet, even if it meant withholding details important to the police investigation?

Colin and Vaughan made one-way journeys on foot right through Chortleford to White Cottage and only the former was spotted by a possibly unreliable witness? The same witness who also saw Rita twice, also on foot, and nobody else did?

Secrets.

A village full of secrets.

After all, it harboured a renowned and prolific popular author who managed to keep his pen name a secret.

Did nobody in Chortleford realise that Rita might be a 'bit of a girl' on the quiet? But, of course, maybe she wasn't. Was anybody really the wiser? On the other hand did other villagers suspect she had a miserable, unfulfilled and rather boring life with Colin, a life in which she longed for romance, adventure and who knew what?

Secrets.

What did villagers really make of their pet hate, the Pervis's? Most were pleased to see the back of him in the hope Mrs Pervis would up sticks. But what did the villagers *know* about them? Who passed the time of day with them? Did anyone actually have any dealings, pleasant or unpleasant, with them?

The more he thought about it the more Drype convinced himself there were answers hidden in the village itself. Chortleford was worth opening up, and in reaching that conclusion he was travelling along a similar route to that being pursued by DC Emma Brouding.

Meanwhile DS Charlie Penderfield was on his way to pull the ragged remains of the carpet from under Katie Pervis's feet.

Her mother had arrived, Vaughan's father and brother had arrived, Mandy was still in situ, and all were ready to support the widow and criticize the police for not having yet apprehended the villain. With the possible exception of Mandy, who seemed quite reasonable by comparison, the other four were positively aggressive and determined to be unhelpful.

So Penderfield found himself very alone and surrounded by animosity. It was as if he was on trial with everyone present glaring at him, claws ready to scratch his eyes out, faces filled with anger, mouths filled was nasty voices. In those seconds he regretted ever becoming a policeman although he froze such thoughts quite swiftly and expelled them from his mind.

This was what the job was all about.

He just didn't fancy telling this herd of animals (as he felt they were) that Vaughan wasn't all he appeared to be and furthermore was seriously in debt, which is where Katie Pervis was going to be now.

Everything he revealed was set upon by the pack of baying hounds in a great and serrated cacophony of snarling noise.

Charlie's only taste of personal loss to date had been the sad death of his dear grandfather, a much adored old gentleman who worshipped his grandson and always made such a fuss of him. Charlie was fifteen when a short illness carried 'grandpa' away and Charlie wept, sometimes openly with the family, occasionally quietly in bed, but not in public, not at school and not in the presence of friends.

It was the first funeral he'd attended and he was at his mother's side, her comforter and supporter, being upstanding and brave and an adult behaving as a man should in his eyes. In such a role he held it all together until they were leaving the crematorium.

Then he happened to look back and saw the tiniest, almost indiscernible whiff of black smoke and he burst into uncontrollable tears. It was now his mother's turn to comfort.

He recalled the incident now as the row going on around him seemed to condense into a distant dark cloud and reduce in volume. He was alone with his own memories, the sadness of his loss, the wretchedness and emptiness of death, the hopeless void that replaces life.

And he looked at this group, and the noise was again ear-splitting, vivid and fuming.

Where, oh where, was the mourning for a lost soul? Where were the tears for a husband, a son and a brother? These wild creatures were overcome by a sense of loss, most certainly, but not for a fellow human being.

Money.

Or, in this case, the lack of it.

Charlie insisted the information was correct and that Mrs Pervis's solicitor would obviously have access to it. He wasn't interested in their suffering. The Sergeant wanted background detail that might be vital to apprehending the perpetrator of the nefarious crime of murder.

Did they want Vaughan's killer brought to justice or not?

And that's what he cried out in vexation and exasperation. His raised voice silenced the others and there was nothing left to hear but the birds singing in the garden and the distant sound of a motor mower.

Mr Pervis senior went to speak, probably to admonish him for his rudeness, but Charlie stopped him in his tracks.

"Look," he bellowed, "you've complained we're not doing anything but we need your help, and I need to find out all I can about what's behind his finances and his business dealings, such as why everything's in the state it is." By now his voice had dropped and the eyes of his watchers, indignantly wide after his outburst, were returning to normality.

Katie's mother, Jackie Waylind, flopped down in an armchair, the first sign of surrender.

"Better listen to the constable," she shouted, deliberately using the wrong rank for humiliation and sarcasm purposes, "as he might, *might* be able to help us find out what's going on. As well as catch poor Vaughan's killer." The last point sounded like an afterthought but it managed to launch Katie into a flood of instant tears and horrible wailing.

At least it broke the spell.

Mandy used the opportunity to offer drinks and ended up providing champagne, whisky, tea and coffee, probably not quite what she had in mind, but she did give Charlie a knowing wink as she handed him his tea.

Charlie, being Charlie, added his own caustic comment as if to demonstrate to Mrs Waylind that he too was capable of being cutting.

"Just a reminder, if any of you drinking alcohol are thinking of driving forget it now. No excuses. Right let's get on, shall we?"

Suitably chastened and chastised, and insulted by his impertinence, the party seemed to relax and become less vociferous, even if their faces retained their fury.

"Mrs Pervis, do you know anything at all whatsoever about your late husband's business arrangements and in particular about the situation with this house?"

Katie wailed, but her acting ability was failing her and seemingly realising this she pulled herself together, perhaps knowing it would all be lost on the officer.

"This house is going to be sold from under me, Sergeant, and I'll be out on the street. And that bast .... my dear husband has left me with virtually no money at all. How am I going to pay them, tell me that?" Her voice ground into Charlie's mind, a whining, squealing, pleading voice.

"Pay who?" he asked.

"Pay who? I ... er ... did I say that? Oh yes, y'know, pay the gas and phone and everything. Do wake up officer." He recognised the latter consideration as a kind of distraction but was surprised when she continued uninvited, and with real fear in her voice.

"You guys have got to protect me. You need to protect me. They'll be after me if I can't pay. You know what it's like...."

"No I don't Mrs Pervis. Perhaps you could tell me. I've heard the gas people can be a bit ruthless but I think you'll find they'll threaten to cut you off first." Charlie's turn at the sarcasm well.

"What on earth are you on about, love," queried Vaughan's brother, St John, sensing the champagne might be working its magic on his sister-in-law's feeble mind.

"Singent, oh Singent, I'm so confused, I am so, so upset, I don't know what I'm saying half the time. Please help me," she sobbed without tears. St John came to her rescue.

"Look, Sergeant, can't you see you're upsetting Katie? This is going to have to wait...."

"No sir, it won't. We have a killer to catch and I need answers right now. Sorry, but there it is."

Entering the fray at this point was Vaughan's father, David, with a few classic words of his own.

"Now listen here, you're just a Sergeant, and we won't be addressed like this. I take it you have a Chief Constable or something. Well, your superiors will be hearing from me, I can tell you. Now kindly leave this house and send us someone with real authority. I can't imagine who you think you're dealing with."

Yes I can, thought Charlie. And he pondered how many times lines like that had been uttered in murder mysteries in books, on television and in films. Fancy saddling a son with a name like St John – 'Singent' indeed – yes Mr Pervis, thought Charlie, I know exactly what I'm dealing with!

DS Penderfield left the establishment thinking that his head had been scrambled and his mind burned, but with one thought firmly embedded in the section of his brain marked 'police investigator'. What did Katie mean about needing protection and, just as importantly, about owing someone money, presumably a great deal of it?

Interesting.

**

Emma saw Harold Dunsburn forking over some soil near a low wall at the front of a property.

"Hi," she called out, simultaneously showing her warrant card, "I'm DC Brouding. Do you live here?"

"Why yes, missy, but not this house. Live just along the way there, Treacle Cottage. Do some gardening for people, like. That's why I'm here."

Treacle Cottage, mused Emma, but she elected not to ask.

"Any chance we could have a chat, just you and me, if you've got a few minutes?"

"Well, be delighted. Is it about the murders?"

"Yes, exactly that."

"Well, I've told your lot all I know, which ain't much, missy, but you've got my statement already."

"And you are?"

"Harold Dunsburn, missy, and everyone calls me Harry. You please do that too, eh?"

"Thanks Harry, and I'm Emma. I know we've spoken to everyone and we're grateful, it's all vital for our investigation, but I wanted to have a kind of chat about the village, the people and all that sort of thing. You know, not just about the murders."

Harry was interested. This was right up his street.

"Suits me, suits me fine. Now missy, want to come up to Treacle Cottage and we can talk in private there, cos I 'spect you want to talk all private like. Only a few steps, girlie."

Missy, now girlie. Exactly the type of language she loved. She sighed inwardly and knew she plainly had to suffer it to make progress, and this was precisely the variety of person she needed to chat to. Old boy, village stalwart, old-fashioned, gardened for residents, bound to be a bit of a gossip. He'd see things and hear things, that's for sure.

He knocked at the bungalow's front door and explained to the lady who opened it he was going to talk to a policewoman and would be back later. Then he led Emma along the road and over a distance well in excess of a few steps.

He stood back at the gate to allow her to pass and looked up at the sign above it. Treacle Cottage, it read. Instinctively she knew he wanted her to ask and she wasn't going to give him the satisfaction.

Treacle was the end cottage of a terraced five, presumably once farm workers abodes, and they looked small and insignificant, yet all five appeared loved and cherished by their owners. Harry lived alone and the place seemed barely large enough for one. Indeed, Emma instinctively ducked when going from hall to lounge although there was no need for her to do so.

He'd managed to cram an appreciable amount of furniture into a very limited space so that even though they sat at opposite ends of the room their knees were not that far apart. She was pleased that at least he didn't give the impression of being in any way lecherous. If truth be told he exuded a kind of pride in his modest accommodation.

"Wife died a few years back, never re-married, y'know how it is, but I keep the place nice and clean and tidy for her, the way she'd have wanted. Like that, was Clara, everything clean, a place for everything and everything in its place." And he gave a little chuckle and suddenly Emma felt immeasurably sorry for him. He must've loved his Clara.

"Married long, Harry?" She had a feeling she knew the answer and the reaction it would bring.

"Aye, lassie, forty-nine years, my one and only," and his eyes watered as the memories flooded back. Emma, saddened for all that, had to bring this chat back on course, if only to spare the old man further pain. Lassie, she thought. Sounds like a dog. Anyway, to business.

"Harry, about these murders. Any theories of your own, anyone else talking? I'm not making notes, just nattering." This not only moved Harry away from his memories but left him warming excitedly to a discourse on scandalous matters, much to Emma's satisfaction.

"Funny goin' ons in this village, missy. First of all that Martyn fellow. Saw 'im dressed as a woman long before story came out. Never told anyone. Not my business what he does in his spare time. Live and let live, I say. But a bit odd that, not that we're allowed to say so any more, eh, missy?

"Have to be, what's it called, politically correct, ain't it?"

"I take it you didn't approve, Harry, and as this talk is off the record please feel free to speak as you find."

"No ... no ... I didn't. Have to be honest, I know it's all the rage today, but, no, I didn't approve. Thought it was disgusting. Then there's that Nash-Perry woman. Colin was the salt of the earth, straight as a dye, a very good friend, decent bloke. I wasn't surprised to read she was handing her favours around. Floozy. He didn't deserve that. I sees a bloke going into her place once, Colin was out, and he stayed over an hour.

"Came out without his tie and his ... er ... his ...fly was undone, if you don't mind me putting it like that, missy." Emma minded more about being called missy than Rita's visitor being described as having an open fly. She'd been out with a guy for a meal a couple of years ago, and he'd come back from the Gents wide open and she had no idea how to tell him.

"Please don't be embarrassed or think it incorrect to use my first name. It's Emma and it's all quite in order these days," she advised, "and the same goes for anything you tell me. Just say it like it is, Harry, it's just between you and me."

So this old gentleman had somehow observed comings and goings at Rita's home. What else had he seen, or was he given to romancing and making up stories to share as gossip?

What she did realise was that this mission was going to be very time-consuming if the other villagers were the same as Harry. Not at all what she'd hoped for, but a very revealing encounter. It merely meant sorting the wheat from the chaff and perhaps she might hit on a nugget of value.

What Harry had incidentally confirmed was that, yes, villagers *did* notice things, especially if there was a hint of scandal. And if Harry did see Martyn dressed as a woman *did* he mention it to anyone? Did someone else know about Martyn's predilection?

Drype had wholeheartedly approved of her taking this line of enquiry, praising her for the suggestion, yet somehow giving her the notion that he welcomed the chance of being rid of her for a long while. Typical male. Typical male officer. Of course she was unaware that, whatever else he was, Drype was not sexist, and he also valued Emma and wanted her to get on in the force, even if she ended up senior to him.

He was willing to let her take the lead knowing it was both good experience and that there was every chance she find an answer.

Harry handed out other snippets all of which confirmed that he was on the ball and cognisant of all manner of happenings in his locality, a trait he must surely share with a good number of other villagers. This had to be a worthwhile route. Proof, to Emma, that not much could pass unnoticed in this close-knit community.

Her conclusion was that out there somewhere vital data were lying hidden.

This village had its secrets, and it was time to bare them to police scrutiny.

Chapter Fourteen

Olivia Handest was gloating.

Even more so now that she'd received a call from a national. The idea of being head-hunted appealed. Would it be name-your-price? Did they want her that much?

To her credit her editor had lavished praise on Olivia for the successful digging and incredible revelations and stories produced. The journalist had a way with words too; she wrote superbly, in a way that attracted readers, held their attention, and left them demanding more.

Mia Cundy rarely had to do anything more than dream up the headlines and re-arrange a few words here and there so that the article fitted the space available. She loved Olivia and respected her professionalism and aptitude, and was rewarded with improved circulation figures.

Not only that, certain advertisers wanted their promotions on any page where one of Olivia's splendid exposes was printed. So advertising revenue increased. Everybody happy.

Today the pair were taking a welcome break and making the most of something that claimed to be coffee, and doing so in Mia's cramped office.

"Y'know, Mia, this is exactly how I thought an editor's office should look. Paperwork everywhere, not enough room to swing a cat, and empty cardboard cups. No offence..."

"Every offence taken, Olly, and I'll have you know I can lay my hands on anything I want, instantly. Quite often anyway! When I can't you want to hear the language!"

Both ladies grinned and smirked and tried to enjoy their drinks. And failed.

"Oh Olly, Olly, so now you might be off, but I trust you'll finish this Chortleford affair first."

"You betcha, Mia. This one's juicy and I sense there's more, and I'm going to do some more digging asap. Mind, I'm not very popular down that way, like, and people are more reluctant to speak now. So I'm keeping tabs on Drype and his flock, hoping they'll lead me to the promised land."

"Well, Olly, go girl go, and if you need anything from me, anything at all, just squawk. We're in competition with the world and its brother, so exclusives figure high in my bucket list. Anyway, what's your theory? Two murders to solve, and I don't think we'll get a sniff of anything on Kerbidge now."

Olivia nodded in agreement as Mia continued.

"It's yesterday's story. Today is Nash-Perry and Pervis. Sounds like a firm of solicitors. Have you thought about looking behind the Pervis facade? They were such a false couple, especially her, so perhaps he had hidden qualities of interest to a backwater rag like ours."

More nodding, then Olivia's comment.

"Yeah, and if there's a few bob in the pot I reckon an exclusive deal with Madam Pervis might be worth a shout, particularly if I take Sam with me."

"Yep, he caught Rita good and proper, didn't he, and I bet Katie Pervis would fall for the same tricks. Yes, y'know she might be ripe for plucking, y'could well be right on that, Olly. So fine, there's some loose change rolling around the petty cash tin, so do a deal, but make sure we get value for money."

"Didn't I last time? Leave it to me. And Sam, of course."

"Seriously, any thoughts on whodunit?"

"No Mia. I don't reckon we're any closer, but I'll tell you what, I don't think the police are either. And I think old drippy-Drype might be a trifle incensed that Martyn's off the hook for Kerbidge and I wouldn't mind betting he'd give his right arm to nail him for Nash-Perry.

"Perhaps I'll give him a friendly push. What friends are for."

"Go as far as you like, babes, and I'll support you all the way."

"Cheers, Mia. I'll be away then. Katie darling, auntie Olivia's coming to con you!"

And there was cynical laughter in the office as they parted company.

* * *

Gladys Frobisher was looking at the remains of a dahlia that sister-in-law Edna had just accidently mowed.

Planted very close to the lawn edge it must've been leaning slightly the wrong way and Edna, in a moment of loose control with the hover mower, pruned it.

Fearing the pruning might not end with the plant Edna threw her hands to her face and cried out her heartfelt apologies.

What might have saved her bacon, possibly only in the short term, was the arrival of Emma Brouding. Two more locals busy gardening and at the front of their property where they would be able to see a good distance along the main street, both ways.

Having introduced herself and gone through the ritual of explaining her visit, including the fact the ladies had been questioned by the police before but this was different, they eagerly invited her into their most pleasant cottage and its comfortable, spacious lounge.

A contrast to Treacle Cottage.

Emma noticed straight away that, even from behind the net curtains in the lounge, they would still have a fair sighting of the road outside to the left and to the right. Gladys set about doing all the talking, and provided the impetus for supplying answers by actually asking herself questions in the first place.

"I ask you, young lady, that Nash-Perry woman, carrying on like that in Chortleford, of all places. Poor Mr Nash-Perry, deceived by the wife he adored. Shocking." And more, much more, of the same.

Eventually she temporarily ran out of steam and paused for an intake of breath, an occurrence that allowed Edna to intervene and do so at her peril.

"I think you remember, Gladys, we did have our doubts about Mr Nash-Perry himself..."

Emma noticed the look of horror on Gladys's face, followed swiftly by a glance in her sister-in-law's direction that would've stopped and disarmed a Sherman tank in its tracks.

"No, I do not remember any such thing, Edna. Pull yourself together and don't mislead the officer. You could get into serious trouble and go to prison, you silly woman." Edna looked crestfallen and hurt at such admonishment, and spoke quickly.

"Yes, you're right, Gladys. I'm so sorry officer, I'm afraid I have mixed things up a little. Sorry." She looked close to tears. Mrs Frobisher regained her own main theme and moved into top gear.

Emma waited for her to draw breath again but waited in vain.

Like Harry, she was just the sort of village gossip she wanted to interview but understood only too well it would always, always be a long and painful and largely boring process. But how could these people see so much yet none see anything at all on the days of the murders?

"Miss Frobisher," Emma eventually interrupted, "can you tell me anything about Katie Pervis, widow of Vaughan? Did she integrate into village life, that sort of thing? Not asking about the victim; his wife." Gladys started answering before poor Edna could even begin to think about what she might say. Edna looked at Emma, shook her head and gently lowered it, her eyes now focused on her hands in her lap.

Having listened to Gladys's complete destruction of Katie Pervis, inclusive of suggestions of what sounded like bacchanalian orgies (Emma's private terminology) being held just up the road, and on a frequent all-night basis, she turned to Edna.

"What are your views on all this, Miss Frobisher?" and in asking in a loud voice simultaneously raised a hand in Gladys's direction, her indignant response being 'well, really'.

Of course, Edna said Gladys spoke for both of them, she had nothing to add and, to further ingratiate herself with her sister-in-law, added that she thought she had spoken rather well and with a high degree of accuracy. Bacon saved for now, she hoped.

Both women denied seeing anyone at all abroad on the days of the murders. Yet quite clearly, like Harry, they saw so much, unless they were making mischief by inventing tales, a distinct possibility. Even if they were, Emma reasoned, they must still see so much that goes on here.

Was this realistically a village with all too many secrets?

Worn down by her two interviews she determined to talk to one more villager today. Any more and she'd be ripe for sectioning, her poor head was in such a daze! But it had so far been a worthwhile effort. They loved their gossip and scandal and that meant they kept their eyes open.

So just why had nobody seen anything at the vital times?

* * *

Drype and Penderfield were nursing sore heads, but not as a result of alcohol intake.

The DCI had tried breaking, as he put it, the witness Glen Bardrew, but the man was sticking to his version of events. Penderfield felt as if his mind had been broken by the moaning-mourners at the Pervis's.

Two sore heads being better than one they had met at a roadside eatery where Charlie had been tempted into a bacon roll. This came piping hot with butter dripping from its sides and large rashers of the aforementioned meat hanging out as if trying to make good their escape.

Consuming this delicacy took some time and provided endless amusement for Henry Drype.

He looked down at the curious concoction masquerading as tea, risked a few sips, decided it was bearable and thereupon drank it as if it was fine wine, no doubt wishing it was. Charlie ended the battle with the roll and tried his own tea. The face he pulled told its own story.

They moved away from the wagon to speak in relative peace and privacy.

"I'm moving along the lines that Pervis was taken out, and that means a hit man. Somebody paid and somebody killed. A pro, if you ask me, sir. We need to get at that family, but I'll say this, I really don't think Katie knew what she'd married into. I think her distress at her revised financial position is genuine. How's Emma getting on?"

"Famously! Talkie-talkie with the residents, the world famous rumour-mongers of Chortleford. And they are almost world famous now!

"I agree with her that for a whole village of chatterers, curtain-twitchers, nosey-parkers, the fact nobody saw anything at all worth mentioning when Nash-Perry and Pervis were done in doesn't make sense. I asked Bardrew who else he saw and he said nobody he knew but there were one or two other people out and about, both journeys, and one or two in their gardens. Also, on his return, when he claims he saw Rita a second time, he saw two women coming out of the butchers and one going in.

"Remembers that clearly because one of the women was, well, let me say desirable, Charlie, but that's not how unexcitingly *he* described her!"

Both men shared a brief laugh in the time-honoured manner of two men sharing a schoolboy-ish expression of humour about the opposite sex.

"Okay, Charlie, I'll tackle your Pervis family."

"Just a moment, sir. Something's just rumbled into my station. Here, that's a good expression. Must remember that." He saw the look of irritation on his superior's face and hurried on.

"Katie exclaimed, and she looked frightened, sir, about not having the money to pay someone. Then, when I challenged her, she tried to back-track. Said she was talking about the gas and phone bills, but I don't think she was, because she'd squealed that she needed our protection."

"I know what you're thinking, Charlie. Did she arrange your hit man? Right, well, we'll keep an open mind as ever, but it's a valid point. I'll quiz her about her needing protection."

They finished their gourmet refreshments and went on their individual ways, Drype very nearly running down a lycra-clad cyclist going past at high speed. The two exchanged the customary hand-signals.

* * *

Dr Monroe looked at Cheryl Maperly who had been articulating her views and concerns about the recent events. She was worried the killer had selected only men so far, and when might he start on the women?

These were typical of the fears of the village, he knew, and mostly unwarranted and probably groundless, but that was the way people were.

Cheryl gave a little stifled squeal as the syringe pierced her flesh. She hated injections even though, on this occasion, she couldn't see what was going on. It didn't prevent her waxing enthusiastically about how frightened she was, that nobody was safe, and that the police didn't seem to have a clue.

The doctor sighed quietly; it was all he seemed to hear these days, and most of it was nonsense.

The qualms patients experienced always overlooked the fact it had now been officially decided William Kerbidge took his own life, and always concentrated on the concept that Martyn must, simply must, be guilty of Nash-Perry's killing.

One or two patients even harboured the preposterous idea that Martyn was also guilty of strangling Vaughan Pervis despite the knowledge he was with a police officer at the time.

"Perhaps when he or she starts on the ladies," he began, entering a period of mischief born of exasperation, "he'll use lethal injections." He smiled as he withdrew the needle, knowing that he couldn't be seen behind her back, but the humour, if it could be called that, was lost on Mrs Maperly.

"I don't want him, that Martyn bloke, anywhere near me, thank you very much." And she yanked up her knickers in an almost indignant fashion while Monroe wiped the smile from his face and just in time.

"I don't think we should judge people like that, Mrs Maperly. We are supposed to be innocent until proved guilty, and then beyond reasonable doubt."

"Well, doctor, you have it your way. I just reckon he's got a temper on him and he lashes out, and whatever he's said, I still think he did for his step-dad. And I bet he lost his rag with Colin, what with the poor sod keep going there and annoying him. Must've got on his nerves."

"Kept going there?"

"Yeah, well, what I've heard, like."

"Have you mentioned that to the police?"

"No, only rumour, isn't it?" Cheryl was speaking nervously and there was a hint of regret in her voice, regret that she'd spoken.

"I think you should tell them anyway. They need all the information they can get. Perhaps let them know where you heard it?"

"Erm ... I don't know, doctor, not my business really, is it?"

"I would if I were you. Leave it up to you."

"Yeah, I'll think about it. Anyway, what's the big deal? They must know Colin was a frequent caller. Not important is it? Don't want to be seen as a gossiper."

Dr Monroe suppressed the laugh that had risen in his throat. You couldn't make it up, he felt. Gossip kept them all going, it was their life-support system and the murders had ramped up the flow of basic data needed to fuel such daily pleasures.

He smiled as she left the surgery, then wondered if she would talk to the police.

Everything he'd heard suggested the officers thought Colin had paid just that one fateful visit to White Cottage. Was there more to this business than anyone knew?

* * *

Rita Nash-Perry was settling down to widowhood accompanied by lashings of brandy.

She looked at the photo of her wedding day.

"I look so pure in that white dress," she commented out loud, "shame I stayed so pure for so much of my life. Wouldn't happen today. Young people nowadays get a better idea of the creatures they're going to marry, if they marry at all.

"In those days it was all take a chance. It was doing the right thing. You got to know your husband after you married him. I was a young girl, head full of romantic rubbish. Thought he was Mr Wonderful, so well spoken, always charming and polite, so courteous. Didn't realise it was never going to get any better.

"Didn't understand the real reason why. Not then. You didn't talk about things like they do these days. Everything was 'right and proper'. God, how I hate that expression." And she picked up the photo and flung it across the room, the glass breaking into many pieces when the frame made contact with the coffee table. She looked away and folded her arms.

"Right and bloody proper. God damn you, Colin. You took my life, you strangled the life out of me, you killed me, left me for dead, a living death." And she collapsed in a heap on the floor yelling out the words, "You deserved to die," as the emotional tide bounded up inside her, smothered her heart and mind, leaving her heaving as the storm of tears thrust their way from her eyes.

Not far away there was similar suffering being endured.

Katie Pervis was settling down to widowhood accompanied by lashings of Bollinger.

She was also damning her husband but for very different reasons.

"Surely that copper can't be right, surely he can't?" But her associates in mourning sadly assured her he was.

The violent histrionics had died out and, thanks to the intervention of her mother and her friend Mandy, she was no longer throwing things and charging around the house. Feeling that a degree of calmness was upon them Mandy decided to chance her arm.

"Katie, what did you mean about the police protecting you, and you couldn't pay someone?"

Mrs Pervis gave Mandy a look that might have led to another funeral.

"Oh, forget it Mand. I was all chewed up, babes, like, and I didn't know what I was saying. Let's leave it out, eh?" And so Mandy left it out, but retained it in her mind.

Shortly after that they had a visit from Olivia Handest and Katie finally found something to perk her up. All was not lost. An exclusive deal, photos. The sun was suddenly shining in her life again.

"If I tell you everything, you know, everything, don't tell lies but let you have all the details, especially as some of its right saucy, if you know what I mean, is there more money?"

Even Olivia, who had been acquainted with all kinds of mercenary requests from those eager to earn some cash at any price, looked aghast but rallied swiftly. It was her way.

"Yes, of course, as long as what you tell us is indeed truthful, we're interested in anything that's newsworthy. But I've got to be honest, Katie, it's got to be something special, not what we might call 'yesterday's news' or run of the mill stuff, if you get my meaning."

Katie did and was already mentally preparing her photo-shoot.

To that end, which seemed more imperative to Katie than telling her story, an appointment was made for Sam to get some pics.

"He'll want you in sad widow mode, Katie. He does a few general shots to start with, making sure the camera angles and lighting is okay, like, then he'll do the ones we'll choose from, the sad, forlorn ones."

Katie was on the edge of her seat, excited and boasting wide, bright eyes aglow with anticipation.

"I've turned out some photos of me and Vaughan together as a happy couple, babes, would you be interested in them?"

"Oh yes, Katie, yes indeed. Happy relationship destroyed by ruthless killer always goes down well." Ms Handest was well and truly warming to this one for, as she had suspected, Katie was not a grieving woman, and was all too keen to unwittingly follow Rita's headlong dash to oblivion.

She looked upwards for a brief second and thought to herself if there's a God, thank you for making such vain, stupid and gullible people for me to tear to shreds. I'm sure Sam will thank you too for he's bound to get some eye-watering pictures of this bitch!

* * *

Charlie Penderfield had found an opportunity to ask Emma about her interview with Martyn.

She could recall very little of the surroundings, and wasn't sure if the windows were open or not. They had been engaged in an emotionally charged discussion in which Martyn eventually folded and issued the truth they had been seeking. There would forever be doubt nonetheless, but there being no forensic support for murder it looked as if suicide, that is, accidental death, had to be the sorry outcome.

Similarly there was no forensic evidence to convict Martyn of Nash-Perry's murder, and none to suggest anyone else had been involved in Vaughan Pervis's killing.

Could they conceivably be looking at two suicides?

But why would Colin Nash-Perry want to do away with himself?

Did he intend to commit suicide and opted to implicate Martyn out of sheer bloody cussedness, or because he hated the man for some reason?

Charlie settled for Schubert as musical accompaniment as he once again plodded through his notes, a second evening passing quietly in his own personal domain.

It was abundantly clear Pervis had been slain. You can't strangle yourself and then dispose of the murder weapon ..... unless you had someone to subsequently dispose of it for you! Unlikely nonsense, thought Charlie.

Now Pervis was the only one of the three whose death might not be connected with the village.

Emma hadn't heard anything that she could remember, but said she would try and go back through her memory of the occasion just in case something lying dormant in her mind might spring to life on closer inspection.

When Charlie said he was going to go through his notes that evening Emma's ears pricked up and she asked him what he got up to. Quite embarrassed he explained how he approached things, with soft background music, peace and tranquillity, and the sense that he was temporarily cut off from the outside world. This intrigued and enthralled the Detective Constable.

"Like some company, Charlie? I could pop round and we could, sort of like, put our heads together." Sensing she may have hit a nerve she added quickly "I won't be in the way, or outstay my welcome, or talk when I shouldn't," and made a nervous giggle sound encouragingly seductive.

Still recovering from embarrassment this new scheme made him blush a deep red to add to his bewilderment, and Emma found it all very attractive in a charming, romantic kind of way.

Not realising Emma had seductive aspirations, as it might be put, he took her offer at face value and invited her round to discuss the case, hoping mum and dad wouldn't mind.

She could barely conceal her excitement.

Innocently he checked his paperwork and computer, trusting it would in order for her, totally ignoring that this was his bedroom and therefore equipped with a bed. In a less naive man where women were concerned it would've become obvious that his visitor might be put off by such a brazen approach, but it would not have occurred to Charlie that the presence of a bed could be misconstrued.

For that matter he'd unknowingly overlooked the small matter of offending his parents in their own home in taking a girl to his bedroom.

It was his study, she was a professional colleague on business, and they were two adults behaving properly.

When he told his parents they had admittedly looked a wee bit shocked, but agreed to the invitation. After all, this was no teenage boy in the throws of wanting to try out adulthood. They trusted their son implicitly, especially where girls were involved, but still felt uneasy about him taking a lass upstairs.

Still, it might do him good, Mr Penderfield said, sporting a wicked grin to enhance his comment. Although his wife ticked him off in light-hearted fashion, she did wonder if this was Charlie's big moment and whether she and Mr P ought to go out! But she decided to draw the line at that idea and made no utterance on the issue.

Now the moment of truth.

Emma found the formality rather twee yet pleasantly delightful. Introductions, handshakes, fine words, kindness. A warm, friendly welcome indeed, and a marked change from the way she occasionally met parents of boyfriends. There was something so deliciously old-fashioned about Charlie and his mum and dad, and she knew it was endearing.

But nothing could've prepared her for his room.

Pastel shades, a spacious place indeed, and one instantly calming.

"Do you like Schubert?" he asked.

"Mmm ... well I'm happy with wine or a beer or something actually," she replied. "Just the one, driving y'know," and she giggled in a way he liked.

"We can have a beer each, if you like, unless you'd prefer tea or coffee?"

"Nah, let's push the boat out. Beer each." He went downstairs and returned with two cans, still amused by her view of Schubert. Probably thinks it's a spirit, he thought.

They drank from the cans in the way of the young, chatted about things in general, laughed when laughter was appropriate, and duly set about their main task, the case.

Sitting side by side she was electrified by his close proximity, whereas for his part he was slightly terrified, had he been forced to admit it.

But for the moment, work. And work might just prove productive in a case that was difficult to crack.

Chapter Fifteen

Having explained his system to Emma, who looked and sounded truly impressed, they went through their notes and then entered a period of wide ranging discussion.

By common consent they chose to ignore the William Kerbidge affair. Unless at some time in the future other evidence came to light, or Michael Martyn confessed to murder, it was unlikely the situation would change.

Charlie wanted him charged and for a jury to decide, but Emma was with the establishment.

"Been some miscarriages of justice, and I think juries are worldly-wise now, Charlie. There's been a few put away, like, when there's been real doubt. I reckon the courts these days are a bit cuter and more cautious about circumstantial evidence, especially when that's all there is."

They agreed to differ, put the Kerbidge case on the proverbial back-burner, and concentrated on the loss of Nash-Perry and Pervis.

"Right," announced Charlie, "let's start with Colin and what we know. According to his computer and his wife, who we might want to regard as a unreliable witness as well as a suspect, he got all hot and bothered about the murder of William Kerbidge.

"It became an obsession. He wanted to solve the crime and tried every which way he could, but knowing he was probably missing vital information only the police held. Very frustrating! Then one day he storms out of the house and off to White Cottage to confront Martyn.

"Maybe they had an almighty dust-up, perhaps it came to blows, possibly a violent struggle. Let's assume that a man with that sort of obsession might easily have a temper on him, be in a rage when he got there, and overheated. What would you say about Michael Martyn, Emma? Capable of losing his temper, being violent even?"

"I don't know, Charlie. But we do know he took his work very seriously and felt all the emotions his heroines suffered, and those sort of emotions can be, in their way, violent I suppose, if you know what I mean. Here's a thought: Colin didn't know about Glynis, so supposing Martyn opened the door dressed as a woman. Enough to pitch a fine upstanding right-and-proper Colin right over the edge?"

"Don't think so, that is I can't see Martyn opening the door as Glynis, that'd give the game away. And I'm not sure I really buy into a fight, Emma."

"Call me Em, all my mates do."

"Thanks ..... Em. Anyway, if Martyn did it then he'd have to strangle Colin, presumably on the doorstep..."

"Unless, Charlie, the murder took place inside and Martyn propped him up against the door."

"Forensics, Em, I don't think we've got anything to support that. Colin looked a strong lad. Do you reckon Martyn was strong enough to overpower him. And don't forget he was strangled with his tie wound round his neck, it wasn't on his shirt."

"Good point Charlie. The tie was removed before it could be used as a weapon. Picture the scene. Martyn says to him 'stand still Colin, I'm just going to take your tie off and then throttle you with it'. Yeah, right." And the two laughed and were serious again.

"So how did the tie get taken off? Em, it looks more to me like someone else was involved, someone a lot stronger than Colin, and I reckon that rules Rita out. In a struggle she'd come off second best."

"Well, how about this, Charlie. We believe Rita may have been following Colin, so how about she and Martyn killed him between them, taking care to leave no traces."

"Far-fetched, but .... but .... supposing they were prepared. This was the chance they'd been waiting for, Em. That kind of thing. Colin sets off, Rita calls Martyn and alerts him, and they're ready for murder."

"And ... and ... and, Charlie," Emma was getting breathless, "she takes the tie with her. Glen Bardrew insists Colin wasn't wearing one."

"I think we're getting carried away, Em, but who knows? Anyway, let's get this all down on our records and move on to Vaughan Pervis, in some ways the perfect murder. At least you gave Martyn a cast iron alibi for once!"

With the great care normally associated with his analysis Charlie, ably assisted by Emma, updated their records and referencing system. She was exhilarated by the combination of fascinating police work and being with a man who was making her tingle without actually touching her.

Charlie felt warm inside but failed to recognise why.

"We're not actually sure why Vaughan Pervis went to White Cottage, other than what Martyn told us, and that may lack some accuracy, Em."

"Yes, sadly he's also an unreliable witness and we seem to be loaded with them! Martyn said Vaughan just wanted a natter, wanted to offer support and say that he didn't believe he'd committed murder. Strange that, Charlie, I mean, why bother, like? I think he had a different reason for going and may have used that gambit as a way of, well, ingratiating himself with Martyn and perhaps getting invited in.

"Clever man, that Pervis, Charlie. Clever man. Might've tied Martyn up in knots, not literally of course, but got him to say all kinds of things, things that might have made him look guilty. Perhaps that was the purpose of the visit."

"And what, Em, was he doing skulking around in the fields outside? Was that before or after his visit? But we do know Martyn didn't kill him and, given the shady business world he lived in, my money's on a hit-man. That would mean someone paid for his death. How ... ever ... I think there's an outside chance Mrs Pervis might have booked the killer.

"Her only trouble now is that she hasn't got the money to pay him. Got to be male. Pervis was a big strong guy. Some puny little bloke wouldn't stand a chance."

"Neither would some puny girl, eh Charlie?"

"You know I didn't mean that...." And they dissolved into fits of laughter, capped by her spontaneous gesture of putting an arm briefly around his shoulder and giving him a quick kiss on the cheek.

"Do you think I'm puny, Charlie? Do you?" There was so much mischief and fun in her eyes and her face radiated happiness and excitement. And anticipation.

"Of course you're not puny, you're ..... you're .... you're .... well, you're lovely Em, just lovely."

The laughter stopped and his head sank in embarrassment.

"Don't be shy, Detective Sergeant. Come and give this lovely Detective Constable a nice big kiss. Detective Constables taste *very* nice, Charlie. Charlie? Charrrrrrrrrrleeeeeeee?"

It was a good ten minutes before they disentangled themselves and returned their attentions to Vaughan Pervis, deceased.

A very good ten minutes.

"Now Charlie, Katie Pervis paying to have her husband taken out. Why would she do that? He was her bank-of-England, her cash cow, her sugar daddy. Why kill the golden goose? Did she really think she'd come into loads of dosh?"

"Yep, she's that stupid, Em."

" Y'know, motives do seem to be in short supply for both murders and, for very different reasons, women wanting to do away with their other halves seem to have some prominent value here. But it's still not adding up, Em."

"Well maybe it's because it's so obvious we think it can't be true. It might be staring us in the face. Sometime truth is stranger than fact. In Rita's case we could be looking at a crime of passion, or in this case a crime of a lack of passion!" And they laughed again and kissed again.

"Charlie, Charlie, I'd love to commit a crime of passion with you," she smouldered heavily in his direction. In his shyness, a shyness still far from overcome, he went a very dark red, and for a second Emma wondered if he was having an attack.

"Um ... Em ... er ... er .... " he spluttered.

"I'll take that as a yes," she giggled, "but not with mummy and daddy downstairs, is that right?"

"Correct. But they're not always here." It is possible he didn't realise what he was saying or what he was agreeing to, but he thought it was a journey that it was high time he made, and besides, it bought him some thinking time. Emma responded in her best Mae West voice.

"Well, Charrrrleeee, I have my own flat. Come up and see me sometime." This statement enabled Charlie to experience embarrassment at the next level.

There was a knock at the door.

"Either of you fancy a cuppa or some coffee or Ovaltine or something," mum enquired, "as it's getting late." This was clearly a warning recognised by both officers. Drinks were declined as Emma said she'd be on her way soon, and she waited until mum had closed the door and retreated a safe distance.

"Bedtime, Charrrleeee. No little Em for you to cuddle tonight."

Entering into the humorous spirit of things he playfully pushed her, called her a right little tease, and then seized her in his arms for a generous, full-bloodied and enlivening kiss.

They somehow found time and inclination to finalise their notes and then went downstairs, but not before sharing yet another fervent and fiery kiss at the door to his room.

The seeds of friendship were not the only seeds they had sown, however, and their inquisitive minds had laid the foundations for success in their investigations. Not that it was obvious just yet.

"Enjoy your Ovaltine with mummy," she called out impishly as she climbed into her car.

***

Katie Pervis was re-born.

Here was her big chance after all.

Tonight Sam was coming to take photos and she was busy deciding what to wear for her much sought after opportunity. The surprise was that selection took so long given that there was so little of it in the end.

Her attire wasn't so much off-the-shoulder as off-the-body. Revealing would be the wrong word since the miniscule amount of material involved hid virtually nothing.

Mandy had departed. She had her own life and wasn't certain the direction Katie was taking was the approved one for widows in any circumstances, but definitely not where ruthless killing was involved.

In fact, Katie was going to be alone.

Her mother, Mr Pervis senior and St. John Pervis decided to go out for a meal so that Katie could get on with her photo-shoot. They left minutes before Sam arrived.

It was in those minutes that her mobile rang and she received the call she'd been dreading.

Meanwhile, just along the road, Cheryl Maperly was preparing pizza for herself and Mr Maperly and thinking back over her chat with the doctor, and beginning to wonder if she should talk to the police. It was only rumour, of course, but supposing the doc was right and it turned out to be important.

It was bothering her and she didn't like being disturbed in that way. She was also being bothered by the injection site which was sore, and which received gentle rubbings from time to time, these being useless as a medium for relief.

The police will think I'm just another village gossip, she thought. No, forget it, I won't tell them. Now where's my Savlon?

Not far from this scene of discomfort Martha, church organist, was eating her salad which was being washed down with a glass of a particularly encouraging Chablis. The wine was her secret. It wasn't the only secret she had. She was also recalling a conversation from earlier in the day, and with that charming detective, Miss Brouding.

How gorgeous to be able to talk about her own judgments about the murders without feeling inhibited in any way. It was confidential, off the record, and just a general chinwag after all.

Happily, from her own point of view, she'd kept one or two other secrets under wraps, for it wouldn't do to tell the police everything. Her chief reason was that the police had not always been her friend, and she didn't feel she should give up all her knowledge over matters that were none of their business and probably of no value to them anyway.

She'd talked in very general terms about the deaths. That would have to do. Just what was commonly discussed by villagers, that was all.

Still, it had been a good time, and she was a fine girl. Not like that policeman all those years ago who had refused to help her look for her watch in her garden. He'd been quite rude about her dialling 999. Not what it was for, he'd said. Emergencies only. Well, it was an emergency to Martha and calling the police was why she paid her taxes.

She was disappointed with the service and said so.

That wasn't her only unpleasant brush with unhelpful hands of the law.

It was behind her, but she was blowed if she'd help them now *they* needed assistance.

* * *

Having watched one of their favourite TV shows the Drype's were relaxing on their settee.

They usually sat together and occasionally held hands, although whether this was a romantic gesture or a means of avoiding one or other escaping was open to debate.

Corinne Drype wanted an update on DCI Drype's investigation, and he deemed a few comments worthy of imparting for two reasons. It might hopefully satisfy his wife and it might also generate a good idea or two. So he put forward the theories on village gossip and how the people there might be hiding something, perhaps, he added generously with a generosity he didn't feel, even if they were doing so unwittingly.

"They see so much yet saw nothing on the days of the murders."

"Did you say there was a doctor in the village, dear?" Drype's mind had wandered and he had to ask Corinne to repeat the question, and applied to it a one word answer.

"Yes."

"I'd have a chat with him if I were you. Out of curiosity what's a small village like Chortleford doing with a doctor?"

"Think he's been there forever, dear. Probably there before the NHS, probably still uses leeches!"

"That's a vulgar thought, Henry Drype. But he'd be ideal for your purpose what with all those old dears as patients. He'll hear all the gossip, mark my words, and patients tell their doctors things they tell nobody else.

"I've told our doc one or two things I've never told you."

His look of horror gave rise to an outburst of laughter.

"Thought that'd wind you up, you daft thing," and they chuckled together. "No, seriously Harry, he's worth a punt."

"It wouldn't be any good, dear, because he'd have to respect patient confidentiality...."

"No, no, no," she interrupted, "he doesn't have to give anything away, just share surgery tittle-tattle with you, that's all. Sometimes all it needs is a sign like a nod in the right place to send you searching in the right direction. There's the added advantage that he's not going to talk about *you* to his patients, is he?"

"Okay, I'll buy into that. As you say, worth a try."

* * *

Rita was bored.

There was nothing she wanted to read, nothing she wanted to watch, nothing she wanted to do.

Now that wasn't strictly true, because in an ideal world she would've loved to be out on the town, and why not?

Exposed as the Chortleford Minx, why not live down to her reputation? Colin would not have wanted her to discard her widow's weeds this early, and the contemplation of how Mr Prim-and- Proper would've expected things done properly only served to make her want to break out of her shell more.

She'd enjoyed her kisses with Harry Drype for more than one reason. It represented escape from her repressed past and subservience to her overbearing husband, and it was an achievement, a goal, a target, seducing not only a married man, but a police officer investigating a serious crime.

Rita was pleased with herself, but now she wanted to capitalise on her success.

There must be other men who would love to fill the void created by Colin vacating his post.

If Drype had been so easily won over, why then there must be other men who would find her attractive and desirable. They would unquestionably find her willing! She wriggled her nose as if to show disgust as she dismissed the concept of Michael Martyn stepping into Colin's shoes, or in this case his bed.

"I'm ready to rock and roll," she bellowed, "and life's too short. Find me a man, have him stripped, washed and brought to my tent." Laughter came first, ironic laughter, then laughter mixed with tears, and finally tears alone, and she sank to the floor once more, weeping for all she was worth. But this evening there had been no brandy as the bottle was empty.

That decided her.

She'd dress to kill and go up the *Log and Weasel* for a drink or three. And that's what she did.

She found the pub poorly patronised. Most drinkers looked at her in surprise and then quickly away. Sally, the barmaid, was equally shocked but regained her composure as Rita arrived at the bar.

"You alright there?" Sally asked.

"Yes. Yes, I'm fine," came the response, Rita unaware that the young had changed the language and Sally's question really meant 'may I help you' or 'what would you like to drink'. "May I have .... now let me see .... I know, I'll have a pint of Bishop's Finger, please."

Furnished with her refreshments she went to a small table near the window and sat quietly sipping and looking all around her. It was dark out so there was nothing to see through the glass, and her gaze returned to the bar where she observed Sally talking to a young gentleman.

Mmm ... what a smart, well groomed, good looking young man. Too young for me, she thought, but then her heart missed a beat as she saw him heading her way.

He introduced himself as Marc Rosberry from one of the national papers, she couldn't remember which, but then she'd had enough of media involvement to last a lifetime.

"I'm staying here," he advised, "and I understand you're Mrs Nash-Perry. My condolences, I am very sorry for your loss, but even sadder for the terrible way the press has treated you. It's disgusting when you've suffered such a huge loss in such a terrible way. May I join you?"

Rita considered his introduction, took a mouthful of beer, let it wash around her tonsils, swallowed it too quickly, spluttered, and then invited him to sit.

"That's kind, thank you. I won't take up too much of your time or cause you any distress. Any time you want me to go, just say the word."

"Thank you Mr Rosberry...."

"It's Marc, Mrs Nash-Perry."

"Thank you Marc, and I'm Rita."

"Okay Rita. Now I'm not after a follow up story or anything like that. No interview. I'm pleased to meet you because it gives me the chance to apologise for those dreadful people in my trade who prey on people like you. I can't imagine the pain that article must've caused, and as I read it I realised, being a journo, that there were two sides to the story." He held his hands up in mock surrender.

"No, no, I'm not after a story setting the record straight, don't worry. I'm sure you want your husband's killer caught, and I'd love to help, and that's all I want. The chance to help you.

"To be honest I didn't think I'd get an opportunity to speak to you. I guessed you wouldn't entertain the press after what they did to you. So it's very kind. Now you can send me away with a flea in my ear, or you can let me buy you another drink."

Rita considered the various proposals, and the one covering the supply of drink readily appealed, and decided she had nothing to lose as long as she kept her wits about her. And he was a very nice man. Dishy. Hadn't seemed to notice her exposed cleavage or exposed mid-thighs just yet, but perhaps he was being the perfect gentleman and not staring at her attributes as she considered them to be.

"Another Bishop's Finger, please Marc, but I'll be wise to any nonsense, trust me. The local rag sent me into a darkness I didn't know anyone could sink into, and I'll not be going there again."

"Understood Rita. Back in a mo."

She was not a beer drinker and had selected her tipple on the basis the label on the bottle appealed to her, as did the name. But she'd discovered to her surprise and joy that she liked it, no indeed, loved it.

Marc was back in seconds with his own drink as well. The conversation consisted of fairly safe general matters and Rita started to relax. They began to enjoy each others company and he appeared genuinely interested in her as a person.

The conversation manufactured some gentle laughter from time to time and Rita realised she was enjoying herself. Then came the question.

"Rita, it's a bit difficult in a pub, bars have ears and all that. Any chance I could make an appointment to meet you somewhere, less public, and just run over a few things. Look, seriously, I'm not after causing you more grief, I'd simply like to help find Colin's killer. And I can dig where the police can't.

"If we meet for a chat you call the tune. If I ask anything you don't like, say so. It's as simple as that Rita. And I'd love to set the record straight, you know, one in the eye for the local rag, show you as the loving, caring and devoted wife you are."

"Marc, I live just down the road. We could meet at my place anytime. After all, I needn't worry about scandal anymore. Do you want to come now, for instance, or are you off duty?" He laughed in a kindly way.

"We're never off duty, Rita, but if I leave the pub with you tongues are going to wag like there's no tomorrow."

"Personally I don't care, but I care for *your* reputation Marc. I could leave now and you slip over in, say, half an hour. I'll give you my address."

"Fine with me. And don't worry about my reputation. Probably lost that years ago!"

They chuckled, finished their drinks, Marc noted the address and returned to the bar while Rita slid out of her seat, through the door and along the road, a skip in her step.

* * *

And night deepened over Kent.

The secrets and mysteries of one village in particular lay buried in the blackness of a cloudy and moonless night. The night was as dark as the deeds perpetrated in this otherwise rustic and tranquil part of the Garden of England that epitomised the rural idyll so often in the minds of the town dweller.

People lived their lives here, much as anywhere, went about their daily lives taking their dreams around with them, suffered life's setbacks and rejoiced in its triumphs. In Chortleford as in Canterbury as in Chilham as in Chatham life spread itself through every day and night, and the people took life as it presented itself to each person individually.

No different here from anywhere.

Good souls, those up to no good, those committing offences, those leading blameless lives. Those not breaking the law of the land but breaking life's moral codes. Pillars of society, the brave, the kind and generous, the hardworking, the layabouts.

Those who lived by and respected their religious beliefs, those who simply lived life to the full. Those who would help and befriend anyone, those who do you out of your last penny.

But it was by virtue of being a village that events in Chortleford put it on the national map.

Those events might have happened in a big town or city and been swallowed up in the daily morass of similar news, perhaps forgotten almost as quickly as they'd appeared.

It was the fact that here was a village community, a comparatively small section of society, woven together tightly, bound by the rules of life in the countryside, that captured the public imagination far and wide.

The diversity of the victims and suspects made good reading. That, and all three deaths occurring at White Cottage, this very symbol of the concept of a country cottage on the edge of a delightful country village.

Chortleford's secrets made good reading.

Michael Martyn revealed as best-selling novelist Glynis Parham. Grieving widow Rita Nash-Perry shown up as the sex-crazy Chortleford Minx.

The world held its collective breath.

There had to be more. There really had to be more.

And, of course, there was.

Chapter Sixteen

"Thank you for seeing me. I appreciate your time, doctor."

DCI Drype was, at his wife's suggestion, calling upon Dr Monroe who now sat behind his desk, arms out in front of him, prescription pad at the ready. Not that he was likely to be able to prescribe anything to ease Drype's pain.

"I understand about patient confidentiality, doctor, so I am not asking about any of your patients. All I ask is this. And I stress I am not seeking an actual patient or patients.

"Village gossip. Do you get to hear very much, and if so is there anything at all, anything you may have picked up that might be relevant to the recent murders, even if you yourself don't consider it significant?"

Dr Monroe drummed the fingers of both hands and looked Drype right in the eyes, unmistakably thinking about how he should answer, the Detective realising that he had something to say. After a decent pause the doctor curled his lip sideways seemingly still unsure about what he should reveal and how. Drype was on the verge of feeling excited for he knew Monroe had words to speak, and he hoped they would be useful.

"I'm not sure how to put this, Chief Inspector, but I'll do my best. I cannot provide the source of this. Yes, I have to listen to all kinds of stories, well, observations really, and it goes without saying that many of my patients love a hint of scandal.

"Give them some bare material and they'll add as much as they feel necessary to produce a juicy tidbit. So I have heard much in connection with the murders, most of it utter baloney.

"The only thing that I have heard that you may not know about, and that has any credence in my eyes, is that Colin Nash-Perry's fatal walk to White Cottage was not his first foray. On the contrary, as I believe it he was a more frequent visitor than you may know.

"What I can't do is pass on the name of the person who provided that snippet. But that's just about all I can tell you. Nevertheless, I'll think carefully back over my many consultations and perhaps something else will occur to me."

"Thank you, Doctor, that's splendid. That's more helpful than you could imagine, but I do appreciate you can only go so far, even though I would love to know where that came from."

"Well, it was at least second hand information, Chief Inspector. By the way, changing the subject completely, how far along the main street have you proceeded with your door-to-door enquiries?"

"I heard that, on this side of the road, you'd reached Smuggler's Den."

Drype looked at him uncomprehending, baffled by such a curious question.

"If that's so," Monroe continued, "the next property belongs to Mr and Mrs Maperly. Oddly enough Mrs M was here very recently. Well," he said, rising and offering his hand across the desk, "I must get on. Good luck with your investigation."

"Thank you, Doctor, you've been most helpful." Drype had suddenly seen the light and now comprehended very well. He shook hands and departed heading for Mrs Maperly's residence.

* * *

To Rita Nash-Perry the morning could not have looked better.

She couldn't help smiling and in a very self-satisfied way as she drew back the curtains and drenched herself in the simple beauty of her back garden. Never had it appeared so lovely, so inspiring, so delightful. She nodded sagely to herself. Must do some dead-heading, mow the lawn, weed the borders, have a bit of a clear up she decided.

But the fact these jobs so obviously required urgent attention did not detract from the glorious feeling of overwhelming joy at the beauty of life that had extended itself into the worship of an unattended garden.

Even the most ugly thing would've have had a exquisiteness of its own today.

She'd never felt like this in her whole life. She wanted to sing, she wanted to dance, she wanted to run naked down the street.

At this point the catalyst for this ecstasy and elation snored heavily, coughed and passed wind.

Rita laughed so loud she woke her bedmate and playfully set about clumping him with a pillow.

This was a new Rita.

A stone's throw from Rita's morning glory another recently widowed woman was also in the mood for singing and dancing.

Sam had taken some stunning pictures and been able to offer a fresh level of comfort for the newly bereaved. The newspaper photographer didn't have Vaughan's money, but then again neither did she, but he had something her late husband had never had – the ability to please a woman in a way that left her floating around the universe.

What a night!

And soon the arrival of Olivia Handest to get the story for which Katie Pervis had arranged all her props, including wedding photos (Bermuda, where else?) and other 'happy couple' holiday snaps.

She sat in front of the mirror applying her make up in such a way as to appear to have been crying. At the end of the evening she'd gone through the same routine at Sam's request so that he could grab some photos of her looking heartbroken.

This was her big moment.

She could launch a career and, more importantly, perhaps snare a millionaire looking for a sexy young girl. It pays to advertise.

But not, it would seem, with Olivia's paper.

If she had consulted Rita she'd have realised she was about to be exposed in a way she wasn't anticipating.

* * *

"Good morning, Madam, DCI Drype, could I have a few words, please?"

Drype showed his ID card to the young woman who opened the door and who then spoke.

"Well, yes, that's fine. Is it about the murders? Only I've told your officers all I know."

"Yes it is, or rather it's specifically about Mr Nash-Perry. May I take your name please?"

"Yeah, it's Maperly, Mrs Cheryl Maperly."

"Thanks. I know you've been spoken to before but we're just revisiting our door-to-door enquiries in the light of new information. Just wanted to clarify a few points with local people." He was quite obviously not going to be invited in, so he continued where he was.

"Mr Nash-Perry. We understand from other people in the village that he was a frequent visitor to White Cottage where, as you're undoubtedly aware, he met his death. We're just trying to piece together odds and ends that we've heard and wondered if you knew he often called there?"

Cheryl fell straight into his simple and untruthful trap.

"Yeah, that's what I heard. Well, got it from Mrs Frobisher, if you're going to be talking to her, or is that where you heard it?"

"No, we haven't spoken yet. Any idea if Mrs Frobisher or anyone else could say for sure White Cottage was always his destination?"

"Couldn't tell you. No idea. Just that people, like Mrs Frobisher, always seemed to know that was where he went. Mind you, a long time ago now. Don't think he'd been for a while before he got killed there."

"What makes you say that?"

"Oh ... oh ... er, I suppose it's what Mrs Frobisher said. You'd better ask her."

"Finally, Mrs Maperly, any idea why there was so much interest in Mr Nash-Perry's movements?"

"I ... er ... er ... no, not really, just the way people are in a small village I guess."

He thanked her and departed knowing he wasn't going to learn any more but convinced there was more to learn. Now for Gladys Frobisher.

***

The Team was making interesting inroads into Vaughan Pervis, the life and times of.

Charlie Penderfield was running through some of the details so far unearthed.

He was making enough money in property development to fund his lifestyle, and that of his financially voracious wife, so why did he dabble in, for want of a better term, the black economy?

And those huge sums he withdrew in cash! For what purpose?

Charlie mused on the thought that, yes indeedee, Pervis was a successful property developer. You don't see many of them driving around in battered old second hand Ford Fiestas, do you?

Even allowing for leeway on either side, essential in a police investigation, it all pointed more and more to a professional assassination, and that meant someone paid to have him taken out. The Sergeant couldn't buy into the idea of Katie herself arranging a hit man. It just wouldn't have made sense.

The logical conclusion was that Nash-Perry was local and Pervis was national, much as he and Emma had decided. Effectively they had two separate enquiries. But a doubt continued to nag at his thoughts about Pervis and the more he allowed that doubt the freedom to wander freely in his mind the larger it grew.

A hit-man? *Really*? However, back to other matters.

Pursuing Vaughan's 'business associates' was proving difficult.

Most such numbers in his mobile phone no longer existed.

"Surprise, surprise," he'd said under his breath. Looking into his more genuine business interests was easier and all enquiries produced evidence none was doing well. For example, he had a shop on the coast selling fishing gear.

'VP Fishing Supplies' was run by a one-man band, technically an employee, with the appropriate name Edgar Salmon.

Naturally, Mr Salmon was more interested in his job than Vaughan's death, but he gave a good insight into the workings of Pervis's curious empire.

"He set me up in this job a few years ago. He does, sorry, did a bit of fishing and that's how we met. He never seemed too worried about whether it did any good or not. In fact, he said once, and I thought he was joking, that it suited him if it ran at a loss for tax purposes.

"Left me to get on with it. So I make some sales, go fishing a lot myself, and that means the shop isn't always open, but the customers know that, and up till now that means I have a pretty good life. Now I reckon I'll be out of work. Still, more time for fishing, eh?"

Penderfield saw how this bit of the jigsaw puzzle fitted in with the other small business interests, for he was getting a similar story elsewhere. Tax losses.

But with the money he was earning why did he really need to bother? Yet more to the point was the fact he appeared to be involved in underhand and probably very illegal operations, and that was where Charlie knew they had to dig.

* * *

"Good morning. Mrs Frobisher? I'm DCI Drype. May we have a chat?"

"Actually it's Miss Frobisher. Mrs Frobisher is my sister-in-law and she's at the butchers right now. Was it her you wanted? Oh, where are my manners? Do come in, come in please. Tell me, what does DCI stand for?"

Drype explained. Edna looked impressed.

"Mmm ... you must be a very senior officer to be coming to see us. Please come through to the sitting room and make yourself comfortable. Gladys, I mean Mrs Frobisher, won't be long."

"Thank you, that's very good of you, Miss Frobisher. Do you live here, for if so I'd like to chat to you as well."

"Oh yes, we live together since Mrs Frobisher was widowed. I can't imagine though what use we could be to you, Chief Inspector wasn't it? Would you like some tea?"

"Um no thank you, but again that's very kind. We're looking again at some of the information we gleaned from door-to-door enquiries, and as you were good enough to talk to my colleague, DC Brouding, I thought it might be nice to natter through one or two details. It's often the case that, even after we've spoken to people, the memory only needs a little jar and a vital piece of intelligence comes our way.

"I must admit that, although our lines of investigation are proceeding well, we do need all the help we can get about the sad death of Mr Nash-Perry. How well did you know him, Miss Frobisher?"

"Lovely man, and married to that awful wife of his. I'll never speak to her again. I think it's disgusting. Not the sort of thing we want to encourage in Chortleford. Hopefully you'll soon get enough evidence together to charge her with her husband's murder." Drype's eyes opened wide very briefly to unintentionally express his surprise.

"Now are you going to interrogate us, Chief Inspector? I do have an angle-poise light upstairs, because I think you have to shine it in our faces, don't you? Gladys, Mrs Frobisher, is very keen on murder mysteries so she knows all about interrogation procedures, but it sounds quite dreadful to me...."

Drype didn't know whether to laugh or cry and hoped Edna wasn't serious. As soon as she grinned and chuckled he knew she wasn't.

"No, no, no, just a chat, off the record, that's all. Did you know Mr Nash-Perry very well?"

"We did. A fine gentleman. So few about nowadays, Chief Inspector, and I really fear for future generations. He was the sort of man for whom wearing a shirt and tie was one of the basic rules of life. Excellent etiquette. Ladies first and so on, if you know what I mean."

"Yes I do. I believe the late William Kerbidge was also regarded as a gentleman."

"Oh indeed he was. One of the best, so needless to say he and Mr Nash-Perry got on very well together. Poor Mr Kerbidge, married to that gold-digger, poor Mr Nash-Perry, married to that ... how was she described in the paper? .... that minx."

Drype was delighted. Edna Frobisher was a mine of exactly the sort of information he sought.

"Tell me about Mrs Nash-Perry."

"We always considered her to be precisely the sort of lady Mr Nash-Perry should be married to, until we discovered she'd killed him, and with his own tie, if you ever did, I ask you. Poor, poor man. He didn't deserve her and he didn't deserve to die."

"Have you heard any stories about Mrs Nash-Perry behaving as a minx, or perhaps ever seen anything to suggest that? When you read about her activities did it stir any memories, maybe two and two suddenly made four?"

"Funny you should say that, Chief Inspector...." No need for an anglepoise lamp here, he deduced, and laughed inwardly to himself.

".... when we looked back we did recall occasions when we might have had our doubts. You know how it is, it never occurred to us she was ... well, like that, so we didn't see anything unpleasant. But looking back, ah yes, looking back, we did hear about odd times when men called at the house when presumably Mr Nash-Perry wasn't home."

Like the meter reader for example. And 'presumably' Colin not at home. Village tittle-tattle. How they loved it.

At that juncture Gladys arrived back and was astonished on three counts. Firstly that a police officer was visiting them, secondly that Edna had not made him a drink, and thirdly, and most importantly, that Edna had been talking to him and answering his questions.

Drype was able to reassure her he'd been offered refreshments, and then antagonise her by saying Miss Frobisher had been most helpful. Gladys's eyes were out on stalks.

"What on earth has she said to you, officer? I wouldn't place any reliance on what my sister-in-law says if I were you. Oh Edna, whatever have you done?" Edna looked at her lap knowing she might well be on a bread and water diet and facing a night or two in the garden shed.

It took a fair while for Drype to establish order, during which time he and Edna ran over what had been discussed and Gladys found she was quite happy with Edna's explanations, but extremely upset she hadn't been the one telling the tales.

"You should've kept quiet, Edna. Whatever next! You might have got some of it wrong."

"Well, I didn't, dear, so please don't go on so when we have a guest."

Light the blue touch-paper and retire, thought Drype. Well done Edna!

There being no further information either lady had to impart although, as before, the Detective sensed there might be something else, he took his leave pleased to be away. Poor Edna was left to suffer whatever consequences might have arisen from her openness, and Drype laughed out loud at the thought.

Snippets. The copper's food and drink. Something to go on, something to investigate.

And although he didn't know it yet Edna's version of events was at odds in some respects to the one Gladys shared with Emma Brouding.

* * *

Next stop Katie Pervis.

The back-up group was in situ (with the exception of Mandy) ready to support their Katie and chomping at the bit.

Katie had enjoyed a most successful interview with Olivia Handest and was therefore on an emotional high. Drype arrived on a high of sarcasm.

"Good morning. My name's Drype and I'm a Detective Chief Inspector, which is I hope of high enough rank. Unfortunately the Chief Constable is unable to be with us." Cutting to the chase he rode straight on thus avoiding an outbreak of criticism.

"Now, Mrs Pervis, you told my Sergeant that you wouldn't have the money to pay someone and also pleaded for police protection," Katie's mouth opened and moved up and down but before any words could emerge Drype had charged forward with gusto.

"Apparently you mentioned your phone and gas suppliers. We cannot offer any protection whatsoever from those companies, as you well know, so who were you talking about?"

It was Vaughan's father, David, who answered, or rather didn't answer.

"This is a disgrace, Chief Inspector. How dare you speak to Mrs Pervis like that. Who do you think you are? This lady is recently bereaved and in the most terrifying and appalling circumstances and instead of catching his killer you insult and offend his wife. Shocking.

"And as for your sarcasm your Chief Constable will be hearing from me. Now, control yourself, man."

"And the answers to my questions are...?" Drype looked directly at Katie, who was looking at David for guidance and obtaining none, and who wasn't sure whether she should shed a few tears at this point but wisely decided against such an act. Instead she settled for 'flustered' and 'confused'.

"Look, officer, I was in a bad way. In addition to my poor Vaughan being murdered I then had to listen to your Sergeant telling me all the horrifying news possible, what with Vaughan not providing for me and not even leaving me this house. How would you have felt? I was all wound up, angry and very, very heartbroken."

"That's enough, officer," cut in Pervis senior, sensing Katie wasn't presenting the best front and in danger of digging herself a deeper hole. But Drype held up his hand.

"I want answers to my questions, Mr Pervis, and I want them now. Nobody, no matter how confused and upset they may be, would think they needed police protection from British Gas. So, for the last time, why did you ask for police protection?"

"I told you, I was hurting, like, and didn't know what I was saying. For God's sake leave me alone." And she flung herself face down on the sofa she'd been sitting on, pretending to burst into floods of tears. Her mother rushed to her side.

Both David Pervis and his son, St. John, converged on Drype in a menacing fashion, and it was St John who unwittingly saved the situation.

"Look, Mr Drype, Katie has just been visited by Olivia Handest for an exclusive and she'll be phoning the reporter next. How do you think you're going to come out of it? You'll look an unfeeling fool, a real PC Plod." Pervis senior was nodding furiously like a demented chicken but at least St. John's intervention had stopped him in his tracks before he could get near the DCI.

"I'd be more interested in how Katie is going to come out of it. I happen to know the true story behind her paper's exclusive with Rita Nash-Perry and I can guarantee that if anyone's a laughing stock it'll be her. Did they take photos?"

Katie stopped sobbing abruptly and turned round.

"Yeah, bloke came last night for some photos."

"Well, wait till you see how they use those! Now, I've got more important things to do than waste my time with a loser like you, Mrs Pervis, and I do owe it to Vaughan to catch his killer. I'll be back but get your answers ready. No more play-acting, any of you.

"And if between you there are other things you can tell me in my quest it would be appreciated."

The gang of four stared at each other in silence as Drype let himself out.

"Okay," started David Pervis, "That's a good idea; let's stop the play-acting. Katie, Vaughan was my son, so now I'd like some answers, and they'd better be good." And he ground one clenched fist into the palm of his other hand.

Chapter Seventeen

Drype, Penderfield and Brouding sat in the former's office prior to a Team briefing.

It was time to discuss what they had.

This was also the time that Henry Drype and Emma Brouding discovered a slight discrepancy in the accounts given by Edna and Gladys Frobisher.

First time around there had been a suggestion Colin N-P had been a naughty boy but that idea had been snuffed out and the deceased left back in the ranks of perfect gentlemen, incapable of infidelity.

"The one thing that struck me," Emma announced, "was that Edna's afraid of her sister-in-law. No chance of contradiction."

"Quite so," agreed Drype. "She was quite garrulous before Gladys arrived home and then clammed up immediately. Gladys took over, lock, stock and barrel."

"That's right, sir. I had a feeling Edna might say more on her own. So what are the chances that they know more than they're saying and, with Gladys ruling the roost, Edna has to do as she's told?"

"Very good, I'd say Emma. The one thing we now learn is that Colin often went to White Cottage so his last visit cannot have been a surprise to Martyn."

"Oh sir, this is a village full of secrets, secrets that dare not speak their name."

"That's a quote, isn't it, Emma? Y'know – dare not speak its name," Charlie interjected.

"Yes," said Drype, "attributed to Oscar Wilde, the love that dare not speak its name, gay love as we would say today. It was illegal in his lifetime. Wait a mo, Emma, wait a mo. Is this another angle we've completely overlooked?

"Could we be looking at a gay love affair here somewhere? Or am I adding another and unnecessary aspect to this puzzle?"

"Yes," Charlie kicked in, "we know Michael Martyn dressed as a woman to write as Glynis Parham, so is there more to that than we've considered? Colin was, by all accounts, old-fashioned so may have taken an aggressive attitude to Martyn if he thought he was gay. Maybe, even, he discovered Martyn was, and that added to his anger when he was sure Martyn had killed Kerbidge."

"Good point, Charlie," acknowledged Drype in congratulatory mood, "in fact it might simply point to Martyn being gay and nothing more, so maybe we don't need to consider a gay affair."

"In which case," Emma pointed out, "it doesn't get us any further. In itself it doesn't get us any nearer being sure who murdered Colin."

"Next issue," Drype commanded, ready to move swiftly on, "is Vaughan Pervis. There appears to be an outside chance Katie was involved, but it's a slender one. I'm inclined to agree with Charlie that this was an outside job, a hit man hired in for the purpose.

"I agree totally that she's got an issue here, what with pleading for protection, but if you hire someone to kill your husband you wouldn't get in a tiswas the first time you're questioned by the police. Well, I don't think so."

Charlie was ready to hypothesise.

"Yes, a professional killer would want cash up front, probably at least half the agreed price when dealing with a new customer. He or she isn't going to arrange interest free credit. So if Katie had paid out a great deal of money she'd not be too worried about finding the balance, not when you've got an expensive car, loads of jewellery, blah-blah-blah."

Emma butted in.

"Can I throw a spanner in the works, guys? Is this actually looking like a professional hit? All the pics I've seen of Vaughan Pervis says to me he was a bruiser. A tall, stocky, burly guy, he looks a real thug, and by all accounts we now learn he probably was.

"This wasn't a mouse easily strangled. This was a he-man who would've fought back. Much safer to take out someone like that with a shooter, surely?"

"The trouble we have with the concept of him fighting back," Charlie rejoined, "is that you didn't hear a thing, Emma."

"That's true, but then we're assuming Pervis walked straight up to the front door along that gravel path. I just feel sure I'd have heard something."

"Let's put that one to the test," suggested Drype. "You go with Charlie and sit in Martyn's lounge, where you were, and get someone to walk up that path. Further, get them to make a bit of noise on the doorstep. That's another curious point, of course. Pervis didn't get to ring the doorbell, and that suggests it was a very sudden attack.

"And that would put a pro in the frame, Emma. Someone totally confident about taking out a big, strong, violent man, by strangulation. They're out there, and expensive too. Let's make some underworld enquiries, Charlie. Maybe there's a guy who specialises.

"Okay, let's do the Team meeting and assign some tasks."

* * *

Gladys Frobisher had been discussing tactics with her sister-in-law.

Or, to put it more precisely, she had been explaining her strategy for any future intercourse with the police, and Edna had better be listening.

The latter had been given a verbal equivalent of a hanging, drawing and quartering for suggesting to Drype that Colin Nash-Perry might have deviated from the matrimonial straight and narrow.

"But we think it's true, Gladys, don't we?" she'd protested, all to no avail.

"Edna, we are not going to blacken that poor man's name just to please the police. Whatever the rights and wrongs, we owe it to one of the village's gentlemen to keep his indiscretions buried. No good can come of doing otherwise, you must understand that. It was not relevant to his murder so it is not of value to the law.

"The poor, poor man must've been driven to extremes by his wife's infidelity, and we must allow that he was entitled to share some genuine love."

"I think love is over-rated, Gladys, far better to be practical. I never found a man I would've wanted to share love with, and I have lived a life that is all the better for it."

"Well, Edna, I found love with your brother and we were both practical, as you call it, and managed to live a joyously happy life. So let's put an end to it and think before we speak, especially when addressing police officers."

And an end was put to it. But the Frobishers were not the only ones talking.

Steve the butcher was busy collating village chit-chat.

This was his role in life and he accepted it gladly.

Being a butcher provided him with an income and a base from which he could exercise his greatest talents, making people laugh and analysing and disseminating local information, particularly if the latter was in any way scandalous.

There had been a marked concern amongst his clients about the change in the approach of the police.

Suddenly they were asking about mere gossip, getting people to chat off-the-record, and more than one person was worried that their secrets (nothing to do with the murders) might be revealed and made public.

In this they were simply justifying the view of the police that the place was heavily laden with secrets, some most definitely connected with the murders, whereas most were not.

It would not have occurred to residents that the latter were of no interest to the law whatsoever. People were starting to feel guilty about matters that were not technically illegal but most probably immoral, and there was a wave of fear sweeping through Chortleford.

Steve was making the most of this.

He was already aware of some of it. Rumour had it that the single mother in Hospend Close improved her taxpayer funded existence by charging men for various sexual activities, so frequent were male visits to her house. These visits included calls by two married men from the village.

Scandal suggested Mr Davis at Humpback Cottage occasionally slipped out when his wife wasn't looking and brightened up life for the widow at Hillview Lodge. Tittle-tattle reported that Mrs Hargreaves frequently screamed blue murder at her husband and the popular viewpoint was that she might well be the next murder victim.

The general opinion was that the widower, Benjamin Dillman, was a nasty, unpleasant man who would be better off dead, and that Davey Morgan was very creepy and suspicious. If you believed all you heard you'd know that Mrs Faulkner never washed her hands after going to the toilet, but quite how that story came about was anyone's guess.

And Steve listened, lapped it all up, recycled it, and made sure the news spread far and wide. He called his customers his messenger service and it was easy to see why he might do so.

So his take on police questioning was designed to stoke up the fires.

"What you tell 'em, off the record if you believe it, that'll be turned into fact, mark my words, and innocent folk will get their lives turned upside down, I tell you. One thing villagers sharing rumours, but once the police put it out there for the world to see, well, everyone's going to believe it, stands to reason, and lives will get ruined.

"My advice, for what it's worth, keep mum."

It was possibly good personal advice for even Steve had a secret, one kept from his wife. But that was another matter.

Gillian was starting to dread the days when her duties meant driving her bus through Chortleford, for the latest developments were all the passengers could find to talk about, and she too noticed that people were far more worried about their own guilt being exposed than the crimes being solved.

Keith, the newsagent, had never been keen on adding fuel to the stories by enhancing them and passing them on, and had frequently rejected village condemnation of individuals by those who should know better. He was pleased the police were not prosecuting Martyn over William Kerbidge as he had felt uneasy all along about the way people had made up their minds without a shred of evidence.

At the other end of the spectrum Dave the taxi driver worked on the basis of no smoke without fire, and if there was no smoke it was time to strike a match. Consequently his contribution to the rumour mill was substantial and amplified as he held sway in any conversation with his passengers. A few just let him ramble on, managing to permit his words to drift in one ear and out the other, but most loved to hear his theories.

These theories were then passed on as close to fact as you can get.

And so Chortleford worked itself into a lather. But worse was to come.

Tomorrow Katie Pervis would be given the public Olivia Handest treatment and that really would get the tongues wagging.

*   *   *

By arrangement Emma, Charlie, another detective and a uniform met at White Cottage.

For once Michael Martyn was not purely co-operative but extraordinarily helpful. But then he knew he had nothing to fear in the case of Vaughan Pervis. He remained top of the Colin Nash-Perry list.

Michael and Emma took up the very seats they'd occupied on the day in question and Charlie sat in the seat closest to the hall and therefore the front door. Martyn was certain he'd have had the windows open as he loved the fresh air, and having windows open was a basic feature of life at the cottage.

By agreement he and Emma engaged in a conversation about general matters, as it happened an appreciation of the annual Dickens Festival in Rochester earlier that summer. The other detective strode up the gravel path to the front door, made a muted squeaking noise, and sat down heavily on the doorstep.

Bearing in mind the occupants of the lounge knew what was going to happen, and the talk was intended to replicate the situation on the fateful day, they barely heard a sound. Charlie, sitting right by an open upper window and literally no more than six feet from the front door, was more conscious of the footsteps.

Experiment two. This time the detective walked on the adjacent verge, a narrow grass strip, there being one either side of the path. Once again a squeal on the doorstep, deliberately louder this time.

Nobody heard his approach but this time they all heard the suppressed gurgling noise. Very realistic, thought Emma, but managed to keep a grin from her face.

Experiment three. The detective and the uniformed officer carried out a wrestling match on the doorstep. So little was heard Emma and Charlie agreed any such noise would've been overlooked on the day. Next the wrestling match included tiny little howls; again, it was too muted to have been noted had you been busy with something else as Emma and Michael were at the time.

Finally, the wrestling spilled over onto the gravel path and they all heard it.

Charlie decided it worth taking a chance on. The other detective was willing, but Emma and even Martyn shook their heads and protested. One more experiment, and Charlie pulled rank.

He stood on the doorstep while the other officer threw his trousers belt around Charlie's neck, pulled but not too tight, and Charlie tried to call out and struggle. He hardly made a sound and the officer's actions kept him literally on a short rein. Struggling wasn't noisy, and in the lounge, frightened lest something should go wrong, none heard a thing.

Charlie was fine, much to everyone's relief.

"Won't find *that* in the training manual," he confessed with a half-hearted chuckle.

Sadly all this business seemed to confirm was that it was possible for Vaughan Pervis to reach the doorstep unheard, and that his last moments alive, and the means of his passing could also have slipped by aurally unnoticed.

But, of course, it suggested the mighty Pervis, man of strength and potential brutality, had been dealt with swiftly and almost certainly by someone who knew what they were doing.

The matter had one side effect they hadn't bargained for.

Maud, who cleaned the florist shop, was walking past and looked along the garden path just at the moment Charlie was being strangled. Convinced she'd witnessed the fourth murder she moved like an Olympic sprinter towards the town, and did so in silence in case the killer should hear her and set off in pursuit.

She burst into the doctor's and collapsed in a dead faint before she could speak, an action that prevented the spread of a rumour that would've run amok in a village already on the ragged edge.

Happily she lived to tell her tale.

After she came round and a 999 call was made the uniformed officer came into the surgery to let them know everything was in order. Maud had witnessed a police reconstruction, for which Sergeant Penderfield would later be given a rocket, fully ignited.

At least it gave Chortleford something to talk about when there were plenty of subjects anyway.

Back at base DCI Drype had taken a phone call that was sending him back to the village.

* * *

Trying to explain to her 'guardians' that she wanted to speak to Drype alone was not easy.

They, each and every one of them, wanted to know why.

"Private matter, a girl thing, okay?" But it was an explanation that was treated with disdain, especially by Jackie Waylind, being a female herself. Mr Pervis senior had been trying to keep himself under control for some while, sensing Katie might have had something to do with his son's death.

He'd grabbed hold of her once, shaken her and threatened her, but her mother had proved more than a match kicking him on the shin for his troubles. Things were getting heated.

"Listen, you lot, once more, last time, right? Why would I have anything to do with my Vaughan's murder. I loved him beyond words, like, and if this sounds mercenary I'm sorry, but he was my meal ticket, you all know that. It wasn't the money for me, it was love pure and simple.

"I – did – not – have – any - thing – to – do – with – it," she screamed, one syllable at the time.

St John Pervis didn't believe love came into it but kept his beliefs to himself.

Katie was pleased when Drype arrived and was able to usher the other three out.

"Sit down, Chief Inspector, and I'll tell you.

"Look, it's like this and I don't want them lot to know. I don't want anyone to know. I got pregnant and I didn't want to be. Not me, not my style, and I wasn't sure it was Vaughan's either. So you can see my predicament." Drype remained silent and motionless, waiting for the rest.

"Anyway, I started making enquiries. I found I could get a very quick abortion so that, hopefully, Vaughan would never know. One day, when he was at work in London, I was whisked away to this place near Gravesend. And I had me abortion.

"Now, I don't know if it was legal and it probably wasn't, but I was in a panic. I had to do something. I'd paid this man a grand up front and he arranged the car and the abortion and getting me home, everything, no questions asked. But I owe him the balance, fifteen grand, and he's not the sort of bloke to be sympathetic and offer extended credit, Chief Inspector.

"I can probably get the money in due course, like sell the car, y'know. But I don't think he's the sort to wait unless he can add a lot of interest, and then that makes it worse for me.

"And that's the truth, so help me God. Nothing to do with poor Vaughan's death. But I gotta deal with mum and the other two. Thanks to you they think I've hired a hit man. Can you believe that?"

Drype could.

"Well, Mrs Pervis, thank you. Sixteen thousand down the drain. Some business deal. The best I can suggest is that when you hear from this man contact me or anyone in my team and we'll take it from there. I'd quite like a word him as perhaps you can imagine.

"It's a plausible story but being the bastard I am I'd like some proof. Would you be willing to undergo a medical examination?" She nodded sheepishly. "And as you're so good at telling stories why don't you start thinking straight and make up a convincing tale for your mother and father-in-law?"

The DCI, behaving more kindly than the situation warranted, spoke to Mrs Waylind alone and said he was following up the information Katie had given him, but that he could quite understand why she wanted it kept quiet. It was a female matter but not even for her ears, so perhaps she could make the two men appreciate the fact.

"I don't think Katie arranged Vaughan's death so I'd be grateful if you could all be supportive rather than hostile. She's been though a bad time. Try and remember her husband has been murdered."

Jackie said no words and Drype sensed annoyance, irritation at interference.

With that he took his leave and left the 'Addams Family' as he now called them to their own devices.

In any case they would have a lot more to argue about when Olivia's paper was on the streets in the morning.

Chapter Eighteen

During her time at White Cottage Emma Brouding had taken the opportunity, when she had him alone, to ask Martyn if he was gay or transgender.

The two had quite a rapport established during that interview some time ago now, so he had taken no offence at the query, nor shown any signs of shock when he was asked.

"I did wonder if anyone might suggest that, but no, I'm not gay. I dress as Glynis to feel the part but it all ends there." Emma believed it was a genuine answer as she was studying him when he replied, and relied on her reading of body language and voice tones to correctly assess his response.

She was also looking directly at him when she threw the next question at him.

"We now know Colin was a frequent visitor here. Why did he come here?" Martyn's eyes and expression of amazement told their own story and required no interpretation. He wasn't acting.

"I didn't know he'd ever been here, and I think I might have known. He certainly didn't come to see me. Who told you that, anyway? Someone making mischief, I reckon. No, I don't think he ever came here."

Emma persisted.

"We know for a fact he did. We've verified it, but we can't reveal where the information came from. I'm sure you'll understand. It's not gossip, Michael, so are you sure you don't know?"

The Detective Constable had pushed back the boundaries of truth but was so determined to get at the answer.

"It's news to me. I wasn't always at home, especially after mum died, and I don't know all the friends William had round, but Colin no, definitely not. Truthfully it's news to me, Emma."

She was inclined to believe him, and that meant that Colin must've called to see William, yet all the information they had suggested the two didn't share any sort of friendship. Both were, by common consent, of which there was a wealth in Chortleford, gentlemen of the highest order, so maybe they did know one another for that reason alone.

Emma's old mate 'gossip' insisted Colin and William were merely acquainted by virtue of living in the same village, nothing more. Time to revisit 'gossip'.

But first 'gossip' was going to get its teeth into Katie Pervis.

The next morning the fires of hell were lit at Katie's home as soon as the local paper was delivered, and it fell to David Pervis to be shocked first.

As with Rita very little was printed as fact, most material implying rather than stating positively, and it was left to the readers, so often seekers of scandal, to make their own minds up.

Olivia had produced a masterpiece, a thoroughly believable piece of nonsense, based largely on suggestion and on belittling reality. Those willing to be taken in would be only too ready to see Katie as a star of pornography who also worked as a high-class lady of the night. The paper said nothing of the sort, but the implication was there. As were Sam's almost pornographic photos.

More realistically she was portrayed as a gold-digger and a woman who cared less about the loss of her husband than the loss of his fortune. And there was a picture of Katie sobbing as, according to Olivia, she was informed there was no fortune, quite the reverse in fact.

There was also a photo of Katie wearing next to nowt and a very seductive smile, coincidently right alongside an item explaining how little heartbroken she seemed when told about Vaughan's demise.

David erupted like Mount Etna on a bad day, St John took on the appearance of a pressure cooker reaching bursting point, and Katie and her mother shed enough tears to end a drought had there been one, clutching each other and squealing like stuck pigs.

The story was soon on the websites of the nationals and Chortleford was right in the thick of the news again. 'Gossip' was set for a field day.

* * *

Emma's first stop was Gossip Central, the home of the Frobisher ladies, where she was greeted by two highly charged and excitable talkers, each anxious to debate the latest progressions.

Edna, who was traditionally not allowed to get a word in edgeways, never mind have it inserted surreptitiously into conversation, was on full steam ahead ignoring the best efforts of Gladys to silence her. The latter managed to complete two pieces of work at the same time, namely to continuously have her own say while simultaneously talking over Edna and trying to quieten her.

Emma had to disappoint them.

"I'm sorry ladies, but I don't want to talk about Katie Pervis, I want to talk about Colin Nash-Perry and William Kerbidge and it's more important than you could imagine."

Her words had the effect of muting the Frobishers, no mean feat, and she could see the sadness in Gladys's eyes. However, she also noted Edna blushing and, as usual, looking down at her hands in her lap. She knew, she just *knew*, Edna was the one to tackle.

"Colin and William met quiet often, this we now know." She was getting used to lying. "I need some background information and I need it quick. Why did Colin visit William and never the other way round?" Telling untruths was becoming second nature. Edna went to speak and Gladys shot her a glance. Edna studied her lap again.

"Oh, for pities sake, ladies, tell me what was going on or do you not want us to nail the killer?"

There was a pause and then Edna looked up.

"I'm going to tell the truth. We have to tell the truth, Gladys. And, in any case, it's only hearsay, and you know full well it is."

"Precisely, Edna, it's hearsay and of no interest to the police, so hold your tongue."

"Ladies, it is more than of interest to us, it is *vital*. Miss Frobisher, carry on, please."

"Well really," Gladys exploded, but Edna ignored her.

"There were rumours, rumours I stress, that Michael Martyn had been seen dressed as .... dressed as ... oh, I can't bring myself to say it."

"Dressed as a woman, for heaven's sake, Edna. I'll tell the Constable since you're currently disabled with embarrassment." This was a favourable arrangement for both ladies as it enabled Gladys to tell the story and Edna to be well out of it and silent, her preferred status.

"And, if you want me to be quite frank with you, there were rumours that Mr Nash-Perry, unable to come to terms with his wife's infidelity, not that we knew anything about that at the time, found friendship with Martyn very enjoyable, if you understand what I mean. Rumour had it that he enjoyed friendship with Martyn particularly when Martyn was pretending to be a woman.

"Now Mr Nash-Perry enjoyed the highest reputation as one of life's perfect gentlemen, and Edna and I could not let his name be sullied by exposing these vile rumours to you. We now know he was driven to extremes by that wretch of a wife, and we both felt the need to protect him."

Edna had been nodding and shaking her head at the appropriate moments and issuing forth subdued little shrieks from behind the hand that covered her mouth.

"Where did these rumours come from?" appealed Emma, taking a deep breath as much to calm herself as to express exasperation.

There was an even longer pause this time. Emma prompted them anything but gently.

"Who?" she cried out. Edna jumped back into life.

"Harry, that is, Mr Dunsburn. Mr Harold Dunsburn," she wailed. "Have you met him?"

Indeed she had, and was now going to renew her acquaintance.

* * *

Rita Nash-Perry no longer bothered with papers.

But this morning, having garnered some news from a neighbour who, for once, was prepared to talk to her, she hurried to the newsagent for a copy of the local. They were going like hot cakes.

It seemed to Rita, reading her copy as she walked home, that if you believed all you read in the press you'd think that Chortleford was a hotbed of wicked women and malicious murderers. Small wonder the world at large was growing to like the Kentish village!

There was a weird satisfaction behind Rita's wry grin in learning that another woman was being dragged through the gutter, so wasn't surprised when Marc Rosberry phoned for more inside information. His paper wanted to lift the lid on life in the village. But there was another motive.

"My editor thinks this Olivia Handest is an extremely clever writer but ought to write works of fiction rather than use her skills to ruin people's lives. He wants me to research Ms Handest's involvement, Rita. Any chance we could meet up again, perhaps tonight? Go over a few things?"

She tried so desperately to sound calm and reserved and knew if she sounded reserved at all it was because she was reserved especially for Marc.

The expression 'once bitten, twice shy' never saw the light of day in Rita's mind. He knew he was on a winner. The expression 'one born every minute' was openly running through Marc Rosberry's mind. Another classic story coming, and one to trump Olivia's expose.

That's why I'm on a national and you're stuck on a backwater, gal, he mused.

Rita ended the call, rendezvous made, and floated on a star-spangled pink and silver cloud that carried her around for the next hour. She sang to herself, danced gently and wildly, gently like a ballroom dancer, wildly like a teenager, and stripped naked the better to soak up the ambiance of the moment.

Completely undressed she sang and danced in the kitchen, in the hall, up the stairs, in her bedroom, her bathroom, in her lounge. She stood in front of the full length mirror and admired every aspect of her womanhood, and dreamed and dreamed and dreamed of once more being in Marc's arms.

Unfortunately she was more likely to be in the arms of the law if she was anywhere.

At arm-length from the law right now was Harry Dunsburn.

"Hello Missy, an' what can I do for you?" he called out in his jolly way. "Is it about that Pervis woman? Cor, what a one, eh? Always said there's funny goings on in this place, funny going ons."

"Can we go inside?" Emma's question was more of an order. Within seconds she was once again in Treacle Cottage.

"Tell me about Colin Nash-Perry and Michael Martyn, please, and before you try misleading me understand this. If you get this wrong I'll arrest you for obstructing a police officer. I need to know NOW what you know, including the fact you knew Martyn liked to dress as a woman."

With that she sat on the proffered seat and waited.

Harry rolled his tongue around inside his mouth, finally nodded once and then sat down right opposite.

"Okay, missy, I'm a nosey old so-and-so. I likes a walk I does. I often go for strolls around the village. There was this occasion I just happened to be in the fields behind White Cottage and I just happened to glance through the shrubs, like you do, after I'd lifted myself up onto the fence, that is.

"And there 'e was, Martyn, prancing around like Ginger Rogers. He had this navy skirt on, a white blouse with a black bra under it, pearl necklace. Not that I noticed much, missy." Emma suppressed a desire to laugh out loud. "But it was 'im. No wig or anything, that's how I knew."

"Well, live and let live, that's my view. What he wants to do in private, well it's up to him, so I kept quiet about it. I liked William Kerbidge, good friend he was, a gent, and I kept quiet for him, cos he had a lot to put up with there.

"Anyways, it was about the time I paid more attention to the movements of Mr Nash-Perry, cos I saw him going into White Cottage a day or two later. Then I followed him once or twice and he always went to White Cottage.

"Well, missy, I reckon he liked going to see that Martyn fellow when he was dressed as a woman. There's blokes that like that sort of thing, ain't there?" Emma made no acknowledgement of his comment so he continued.

"Anyways, there's people here you could tell and those you couldn't, if you get me drift. So I kept quiet, like I say, for Mr Kerbidge's sake. But I always regarded it as queer, so to speak. Then we find out about Mrs Nash-Perry and now that Pervis woman. I didn't like her husband, big, horrible bloke he was.

"That's all, missy. Do I get arrested or that lot do you? 'Tis all the truth, God's honour."

"No, you don't get arrested. This time. I'll be off now but thank you for sharing your tidbits with me." There was no disguising the sarcasm in her voice. As she rose she noted the various photos on the mantelpiece.

"If you don't mind me asking, Mr Dunsburn, is that your son proudly holding that trophy?"

"Handsome lad, eh? No missy, it's me, taken centuries ago or so it seems. I was a champion wrestler in my youth, amateur you understand. I couldn't wrestle a spider now and stand any chance of winning!

"Diff'rent world in my day missy. You lot got it easy today. Worked all hours on the farm, seven days a week mostly. But I loved it. Bet you don't work half as 'ard as we had to then.

"Out in the fields in all weathers, then come in fer breakfast. Then back out again. Backbreaking work, but I was a big, strong powerful lad, I was. An' I 'ad me admirers, I can tell yer!

"Had an outdoor privy. And we knew what real poverty was in them days. We'd have bitten yer arm off to be as poor as some what reckons they're in poverty today.

"Some days me mam couldn't put food on the table. We 'ad no central heating, no double glazing, and the roof leaked. I shared a tiny bed with two o' me brothers. No state support. Your generation got it easy, missy....."

Emma interrupted brusquely, her voice rising as she delivered her response.

"Actually I know what an eighteen hour day looks like, I know what a seven day week looks like, I know how it feels to have my leave cancelled at the last moment. And out on surveillance in the country I've been known to have to crouch behind a bush to have a pee, and without the luxury of a sheet of newspaper to wipe me bum."

And leaving that statement to waft in the air and ferment in Harry's mind she stormed out.

Pleased to get away she sat quietly in her car and considered the sum of her knowledge. Every day appeared to open up new angles as every day more evidence surfaced, but would any of this help them get any nearer their quarry?

And then she mused on Harry's comments on poverty. An outside toilet, eh? Wow! And just how did Harry's generation ever manage without mobile phones.....?

* * *

Olivia Handest and Mia Cundy had broken open a bottle of champagne.

To some drinking mid-morning might seem a trifle early, but they felt they had something to celebrate. Plus there was the news Olivia had been summoned for an interview with the national that had shown an interest in her.

"If you're free tonight, Olly, let's open a bottle at my place. Got a spare bed so stay over. Have more to drink!"

"Cheers, Mia, hold you to that. I'm free and I'll be there. Gawd, what a success! You wanna watch out, even Sam might get head-hunted! How on earth he persuaded that cat to pose in that fashion I'll never know."

"Used his manly charms, my girl. They'd be lost on us, but they obviously worked a dream on randy Katie. Bet she's as sick as a pig today. Probably not content with wanting to kill you I bet she'd roast Sam over red hot coals if she could."

They laughed, raised their glasses, toasted each other and Sam, drank, and then went about their individual business, Mia back to her desk, Olivia back to her car to try and tail Drype.

* * *

For the present DCI Drype was not for tailing.

He was in his office with DS Penderfield and both had been taking a brief look at the local rag.

"The important thing, Charlie, is not to behave like typical males and drool all over this dross. I think there's a hint of nemesis here, first of all Katie finding out that there's virtually no money and then falling victim to Kent's largest bird of prey." They both laughed.

"She's a bit of a stunner, whatever you say, Charlie, and not afraid to spread her sunshine around." Charlie had nothing to say because he had never seen women as sex objects and wasn't one for being warmed by risqué photos of the female of the species. There was zero chance of him drooling over any dross, as Drype had dismissed it.

Besides, he was in danger of coming of age if Emma had anything to do with it.

"Emma's on her way," the DCI announced, "and she's got some news. Might be yet another side to this story, certainly where the Nash-Perrys are concerned. A policeman's lot, eh Charlie? Now, how are things going with Vaughan Pervis?"

"Well sir, it's not so much about finding people who don't really want to talk to us as finding anyone in the first place. His sidelines were shady whichever way you look at them, definitely the wrong side of the law, but we just can't find anything to paste onto his cv. Covered his tracks well.

"The guys at Gravesend have come up with a possibility for Katie's abortion clinic, and certainly not the sort of establishment to attract NHS funding. A raid's a-coming.

East Sussex reckon they might have a rent-a-killer who specialises in swift, quiet strangulations and they're getting back to us."

"Wouldn't have thought East Sussex was a place to harbour such criminals. A lovely part of the country, really," Drype eulogised. Penderfield looked askew at his boss until Drype's face cracked into a grin which was followed by a smirk. There was a knock at the door.

Upon being invited to do so Emma entered and grabbed a seat without waiting to be asked.

"See Katie got her come-uppance," she began, ignoring protocol, good manners and etiquette.

"Good morning, Emma," Drype said very pointedly.

"Oh, morning sir, morning Charlie. Now here's what I've got." Both Drype and Penderfield stared at her for a second or two, and then allowed her enthusiasm to wash over them and settled down to hear her news."

* * *

Martha, whose playing of the church organ was beginning to attract criticism, listened intently to Harry's tale, for he had added some robust adornments likely to make the story more exciting and newsworthy. Emma's visit had livened things up on 'Gossip Route One'.

Edna had been rebuked by Gladys but both had set about spreading the word following the Detective Constable's visit, and were stitching on suitable decorations to make their version of events even more scandalous.

No other broadcasting medium could've despatched rumour so completely, so fervently and so thoroughly around a community. And, as ever, Steve the butcher was the communications centre.

In a village where surprise was becoming a dead word it would've been difficult to imagine anything lying dormant, yet to be brought to life, causing so much as a mild shock. Chortleford was becoming shock-proof in that respect. Of course, there was always the chance of a genuine bolt from the blue shaking everyone to their cores, but by and large the residents were immune.

Now they simply lapped up each saga as it came their way, bathed in the pleasure it gave them, and eagerly awaited the next instalment.

However, the next instalment was destined to be a total bombshell.

Chapter Nineteen

DC Emma Brouding was looking at a magazine.

It was an article on Glynis Parham in the light of the disclosure that the famous author was the nom-de-plume of Michael Martyn.

The accompanying photo showed him with the managing director of his publishers and was taken before the whole Chortleford affair kicked off. She'd taken the trouble to contact the publishers to find out the date.

At that time there was no question of publication, of course.

Now she studied the picture without knowing why.

There was something, *something*. What the hell was it? The picture was trying to tell her *something* but she wasn't hearing.

She'd shown it to Drype, to Charlie and to two other detectives, but none could see anything unusual or pointed. Yet she knew it was there. The picture itself was a clue, she just knew it.

"Oh picture, picture, tell me your story," she pleaded and still received no response. So she memorised the photo and put the magazine away, and allowed the image to haunt her. If there was one thing she'd learned as a detective it was that time can be wasted searching out false clues and clues that don't exist.

The maelstrom that was the Pervis household was gathering a momentum of hatred, epitomised by David Pervis ordering his solicitor to Kent at such speed that he should arrive 'yesterday'. Even now the poor man was risking trouble by hitting 95 mph in his BMW on the M20.

Pervis senior, having decided to sue everyone, was now getting his 'sue-age' plans into some sort of order with specific targets in mind.

Olivia's outfit was going to be screwed into the ground and burned to a cinder with Ms Handest aflame on top. In his rage he was not only delivering an appalling monologue of horrible acts to be performed on various people and organisations, but littering his dialogue with a host of filthy language which Jackie Waylind did not take kindly to at all.

Having previously been kicked in the shin by Katie's mother, and now being threatened with another and worse, he wisely desisted from his tirade and ended up muttering profusely, but in a quieter tone devoid of bad language.

In complete contrast Rita Nash-Perry was on cloud nine, still revelling in her nakedness about her home, and the sensual feelings of sexual animation it gave her, and anticipating the fun of a another night with Marc Rosberry. It was an evening they were not going to spend together.

Harry Dunsburn popped into the *Log and Weasel* for a pint, tendering his now usual twenty pound note, ready to regale anyone who would listen (and there were actually precious few) with his tales of meeting the delightful and exciting 'maiden' DC Emma Brouding. Emma, who did not like being called missy or luvvie, would most certainly not want to be called a maiden, least of all in the lecherous tone he employed.

Meanwhile one news website was showing a picture of both Rita and Katie with the caption 'Randy Rita and Kitten Katie, Chortleford ladies, catering for all ages'. Mrs Pervis, catching sight of that, threw herself face down on the bed, pillow clutched over her head, for one of her weeping and wailing sessions that nobody was taking any notice of any more.

Social media went into overdrive with its usual unpleasant drivel, much comment reflecting the illiteracy and poor intelligence of the writers, an odd but often anonymous way of publicly demonstrating one's deprived and limited mental capacity.

Steve was capitalising on his business and his own reputation.

A chalk-board appeared outside his shop advertising 'Gammon with Gossip, Ham with Hearsay, Pork with Porkies, Sausages with Scandal, Rump-steak with Rumour - full service for Chortleford Chatterboxes and Chop lovers!'.

Martha, whose playing of the church organ had been rudely likened to a dog taking its owner for a walk, was sickened, disgusted, horrified, mortified, dismayed and repulsed by the news and privately, secretly adoring every morsel she could lay her hands on.

In this her excitement, kept to herself, was matched by that of a great many villagers who publicly poured scorn on Chortleford's happenings, and condemned those who had brought the place into disrepute.

When the bar of the *Log and Weasel* was occupied exclusively by local men one or two expressed their sorrow at not realising such gifts had been on offer, and their regret at not being able to take advantage.

Natasha's mum, who had neither heard from nor seen Glen Bardrew of late, felt let down and started to wonder if Glen himself had been naughty elsewhere. She hated the idea of being a notch on someone's bedpost, but was grateful Olivia Handest hadn't caught up with her again. Imagine being tarred with the same brush as Rita and Katie!

Edna was in trouble again. She'd managed to start an unpleasant rumour about Gladys by merely telling Harry Dunsburn that her sister-in-law now had a gunnera, and he mistook the word for one of the nasty social diseases that can result from personal intimacy. Edna tried to pooh-pooh the nonsense, telling Gladys that a keen gardener like Harry would know what a gunnera was, and that he was, in all probability, making mischief.

Gladys had some palpitations, as was her wont, and sprawled in an armchair where Edna fanned her with a copy of the Daily Mail. This procedure was becoming something of a regular activity in the Frobisher household (although not always involving the Daily Mail) where Gladys liked to be shocked and on a frequent basis. What she didn't like was finding herself the centre of tittle-tattle, and she determined to put a stop to it, thank you very much Harry.

She had no intention of her photo appearing alongside those of Rita and Katie, little realising that such a venture would have no attractiveness whatsoever for the news media.

Back at base DC Emma Brouding had her eureka moment and charged off towards Drype's office.

* * *

Charlie Penderfield had been putting forward an idea.

The other updates they'd received advised that, following a tip-off, there had been a raid outside Gravesend resulting in the closure of premises used for all kinds of illegal activity. This was where Katie Pervis had gone. Arrests had been made.

Also East Sussex confirmed that at the time of Vaughan's murder their known hit-man had been lying in a hospital bed in Leicestershire. It transpired he had become a victim of his own trade, one of his colleagues in death having tried, unsuccessfully, to complete a contract by shooting the strangler. He'd survived but knew he was a marked man, in more senses than one.

Charlie had methodically and analytically arrived at a possibility, and it was time to expound his work.

"Look sir, if we take one of our new angles and explore it thoroughly I reckon we might just get to pin something on Martyn. Here's my theory." And he set about explaining his point of view. The DCI listened intently, weighed up the possibilities, and then came to a decision.

"Two possible directions of attack there, Charlie, and they're Rita and Michael Martyn. Now Martyn, maybe because he's a successful author, has led us a merry dance and is quite capable of holding us at bay. An accomplished liar, and perhaps he has trouble distinguishing between fiction and fact, but he's too clever by half.

"That leaves Rita. I'll phone her and I'll take Emma with me....."

Emma burst through the door like a racing car approaching the checkered flag and paced straight to the front of Drype's desk.

The DCI looked up and quietly and coolly said, "Come in." Charlie sniggered.

"Sorry, sir, but I haven't time for niceties. Look here, see this picture, it's Michael Martyn, and it was taken before the deaths in Chortleford." The men glanced at the photo, intrigued. "The tie. He's wearing an identical one to the tie used to throttle Nash-Perry. Unusual design. Anyway, I've checked and the design matches."

"Might solve one thing. If Martyn was wearing it then he must've used it to kill Nash-Perry, leaving it on the corpse. And as Rita identified the tie as Colin's that means she must be implicated .... Sir."

With that she took a step back, breathing vigorously with excitement, face aglow with pride and pleasure, and placed her hands behind her back as if awaiting the plaudits she was sure would follow.

And they did.

"Well done, Emma. Let Charlie tell you his theory, and you can add your two-penneth. Then you and I are going to see Rita. Charlie, track down Glen Bardrew but don't let on. Tell him that we now have verified information that shows us he's been less than honest with us. Advise him of the dire consequences of deliberately misleading the police and grill him mercilessly."

"I understand lighted matches under the fingernails can be quite effective. Phone Emma; I don't want mine on when we interview Rita as I won't want to be directly interrupted."

DS Penderfield explained his idea, and Emma agreed at once.

"Martyn told me he wasn't gay and I believed him, as I've told you, so what you're saying Charlie makes sense."

"Okay guys," Drype began, "and be aware how much I value your input. You've both worked your socks off on this and if it scores a direct hit it'll be largely down to the two of you. That will be noted in the right places, I assure you." And with that he picked up the phone to call Rita.

Emma smiled at Charlie with a look of joyous satisfaction and Charlie smiled back the same way.

"By the way," the DCI added, "nobody below the rank of Chief Inspector crashes into my office without knocking." Rita answered the phone at that moment and Drype looked away leaving Emma and Charlie to exchange more smiles.

* * *

Dave the taxi driver was also smiling with satisfaction.

He'd been sent to Canterbury East station to collect two people who were travelling to Chortleford's only B&B. This would be a nice little earner.

The couple seemed nice enough. Middle-aged, smartly dressed, polite and well-spoken, carrying a small suitcase each, these being loaded into the boot.

Setting off, Dave, being a taxi driver, started conversation as you might expect.

"On holiday, having a break in the village?" he queried in his usual bright, merry voice.

"To tell you the truth," the lady replied, "we just wanted to see this extraordinary village where so much has happened, and where there seems to be so much going on." Before Dave could comment the man spoke.

"The main reason why we wanted a local taxi, not one from Canterbury. Thought you might know the village and its inhabitants well and could be useful to us." Dave was amazed. Tourists flocking to Chortleford! Tourism would certainly boost his income.

"Yeah, I live there. Emigrated from south London years ago. Driven most of the villagers at some time or other. And yes, I've driven all the deceased and all the suspects. So anything else you want to know just ask old Dave here.

"People talk to me, so I get all the local gossip as well as the true stuff, if you know what I mean."

"Thank you, Dave. That's very helpful. Now, please don't be offended, but we'd like to continue our journey in silence, simply taking in this beautiful Kent countryside. Hope that's okay?"

Dave said it was but found himself puzzling his fares.

Strange people. Very strange.

When they arrived at the B&B Dave took the cases in, accepted the fare complete with a handsome tip, and almost touched his forelock in deference. The man spoke.

"Thank you Dave. I'll be in touch. We need your help and we're willing to pay, if you know what *I* mean?" Dave did, and he pocketed the cash and regained the driver's seat, whistling a happy tune as he went. He'd landed. His chance to earn some real dosh.

He looked in his mirror. You little rascal, you, he muttered, and he saw his reflection beaming back with great self-satisfaction and smugness.

But these were no tourists. And Dave was just the sort of gullible village idiot they were looking for.

* * *

Oscar Falhaven didn't like it one bit.

But he didn't have any choice.

His firm had sent him for three reasons. He was available, he was good enough and bright enough and sharp enough, and David Pervis had taken a shine to him on a previous occasion.

What had upset Oscar right now was that, having zoomed along the M20 at nearly 100 mph with impunity, he had been caught doing 45 in a 30 when he was just a few miles from Chortleford. And all so that he might please Pervis and arrive promptly.

To listen to Mr Pervis senior you might have believed Mr Falhaven had ambled in three or four days behind schedule, and done so with a casualness designed to annoy his client.

Now he had to listen to his client ranting and raving, and the various interjections of the gang of three which were made at any time when David Pervis paused to inhale, as well as when he was in mid-stream. Oscar likened it to a radio not quite tuned to a station when there is interference as well as hints of other nearby stations breaking in.

What a cacophony!

He had a laptop open and was trying to make notes, these becoming copious without being placed in any order. But he'd sort that out later; he was good at that.

"Who shall we sue first?" David boomed.

"I think we have to kick off with the local rag," Oscar replied, trying to sound confident and positive, "but with your agreement I'd like time to study my notes and then advise you on courses of action open to us." All very professional but not what Mr Pervis wanted. St. John piped up.

"We want Katie's name cleared, we want apologies, but mostly we want compensation, and I mean real, live compensation. Thousands, thousands and then thousands after that." Oscar nodded as if offering approval and that seemed to satisfy Vaughan's brother. He queried one point.

"And Vaughan's killer?"

"Leave that to me," cried David Pervis, "I'll find him and deal with him, be sure of that. Now don't you worry about that. That's our business, not yours. And I'm employing someone else to lead me to my destination. You'd better be good enough at your job, Oscar, or maybe I'll be after you too." Oscar felt a tingling sensation run up his spine.

He didn't doubt Pervis meant every word.

"There's another matter going to be settled out of court, Oscar.

"My powers of persuasion are undiminished and I coaxed my daughter-in-law to reveal that she'd had a back-street abortion." His voice rose as he spoke and the final words were all but screamed. Oscar could've sworn he saw sparks fly from Pervis's mouth.

"Just let that joker come for the outstanding, just let him." And Oscar's tingling spine made his whole body shake. This guy's serious, he concluded.

The solicitor glued his eyes to his screen in a show of concentration and tried to fight off the feelings of raw fear. He was far from pleased with this assignment. Gold-plated five-star success was the very minimum required of him.

Even being booked for speeding was of nought compared to disappointing Mr Pervis. No, he was far, far from pleased.

And Pervis himself was going to be far from pleased to learn Kent Police had the man who arranged the abortion under lock and key, and beyond the grasp of Pervis vengeance.

* * *

In a way Keith the newsagent *was* pleased.

He was upping his orders for papers now that demand was increasing, and naturally he was looking forward to improved earnings.

Most locals were buying more than one per day now, and some were investing in expensive and colourful magazines that normally sold in miniscule numbers. It was just that he wasn't sure he liked the way Chortleford was going.

Harry Dunsburn bustled in and bought a ladies mag, and all because it advertised an update on the Chortleford ladies.

"Funny goings on here, Keith, funny going ons, if you ask me." Keith felt compelled to nod but he did so not so much in agreement with Harry as with his unhappiness with his village. He gave Harry the change from the twenty pound note and asked him a question.

"Harry, how well did you know William Kerbidge?" This brought Harry to a stand. It was a most unexpected enquiry.

"Knew him as a friend, as one of life's gentleman. Colin Nash-Perry too. It was that Pervis fella, nasty piece of work, pleased to see 'im gone, and hopefully that vixen he married will be gone soon too. Word has it she ain't got no money of her own an' he ain't left her none. Well, that's what it says in them there papers but you can't believe everything you read."

"Do you think Mr Kerbidge took his own life, Harry?"

"Nah, an' them daft police, they'll never do that Martyn fella, will they? You mark my words, guilty as charged!" He said a cheery goodbye, waved in a friendly manner, and left Keith standing behind his counter reflecting that Harry's viewpoint had been echoed by most of the village.

However, there had never been quite the same conviction, in a manner of speaking, over Colin's murder, almost as if people couldn't accept the premise that Martyn might be a double-killer. Also there didn't seem to be the same sympathy for Nash-Perry as for Kerbidge.

And nobody seemed sympathetic to Vaughan Pervis at all. Funny goings on indeed Harry, Keith thought to himself.

At that minute St John Pervis walked in. Keith recognised him.

He purchased a cold drink.

"Do you know who I am?" he suddenly asked as he accepted his change. Keith settled for safety.

"No, I don't."

"The name's Pervis. And I'm a bit sad to find you're peddling all this rubbish about my sister-in-law. I expect you exchange views with your customers too. Am I right?"

"No, most people are in and out in a flash, so I don't get much time to talk." St John approached the counter and Keith saw the menace in his eyes.

"Just don't be meddling, my son. I want an end to village chit-chat. I'm just putting the word about so there's no misunderstanding. I can't stop you selling this filth but you can discourage gossip. *Can't* you?"

"I don't gossip, but I'm not afraid of you, and I don't respond to threats."

"As long as we understand the situation I'll leave you in peace, my son. But please, I'm not threatening you. Good God, whatever would those nice policemen say?"

Keith shuddered as St John left, and decided he'd find out exactly what those nice policemen would say.

* * *

Rita invited her guests into the lounge and offered to make drinks, hot or cold, an offer politely refused.

"Well, two of you today. What have I done to deserve this?"

"Rita," Drype started, "I want to have a good talk with you. It won't be easy for you, I know that, and I'm sorry for any distress...."

"There'll be no distress over Colin, Harry, you know that."

"Yes, but this is a far-reaching matter, and it means going beyond issues we've already discussed. But I do want to urge you to be open and honest. Certain knowledge has come our way and we now have to press ahead with this.

"I'm genuinely sorry, Rita, but there are things we must talk about and I feel confident you'll find them distressing."

"We're not going back over the woman in the black coat are we? You can't prove it was me, because it wasn't. I wasn't there. Full stop."

"No, Rita, this concerns your husband. Once again I'm sorry it has to be like this, but I need the truth and the whole picture, and there's no point lying about it anymore."

She stared into his eyes.

Suddenly she was dreading what was coming. All her reserve deserted her and she felt herself shake inwardly. Her confidence drained utterly. It was truly the moment of truth and she knew it.

She was suddenly very alone.

Chapter Twenty

Having settled into their accommodation, showered and changed, Mr and Mrs Hopetown went walkabout.

There was something so remarkably Kentish about Chortleford, with its features that would relate it to the county such as the converted oast houses, and yet it was exactly how any charming English village should be.

The narrow roads swung this way and that, with little undulations, and were lined with grass verges, hedges, climbing roses, pretty cottages, weatherboarded properties, trees, shrubs, brick walls and fences. Quintessentially English, outstandingly Kentish.

The church, so they learned, dated back eight centuries. The pub, the *Log and Weasel*, looked both quaint and quirky, the hanging baskets both adding to its attractiveness and managing to look completely naff at the same time.

They also discovered that, friendly though the natives were, and as much as they liked talking to each other, they were now extremely wary of strangers and not prepared to go beyond brief discussions on the weather and other harmless topics. Yes, they would need their taxi driver Dave to make any inroads here.

Time to find him.

They bumped into a reporter who hoped they were local and ready to comment on developments, and who expressed her disappointment quite openly. Probably finding, as the Hopetown's had, that people were holding their tongues where visitors were concerned.

Dave was free an hour later and they arranged to meet him, at his suggestion, at the *Log and Weasel*. They said they would pay for his time so he decided that he would abandon his taxi for the rest of the day at that point. A nice little earner was beckoning. Definitely.

Mrs Hopetown's eyes lit upon the butcher's shop but there was nothing she wanted to buy. She looked about her, realised the church could not be seen, and elected to go and ask where it was, as good an excuse as any.

Steve was engaged in conversation with Mrs Kendrick who had noted a recent occurrence.

"See that bigwig copper's back at Rita's. Recognise the brown Hyundai. I thought he might have come for his afters but he's got that nosey woman detective with him, y'know, the one who's been asking lots of questions lately."

"Yep, Mrs Kendrick, he doesn't want to leave her alone, does he? Tell you what, I bet he's so keen to prove she wasn't involved in Colin's death because I reckon she'd be right grateful." And he winked so that she might understand if she didn't already. Seeing a stranger on the premises he winked again, to try and draw Mrs Kendrick's attention to it, and then spoke.

"Hello love, what can I do you for?"

"I am so sorry, but I'm a stranger here and I'm looking for the church." He gave directions and she continued.

"Your village has been headline news, hasn't it? I suppose you get fed up with it all. And yet it's such a lovely village. A great shame. Did you know the deceased?"

That did it for Steve. The wrong question.

"You one of them reporters?" he asked outright. "Had enough of reporters and people pretending to be what they're not. Sorry love, I don't talk about it anymore. Sorry." She nodded and turned and left, rejoined her husband and walked the opposite way to the church, thus confirming Steve's suspicions.

"See?" he said to Mrs Kendrick. "You can't trust nobody."

Out in the road Mrs Hopetown reported the news of the 'bigwig copper' visiting Rita Nash-Perry and her husband nodded. By itself it wasn't of interest to them. It wasn't Colin Nash-Perry's death that had brought them to Chortleford. It was Vaughan Pervis's murder.

Nonetheless they went off to seek out the brown Hyundai and found it easily and by that medium decided which house belonged to Rita.

They'd come back and have a word when the coast was clear.

Inside Rita's, the 'bigwig copper' was listening to Mrs Nash-Perry at that very moment.

* * *

"Rita, was your husband gay?"

Her eyes widened for the briefest of seconds and still they stared hard at him, but now there was movement in her lips and he realised she was visibly shaking, and knew the tears were nearly there, just as he appreciated they would be.

She remained silent and he watched intently as the softest of teardrops escaped from those beautiful big eyes and trickled slowly down her cheeks. Then her eyes closed and the tears flowed freely. Drype spoke again, quietly, gently.

"And was he in a close relationship with William Kerbidge?"

The shaking manifested itself fully as she wept openly and dragged a hanky from her sleeve to dab her eyes. Gradually, very gradually, the hearty crying eased, and Drype sensed that at long last Rita was totally overcome with relief, and he knew she would tell him the truth.

She started by nodding. Then she seemed to pull herself together, blew her nose and relaxed back in the armchair, ready to talk. The tears ran down unnoticed, ignored.

"Yes Harry, he was, as you say, gay. Not that we called it that back then. Different era, different values. We never talked about it. I discovered the truth after I gave birth to Vanessa. It was the only possible explanation for his attitude towards me and I challenged him.

"He didn't look ashamed or anything like that, but perhaps it was wrong of me to expect shame. He just appeared quite proud of it. There would be no discussion. I had to accept that intimate relations between us had ended, and they hadn't been anything to write home about at any time. God knows how I got pregnant.

"But that was life back then, Harry, you must understand that. People didn't talk about it. I had nobody to talk to; I couldn't broach the subject with mum and dad and you couldn't get counselling.

"In those days you got married then found out about your partner. I would never have guessed that such a charming gentleman had such a secret. Getting married made it alright for him, don't you see, he was normal and nobody need have any doubts."

Rita paused for more tears, painful for Drype because he knew they genuine, painful for Emma because she sensed the terrible suffering, the lifetime of suffering, and the massive relief now swamping her. Rita recovered, wiped her eyes, blew her nose again, and continued.

"You just accepted things, Harry. You got on with life. No question of divorce. We stayed together anyway so we could raise Vanessa, and then we drifted into staying together for the grandchildren. I was aching inside. I would've had an affair if I'd had any idea of how to go about finding one to have.

"I was naive about everything. And I let life sweep by and sat on the sidelines. What made it worse, of course, was Colin's affairs. I had the added pain of knowing he was seeing men and he made no attempt to hide them from me. I was a housewife and mother and I was dependent on him and he knew I'd not make a fuss, let alone walk out.

"When we moved here I thought things might improve but he started going out and I realised he'd found a friend here, even in a small village like Chortleford. Only by following him did I find out where he was going.

"I wasn't the only one caught out. When Kerbidge married Maisie I thought it might stop, but it didn't. I met Maisie much later and we poured our hearts out to each other. If you listened to gossip round here you'd think she was wearing him out in the bedroom. They only ever *slept* in their bedroom.

"You might ask why she married him. Well, she had no money and was thinking of her son despite the fact he was earning good money as a writer. I suppose you could say she got her revenge by making sure the old boy left everything to Michael Martyn.

"He eventually learned what was going on and was apparently horrified. Well, who wouldn't be? He even threatened Kerbidge but he laughed at his son-in-law. So you can imagine how all that pent up anger came out when

Maisie died. Michael held Kerbidge liable for his mother's death and swore revenge would be his.

"When the old man died I really did think Michael must've killed him. And of course, so did Colin. And that's why my husband became obsessed with Martyn. As far as he was concerned Michael Martyn murdered the man he loved and he determined to bring him to justice. The police weren't doing enough. He was furious and frustrated and heartbroken, a lethal combination.

"Eventually he stormed out of here yelling he was going to kill Martyn. I pleaded with him not to go, but he went. So I followed him, hoping to calm things down when he got to White Cottage.

"When I arrived Michael had just opened the door and Colin was waving his arms, shouting and screaming and all of a sudden he grabbed Martyn and they struggled for a moment or two. I ran up to try and intervene and Colin roughly pushed me to the ground. He turned and got hold of Michael by the throat, but Michael was too strong.

"I got up and tried to pull them apart. Colin let go of Michael and punched me and I fell to the ground winded and in pain. In that moment Michael had whipped his tie off and wrapped it around Colin's neck. He pulled tighter and tighter and tighter. Colin was powerless and so was I.

"He just kept on pulling it tight, his eyes like those of a possessed maniac I suppose. A madman.

"I just lay there watching without comprehending. And as Colin's lifeless body slid slowly to the ground I looked at Michael and saw the face of a ruthless killer. In that one look I saw the man who had murdered William Kerbidge the same way.

"I said to him, you killed your step-father didn't you? And he nodded and said callously, and I've just killed your husband. Done us both a favour, he said. And rid the world of two more of them, he said.

"He went on to say that Kerbidge mocked him time and again, just as he laughed at him in the back garden that day. Kerbidge was kneeling down having said something very unpleasant to Michael. He grabbed the twine, threw it round the old man's neck and strangled him, so he told me

"Then he reminded me I'd just let him kill Colin and done nothing to save him. What could I have done? *What* could I have done?

"He said to me, right Rita, you're an accessory now, so you'll do as I say or end up inside. First up you say it was *his* tie. But you don't say you've been here. I'll sort this out, make sure there's no DNA, because I write crime novels, you know, so I know what I've got to do. He was so callous and cold, Harry. I couldn't believe what I'd just seen and what he wanted me to do.

"But what he said next decided me and chilled me to the bone. He said if I wandered from the script he'd kill me. Looking down at Colin's body he said, there, it's easy, and I'll laugh at you as I strangle the life out of you. And he laughed there and then.

"I made my way home, frightened and shaking. I just collapsed in a chair. I couldn't cry or do anything. I just stared at the floor. Then, later, I heard the sirens and froze with real fear. It was some while before I pulled myself together, made a cup of tea, and waited for someone to come and tell me my husband had been slain."

Emma spoke

"Would you like a cuppa now, Rita? I'll go and make one." Rita nodded.

"And that's the whole truth of it, Harry, and now I expect I'll go to prison. Well, serve me right."

"Rita, you haven't told me about Glen Bardrew. What part did he play?" Rita considered this and then replied.

"He tooted at me and stopped on my way back. I was shocked. I said to him, for God's sake Glen, don't say you've seen me, please I beg you. Try and understand and be a friend to me, for pities sake. If anyone pins you down about seeing me make up a story, throw them off the scent. It'll be on the news tonight but please be a friend and know I didn't do it and I couldn't stop it.

"I hurried off leaving him looking very puzzled. I don't think anyone else saw me. Well, nobody has come forward, have they?"

Emma put her head round the door.

"Charlie says Glen supports what you've just been told," and she vanished back to the kitchen, and then returned with a tray and three mugs of tea. Drype took a few sips and then spoke.

"When Martyn came here, Rita, was it to threaten you, to make sure you were keeping to the script, to use his term?"

"Yes, Harry. He's evil. He'd have killed me then, I know he would. I'm so sorry, but I've been so frightened."

"Well, we'll finish our teas, then sadly I have to arrest you. When we get a statement at the station I will come back and deal with Martyn. My only wish is that you'd confided in me earlier, and you had the chance. I think you trusted me, Rita. It might have gone so much better for you.

"I can't say what will happen now, what the courts will do. I wish I could, Rita, I do so dearly wish I could. But the main thing is that a killer will be behind bars, and you will have much to mitigate your involvement."

They finished their tea in silence. The DCI allowed her to ring her daughter, and then they left the village, Rita thinking she might never return. And the tears came again. At least she hadn't been handcuffed so onlookers would've not realised she'd been arrested.

As they drove along the lanes Rita wasn't persuaded she'd ever want to set foot in Chortleford again, even if she had the chance.

***

Charlie brought in Glen Bardrew.

He wanted a solicitor present for his formal interview so that caused a delay.

With Emma taking care of Rita the men met in Drype's office.

"Charlie, we need a first class job here. We need to do the business on Martyn. So it's all out attack but we have to be clever. I believe Rita one hundred per cent. It was like an enormous weight lifted from her today.

"Can you imagine a married life like that, living a lie? We can't begin to imagine what she went through when Martyn killed Colin in cold blood right in front of her. And what she's been through since, under threat from the murderer, a man obviously prepared to snuff out life on a whim.

"I know it's no excuse, Charlie, but I feel sorry for her.

"And that makes nailing Martyn even more important. We have to get it right first time; he may well deny what Rita's told us."

"Would he know how to remove DNA, sir?"

"His publisher told me that when he started writing his crime novels he had sessions with Kent Police. Heaven knows what valuable info he finished up with. But he's pulled the wool over our eyes and today I'm going to be getting my own back, believe me!"

"This guy writes the most dreadful murder mysteries but we know he thinks the world of them and you can bet your bottom dollar he thinks he can stay one step ahead. After all, he's managed it quite well so far."

"With that in mind, sir, he could just deny everything, and then it's Rita's word against his. With no other evidence we'd be stuffed."

"That's right, Charlie. And that's why we need to be on the ball. We have to contrive to catch him out. So let's have a good think about this and decide on a strategy. One slip on that man's part and I'll have him, so help me God."

***

Back in Chortleford the Hopetown's had been unable to catch up with Mrs Nash-Perry, for obvious reasons, and were finding local people a barrier to their enquiries.

At the appointed time their saviour met them at the pub.

Dave was in good form and keen to make an impression.

They sat outside, hopefully away from prying ears, of which Chortleford had many, and asked seemingly innocent questions of their tame taxi driver.

In his enthusiasm Dave talked freely and endlessly, and gave away far more than he might've intended to. They gave the appearance of being interested and fascinated by what they were hearing, whereas they were largely bored witless and anxious to cast out the nonsense and digest what they really needed to know.

Dave was excited to be handed a plain brown envelope, and a quick inspection of the contents showed it to be stuffed with notes. The meeting ended after Mr Hopetown had furnished them all with another round of drinks, and advised Dave his services would be required again soon.

Back home Dave had a count up. Four hundred quid! He'd have sold his own grandmother for less.

Edna had seen him walking home looking very pleased with himself, a fact she now passed on to Maud. Maud had news.

"Mrs Nash-Perry, gone off with the police again, Edna. Whatever's going on? According to the paper she murdered her poor husband so why don't they just charge her and put her away?"

"Well," Edna responded, "I expect they have to be sure. They've been asking all of us a lot of personal questions, you know, things people shouldn't ask each other, and maybe someone has let the cat out of the bag. Gladys says the police are very good at getting people to confess. She knows all about these things, being a bit of an amateur sleuth herself, Maud."

Maud nodded as she was aware of Gladys's interests, then said her farewells leaving Edna to do some more dead-heading. The next passer-by was Martha who paused by the roadside where Miss Frobisher was working in her garden.

"Hello Martha, I understand Mrs Nash-Perry's been carted off by the police yet again."

"Lord no. Why do they keep doing that? If she's guilty she should be behind bars, not left to lurk around our village, to rub shoulders with innocent folk like you and me. It's frightening. Steve reckons there's more to all this to come out, just you wait and see."

"Well, I feel so sorry for poor Mr Nash-Perry. What he must've had to put up with. And lovely Mr Kerbidge too. And I don't think he killed himself, either."

"Neither do we," concurred Edna, speaking on behalf of herself and her sister-in-law. "Gladys thinks Rita and Michael Martyn were lovers, and they each did away with the obstacles to their partnership. Partners in murder, Gladys says. Dastardly people, shocking if you ask me."

"Wicked. Evil. The pair of them. Hope they rot in hell, Edna." The two shared a little more general dialogue before Martha set off again and Edna, once more, returned to her gardening. She was interrupted this time by Gladys who had arrived back from the newsagent's puffing and panting.

Gladys always fretted when she saw Edna talking to someone, and did so on two counts. She wanted to be involved, and secondly she didn't trust Edna to speak either the truth or words of wisdom. Or perhaps, more to the point, she didn't trust her to utter their agreed words, especially where Chortleford's problems were concerned. So she had made haste, hoping to reach Edna in time.

While Gladys interrogated Edna things were happening elsewhere.

It was quiet in the *Log and Weasel* when Harry Dunsburn nipped in for a pint.

His mission was to try and find out about the middle aged couple staying at the B&B who were asking too many questions for his liking.

They claimed not to be the news media but he couldn't be sure and nobody else was convinced either. With precious few customers in the bar, and barmaid Chloe coming from another village, Harry learned nothing to improve his knowledge past discovering Dave had been drinking there with the couple quite recently.

"Funny going ons, funny goings on," he was heard muttering as he departed and headed hot-footed for Dave's home.

Dave wasn't able to enlighten him much either.

"They just talked about the village and asked me loads of questions about the murders, and all I told them was what was in the papers. No local gossip. That's not for their ears, is it Harry?"

"No son, it certainly isn't. I'm a-thinking they're reporters and we need to be careful, y'know, close ranks. It's our village, not theirs." From the look in Harry's eyes this statement was clearly intended as a warning and it worried Dave, if only because he had indeed shared local gossip.

Much earlier, and a stone's throw from where Dave and Harry were talking, Katie had taken a phone call from the man who'd arranged the abortion. She'd handed the phone to David Pervis who offered to meet the caller.

However, Pervis was not going to be offering him the balance of the money, just a nice, simple beating for his troubles. The rest of the conversation suggested to Katie war was breaking out and she didn't want to be around to witness the outcome.

"Can't we go to the police?" she wailed.

"No, we settle this here. This isn't a police matter, and I've taken Vaughan's murder out of their hands too. I've got private detectives working on that, my dear, and Vaughan's killer's days are numbered, just like those of the joker who reckons he's gonna have a few grand off you."

This terrified his daughter-in-law.

Not more murder, surely?

But the 'joker' *was* police business and he'd been arrested somewhere south of Gravesend, so no more murder. Katie needn't have worried.

Oscar Falhaven, solicitor, had been working feverishly on the information he'd been given, and had made a number of calls to base to ascertain the next courses of action, Mr Pervis senior demanding they be activated immediately. Oscar was extremely concerned overhearing the phone call and the news private eyes had been engaged.

He thought he should talk to the police, but now knew Mr Pervis would frown upon it and do so quite violently.

Elsewhere in the village Michael Martyn was about to talk to the police and he was on his guard. He didn't trust them. He was conscious that he and Rita were prime suspects and Drype would try and goad him. Keep calm, stay focused, remain in control, answer carefully. He was ready.

Or so he thought.

Chapter Twenty One

Drype greeted Martyn like a long lost friend.

He was at pains to stress they just wanted a chat, the chance to run over a few things, and behaved as if he was a kindly uncle cheerily offering a nephew a treat.

This made Martyn even more cagey and distrustful.

He knew only too well that police 'chats' were far from amiable chinwags, and usually came with 'malice aforethought' and a health warning for wrongdoers. In his novels he had often dreamed up conversations between an officer and a suspect where the officer, with a dexterous and cunning approach, had outwitted an otherwise smart villain.

This wasn't going to happen to Michael Martyn, ace murder mystery author.

He looked upon the event as one of those television game shows where, in order to win the prize, you have to get all the answers right and be wiser than the quizmaster. Let the battle commence!

DS Charlie Penderfield was in the starting blocks.

"Just wanted to show you this photo, Mr Martyn. Do you remember it?"

Martyn glanced at the magazine picture and opted for sarcasm.

"I think it's me. Is there any question about it, Sergeant? I'm happy to confirm that's me."

"Your tie sir, it's the same as the one used to strangle Colin Nash-Perry."

Martyn pondered this. It was a bolt from the blue and he needed time to think.

"Yes. So? It's a common enough design, probably Marks and Sparks I should think. Colin must've had an identical one. I didn't notice at the time, had more important things on my mind, like a corpse propped up against my front door."

"Would you mind showing us your tie, sir, the one in the picture?"

"Oh, I'm certain I don't have it anymore. I threw a lot out a short while ago. Sorry and all that."

Beads of sweat were appearing on his forehead, fully noted by Drype who accepted them as a sign of fretting, a give-away for a guilty party telling porkies. But this was only the start, the aperitif, and it was over the main course that they had to derail their man. Oddly enough Drype found himself sweating, probably a sign of nerves knowing he was faced by a master of the dark arts.

Surely there could be no doubt? A ruthless killer, but a conniving one, a man who might yet thwart Drype's attempts to catch him out. Yes, a master criminal with a brain to match. How on earth, then, did he come to write such rubbish about murders?

Charlie held his tongue. This was part of the agreed plan. Normally he might've added a sarcastic comment of his own about how convenient the absence of the tie was. No, don't anger your target. Try and make him feel in control, then he'll be more likely to relax and make a mistake.

"I know you've made a statement, Mr Martyn, but could you briefly run me through Colin's arrival at your door again?" It was the DCI's turn to launch an attack. "You said you were surprised to see him and told him you weren't going to argue on the doorstep, then closed the door. But can you tell me what he came to argue about?"

Martyn took a deep breath, which bought him time and helped him keep his composure. It was going well.

"As I've explained he thought I killed William Kerbidge, just like everyone else around here thought, and he wanted me to confess. That's when I told him to go, and closed the door."

"Why would it bother a complete stranger? Why did he come and confront you?"

"I've no idea, and you can't ask him, can you?"

"Was it because Colin and William were lovers and therefore gay, and Colin believed you'd killed the man he loved?" As expected this stunned Martyn completely. He had to think quickly, but the damage was already done, had he but known it.

"Utter nonsense, Chief Inspector. Utter nonsense. Where did you get that idea from?" Martyn was beginning to realise that Drype had probably got it from Rita. She'd spilled the beans at last to save her own skin. So be it. His word against hers. Let's play the game but give them no satisfaction.

"I want my solicitor."

"Not a formal interview." Drype was now snapping out his words and looking for a fatal quick-fire exchange. "You struggled with Colin, removed your tie and strangled him, right?" Martyn laughed in a hollow fashion. He tried in vain to slow the altercation down.

"Oh, Chief Inspector, you read too many crime novels. Fancy yourself as Morse, do you? No I didn't strangle him."

But the questions and answers were coming thick and fast, staccato style.

"Did Rita try and stop you?"

"Rita wasn't here."

"Did Colin attack you first and you acted in self-defence?"

"No, there was no struggle, no fight, I sent him away and shut the door. How many more times?"

"You removed your tie and wrapped it around Colin's neck and strangled him. Perhaps you didn't mean to kill him but you thought you were fighting for your own life." Martyn laughed again but his confidence was sapping.

"Oh, for God's sake, where's this going, Chief Inspector? I didn't touch him. Has Rita told you all this?"

"Rita? Where does Rita come into this? You told me she wasn't here?"

"She wasn't....."

"Why should she tell me anything, Mr Martyn? If she wasn't here she wouldn't have seen anything."

"This has gone far enough...."

"You'd killed your gay step-father, now you could kill his lover."

"This is preposterous, Drype, you're obsessed with people being gay."

"We know they were lovers, and so did you."

"Oh don't make me laugh."

"We know he wasn't wearing a tie, so you used yours."

"It wasn't mine and no, I didn't kill him."

"Were you shocked when Colin punched his wife so hard she fell to the ground?"

"She was asking for it, she was trying to interfere ..... I mean .... I .... I...."

Martyn knew what had happened.

Game set and match Drype.

And Drype breathed a sigh of relief.

"Okay, okay," said Martyn. "I think I have to say it's a fair cop or something. I don't suppose that happens in real life, eh? Right, I'll come down the station and make a confession, and yes, I really will have my solicitor please."

Unlike Rita, Michael Martyn was handcuffed and taken from the premises where his exit was noted by Harry Dunsburn. Now here was some real gossip! It looked like they'd got Martyn at last, and Harry wanted to be the one to tell Chortleford, to tell Kent, tell the United Kingdom and the rest of the world.

He hastened up to the village as fast as his ancient legs would carry him.

* * *

Olivia Handest was as welcome in Chortleford as a fox in a hen house, so her paper sent a cub reporter on a daily basis just to keep an eye on things.

First of all he was able to advise that Rita Nash-Perry had been whisked away, and then the coup, Michael Martyn arrested.

Having managed to reach Drype Olivia found she had only reached as far as his cold shoulder.

She was referred to Police PR.

"Oh come on, Harry, give, give, give baby. You owe little ol' Olivia one, y'know. You don't take a guy away in handcuffs unless this is a new fun game. And where's Rita?"

"Olivia I have nothing to say. Now I'm busy even if you're not, and frankly you should contact our people in case you miss out. All the truth will be there, unlike in your paper which publishes tripe, peddles scandal as news and glorifies perceived police failure.

"Well this time PC Plod has got to the bottom of the case. Good, old fashioned police work, Olivia. We have what is often termed a result, and we've achieved it without your help. Goodbye."

"Drype, just don't ever, ever ask for my help again, ever." And the call ended leaving the DCI with a haughty grin. Small victories, he thought, small victories.

Another man enjoying (if that was the right word) a small victory was David Pervis, but it brought him little succour. His underworld enquiries had also produced a result alright. Vaughan Pervis was implicated in a gangland killing in which a man in Ilford had been murdered. Did that lead to Vaughan being strangled?

It wasn't justice in David's eyes, but to the rest of the world it might have appeared that way.

Evidence now supported the theory of an assassination rather than any local involvement, and Pervis was relying on the Hopetowns to either be able to confirm that or point the finger. They were good at their job and he'd used them before with very satisfactory upshots.

Thanks to intelligence imparted by Dave the taxi driver, albeit a very inferior and infantile level of intelligence, they were now standing outside the Frobishers very loudly admiring the front garden.

They discussed the flowers and shrubs, demonstrating great knowledge and appreciation, and the amount of effort and skill of the gardeners in creating such a work of art. The purpose was to attract the attention of one or both gardeners in the hope they would come out to soak up the applause.

And Gladys did.

Gladys was as wary as anyone, but Gladys was Gladys and at the end of the proverbial day she was always ready for gossip. Besides, two people falling over themselves to praise the garden was harmless enough.

They seemed to know what they were talking about, and weren't just admiring the prettiness of it all.

Mrs Frobisher felt on safe ground and was soon up and running, and got so carried away that when the conversation turned to the village murders she was in full swing and unable to stop herself from chatting at full tilt. When the Hopetowns finally said their goodbyes and walked away they felt as if their ears had been subjected to a lengthy and thorough beating, but they had gleaned some vital data, and that was most important.

* * *

The next day Chortleford was back on the front pages and adorning news websites.

Martyn had been charged with two murders following his confession, with Rita and Glen facing other charges relating the killing of Nash-Perry. There was nothing to report on the Pervis case beyond the police reiterating that one of their officers was in White Cottage with Martyn when disaster struck on the doorstep.

But the police had commented that they had conducted a number of investigations on site and concluded that a swift execution could be performed on the doorstep with the occupants of the cottage unaware. They appealed for public assistance in providing information leading to the capture of the perpetrator.

David Pervis decided against offering a reward, especially in light of his discovery that Vaughan was up to his eyeballs in dark practices. No need to stir things up. He was also aware, having received a phone call, that the Hopetowns were making progress but in the direction that suggested no locals were mixed up in his son's death.

Yes, this looked like a revenge killing with gangland associations. Perhaps let sleeping dogs lie? Other fish to fry, compensation claims to pursue. Yes, leave well alone and move on.

For DCI Drype the investigation now had one branch only: Pervis. And Drype, whilst keeping an open mind, was leaning towards an external involvement. There was nothing at all, not even local gossip, to attach it to the village. It looked as if the investigation would be taken out of his hands and for once he didn't seem to mind one little bit.

* * *

Charlie looked at Emma and Emma looked at Charlie.

"Was there a moment, Charlie, when you thought Drype wouldn't crack him?"

"Yes, lots of 'em! But he held his nerve. I don't think I'd ever make it to his rank and quite honestly I don't think it's for me anyway. I'm happy where I am. I think I'd have been the one to crack! I thought Martyn was more than holding his own and more than a match for our beloved DCI.

"But I think the DCI would've just kept baiting him until he made a slip up. I was afraid Martyn would clam up and demand his solicitor and then it would've been all over. So credit to Drype for keeping him interested and on message!

"The thing about Drype is he's a bloody good detective, Emma, and I know he thinks the world of you. Hopes you make it right to the top, and so do I. He'll support you all the way. He once said to me that when the day comes that you're senior to him he'll rejoice, and willingly take his orders from you. Don't mention I said that or I'll have to kill you." They both laughed.

Emma blushed to the roots. So these guys weren't the chauvinists she thought they were! Not even drippy Drype.

"Thanks Charlie. You're an angel. I suppose it's true that if we take the trouble to open our eyes and to listen we can learn so much from our seniors and elders. They're not all idiots. After all it was me Martyn fooled. All that training, y'know, body language, facial expressions, voice tones and so on, and I come up against a very good actor.

"And you're correct, Drype's a damn good detective, but you're the damn good detective I want to take home. When y'coming, lover boy?"

Charlie looked flustered, embarrassed, pleased, excited, wary, discomposed and all in one go. Emma giggled and then Charlie giggled.

"How about tonight? I'm free, Em, just have to let mum and dad know I'll be late."

"Nope, you've failed the first test. You tell them you won't be home at all, Charlie." He looked like a child who has been caught with his hand in the chocolate box and Emma giggled all the more. "And, Charlie Penderfield, we are *not* going to discuss the death of Vaughan Pervis."

* * *

It was Mrs Hopetown who made the call.

David Pervis thanked her, wished them a safe journey home, and pressed the 'end' button. He looked ruefully around him, almost thankful that they'd found no evidence that anyone in Chortleford had anything to do with Vaughan's death.

Harry Dunsburn had exhausted himself spreading the news the previous evening but a good night's sleep after a couple of pints of Whitstable Bay had restored him. He'd been a farm labourer most of his life, boasted a strong constitution, and now threw himself into gardening when he wasn't busy gossiping.

He looked at the photo that young missy had admired, the one of him as a champion wrestler. Those were the days, he mused. I'd have won that little missy's heart alright. There might have been one or two wrestling holds I'd have tried out on her! Just gently, just for fun. He smiled and set off for the first garden of the day. Plenty to do at Mrs Greenberg's place.

"Ah," he sighed as he closed the door behind him, "bin some funny goings on here, some funny going ons....."

For once it was Edna Frobisher in pole position, and Gladys looking sheepish and subservient. It wouldn't last, of course, so Edna was making the most of it.

"We did wrong, Gladys, and that's all there is to it. We should've told the police our suspicions. It might be old-fashioned to defend your friends especially when they are such fine gentlemen, but this was very serious, this was murder Gladys. And we misled the police into thinking Mr Nash-Perry was seeing ladies when he was doing nothing of the sort.

"And since we now know that such information would've helped catch that Martyn fellow much sooner, well, we should be ashamed."

"I know, Edna, but we did what we thought was the right thing. You're right, we have an old-fashioned approach to life, old-fashioned standards, and yes, we misused them this time, I accept that. But we felt we needed to defend the reputation of two gentlemen even if they were behaving unnaturally, shall we say."

"And we were defending the reputation of our village as well Edna, don't forget that."

"I think we've learned an important lesson, Gladys, for all that."

"For heaven's sake, Edna, I hope we don't ever find ourselves in a position where we have to draw on such a lesson!" Edna agreed and in so doing surrendered the moral high ground and her temporary post as top dog.

Martha had gone to the church to pray expecting the vicar to be there, as he was.

Having spoken to him briefly she knelt in a pew and prayed for the souls of the dear departed, Mr Kerbidge and Mr Nash-Perry, and for the deliverance of the guilty that they should repent their sins.

Prayers despatched, Martha, with the vicar's permission, decided to play something on the organ, or rather fight the contraption in the worthless pursuit of tuneful pleasure. The vicar looked towards the altar, rolled his eyes, muttered light-heartedly 'Father forgive her, for she knows not what she does' and made for the comparative peace of the vestry.

Epilogue

Michael Martyn went to prison for life.

He thought he'd hoodwinked the police and got away with murder.

His crime writing skills, if they could be called that, had let him down. He thought he'd covered everything, every possible detail, every conceivable angle, and that it was all going to plan.

In particular he was extremely proud of his interview with Emma. One of his fictional criminals could not have played the part any better. Perfectly scripted, brilliantly acted. Police convinced.

But he'd reckoned without a real, live policeman undoing him.

Never confuse fact with fiction.

Rita avoided prison with a suspended sentence, the court showing great leniency in her circumstances. To his credit Martyn did say that he'd threatened and menaced her, and that worked in her favour.

She never returned to Chortleford, going to live with her daughter near Ashford while Vanessa and her husband arranged the sale of her property and helped her choose a new one near them. 'Suburban' Ashford suited her as did the close proximity of her daughter and her family.

To this day there has been no man in her life although she no doubt still dreams.

For folk like Gladys, Edna, Martha et al, life would take on a different shade, for there was a permanent shadow over the place they dwelt in, and recent events would cloud their final years.

Steve still cheeked his customers, but that is the way of butchers, and he stayed very much the focal point for any tittle-tattle remotely connected with scandal. It was just that people didn't seem to talk the way they used to.

Dave was delighted with his 'readies' which he put to poor use as you might expect of such a man, and he saw his earnings evaporate in double-quick time. Keith, the newsagent, carried on as before, as he did more or less every day, and saw his takings drop in direct proportion to Chortleford stories gradually vanishing from papers and magazines.

Olivia Handest started work with a national and was promptly head-hunted by television. A promising career, that had thus far simply nestled on the horizon, was rushing forward, propelling her to potential stardom.

Unfortunately a poor decision in earlier life, allied to drug taking and alcohol abuse, and unwise associations with unpleasant people, led to her being a high profile casualty of a newspaper expose. Hoisted by her own petard she returned to local newspapers and was last heard of in Yorkshire or somewhere.

DCI Henry Drype busied himself with other crimes, ably assisted by DS Penderfield, and Emma Brouding qualified as a Detective Sergeant. She and

Charlie celebrated at her flat while Charlie's mum kept her fingers crossed. They developed a taste for Cava and for each other, and it now seemed most unlikely Angelique Gorling-Parter would get her date with Charlie.

And perhaps that was just as well.

Katie Pervis was awarded substantial damages which enabled her to buy her own home in another part of the county. David Pervis, whose rants must've put him within touching distance of a heart attack, came to the conclusion Vaughan's killer might never be identified and that the pursuit of such a villain might open a can of worms with devastating results. He left well alone.

Besides, Vaughan's business dealings left much to be desired since some were positively shady, others lost in the shadows and few designed to hoodwink HMRC. Not a nice man at all.

Vaughan Pervis's murder remains an unsolved crime, the killer still at large and likely to take his secret to the grave, especially given his advanced years.

Quite accidently he achieved what Martyn hoped *he* had, namely the perfect crime.

With attention focusing on the criminal world and away from Chortleford it left the perpetrator to lead a quiet life in the village where he'd been all the time. Penderfield had never felt easy, right from day one, about there being a hit man, yet all the signs had pointed to it.

White Cottage has new owners, a retired couple from south-east London escaping to the country, and clearly not put off by the property's dark past. The only blot on their "escape" being the church clock chiming all night, the cocks crowing, and the sheep bleating.....

And so Chortleford returned to the serenity, obscurity and near normality it had enjoyed before Mr Kerbidge met his end. Yet some things would never be the same; there would be increased poison gossip and more fingers of suspicion being pointed than previously.

As Vaughan Pervis's killer would've said:

"Funny goings on here, funny going ons."

Author's Afterthoughts

I am sure most readers will have worked out who killed Vaughan Pervis for there are enough clues in the text.

Chortleford is a fictional village in a non-fictional county, and is not intended to represent any other living village (or area) in Kent.

Kent, however, makes a guest appearance as itself, as do its towns and cities and other villages.

Therefore inevitably Kent Police are mentioned, but the officers in the novel are the product of my imagination. The ranks and procedures, and the behaviour of my detectives, are pure fiction to suit the story and are not reflections of real officers and Kent Police.

The countryside is praised throughout and is very much a true representation of my home county, a county I am very proud of.

It would be folly to try and note all the wonderful places you can go to get off the beaten track but I have appended a small list of some of my favourites. The list is by no means exhaustive and I apologise for the many that are missing.

The book mentions four places where the gardens are open to the public at certain times. All have websites where more information can be found. I recommend all four visits! Belmont, Doddington Place, Godinton, Mount Ephraim.

When I wrote my book "Kindale", a tale of treachery, espionage and intrigue set in 18th century east Kent, I mentioned the extraordinarily diverse coast of the county. Surrounded on three sides by water there are few coastlines to match it in the country.

The famous White Cliffs, the sandy beaches of Dymchurch, Margate and Broadstairs, the sloping pebbly shores of Tankerton, Greatstone and Deal, river and creeks a-plenty, islands of all shapes and sizes, and that's just to name a few of the places and features. I haven't even noted Romney Marsh!

When you then add in the countryside revered in this book, and there is a great quantity of that too, you begin to get a picture of an amazing county. The North Downs are not the only hills and not the only places to enjoy spectacular views. The Weald is an area of startling beauty and prettiness with some gloriously explore-worthy towns and villages, and it doesn't even feature at all in this book!

Neither does west Kent, which is also a shame.

If you have read and enjoyed this tale and are unfamiliar with Kent do come and see for yourself.

Appendix I - Off the beaten track

Queendown Warren, south of Hartlip, off the A2 between Rainham and Sittingbourne.
Conservation area with a number of scenic and woodland walks, with splendid views on the open stretches, notably across the valley.

Harty Church to Leysdown, east end of the isle of Sheppey, coastal walk.
Walk along the fields and the northern shore of the Swale, with views across the water to Oare, Faversham, Seasalter and Whitstable.
Fish and chips at Ron Wood's, Leysdown!

Crundale, mentioned in the text.
Awash, as so much of Kent is, with well marked footpaths. Tranquillity and scenic views seemingly miles from anywhere. Choose your walk; short and pleasant, long and thrilling.

Lenham, north of the village and the A20, on the North Downs, and to the east and west.
If all you seek is truly unspoilt undulating countryside and almost total peace, ramble on some of these lanes and footpaths. Every now and then stumble on glorious views south across the weald.
The Pilgrims Way is at the foot of the Downs. Get up the hill and LIVE!
Two highly recommended pubs: eat and drink at the Ringlestone Inn and the Bowl Inn (Charing): (accommodation available at the latter). Two truly remote country pubs.

Knole Park, National Trust, Sevenoaks town
Extensive and attractive deer park with large open spaces and woodland areas in a rolling landscape with delightful views north to the Downs. Open all year.
Other large and beautiful gardens open to the public nearby include Ightham Mote and Emmetts, both NT.

Footpaths!

Miles and miles and miles of well marked paths criss-cross the county and armed with an Ordnance Survey map walks of any length can be enjoyed from almost any point, one-way or circular, the walker can choose.

Guide books and leaflets can be easily found.

Kent County Council's website features an interactive map with a substantial amount of information on routes, not just for walkers but for cyclists too.

My apologies to west Kent, the Weald, Romney Marsh, east Kent, Thanet, the Hoo Peninsula and so many more too numerous to mention specifically here.

Appendix II - Other e-books by Peter Chegwidden

Peter writes across a variety of genres and there's something for everybody.

Plenty of good reads, enough to please most tastes. You can sample them online (Amazon). Two of the books are also available in paperback, *Tom Investigates* and *Kindale*.

Deadened Pain

If you're looking for something very different to the Chortleford Mystery try this.

Deadened Pain is a satirical parody of the crime novel genre full of clichés, stereotypes and typical life and death situations.

There's humour, romance, murder, horror, serious crime, red herrings, a wide range of characters and a team of detectives not always pulling together.

And there are serious messages too, such as those relating to the illegal drugs industry and the misery and crime it causes.

The tale starts with a robbery at a local garage in which very little was taken and escalates as murder most foul is committed, and the body count increases. It's a race against time for the police and not everyone has their brains in gear.

All the ingredients, in fact, for a typical crime story.

Tom Investigates

Follow the adventures of a cat called Tom as he and his friends solve a crime, do a little human match-making, and get involved in narrow scrapes and dangerous situations.

These are not cartoon or animated cats, they are the cats we see in our neighbourhoods every day, behaving just as we see them. But in this story we are allowed into their world and hear them speak and learn what they are thinking.

It's an adult "cat's tail" but without bad language and anything to offend. So get in touch with your feline side and come along for the ride.

(Tom Investigates is also available in paperback from Amazon)

Tom Vanishes

The sequel relates how Tom is accidently lost and the efforts he makes to find his way home.

Needless to say all his friends unite to try and locate him with farcical chaos resulting!

Does he make it? Well, read on and find out.

Sheppey Short Stories

Eighteen short stories, based on Kent's Isle of Sheppey, all with a common theme ... relationships.

There's humour, drama, romance, fun, crime, poignancy and pathos!

Kindale

Set in the late 18th century at a time when England is braced for war with France and Napoleon is rising to power, this is a story of intrigue, espionage and treachery.

The mysterious Oliver Kindale arrives in Kent and he's a man on a mission.

He is not chasing the smugglers who are prolific around this coast but their paths inevitably cross.

Fear is in the air and danger lurks around every corner.

The widely diverse Kent coast has a role to play as a seemingly terrible plot is unearthed and Kindale seeks out the perpetrators before irreparable damage can be done.

But he is totally unprepared for one eventuality that comes to threaten his mission.

However, success is vital, and the very fate of England could lie in his hands.

(Kindale is also available in paperback from Amazon)

To be published

After Hugh

This book follows recently widowed Hannah as she negotiates life alone after her beloved husband Hugh passes away.

Her family test her to the limits and she has to abandon long held beliefs and prejudices as she finally copes and comes to realise how Hugh dominated her thinking for her.

She has no interest in romance and tries in vain to warn her best friend Jayne against online dating.

Sadly it is Hannah herself who falls for the wrong man, and head-first into one of love's pitfalls!

With Jayne's help she gets back on track and then discovers true love in a most unexpected way.

Dead Corrupt and Dead Departed

The sequels to Deadened Pain follow the hopeless efforts of Birkchester's CID as more and more crimes (and murders) pile up on the doorstep.

Printed in Great Britain
by Amazon